LIPGLOSS

LIAM GAMMALLIERE

- Disclaimer -
This work contains scenes of an explicit sexual nature, references
to recreational drugs, use of offensive language, and themes
which may be distressing.
Discretion is advised.

For my Mum & Dad, Brother & Sister, and Nan in providing me
with invaluable love and support.
For Chloe in being the root of my strength and my biggest fan.
For Nancy and our long talks.
For Guy in helping me to walk on air.

I couldn't have done this without you.

Thank you.

Before reading...

Lipgloss was conceptualised in 2012/13 and has been an evolutionary process over subsequent years.

It is my first novel – beginning as a bag of ideas and observations on relationships, with the notable motif being how and why these change across time.

Starting as an eBook uploaded to Amazon Kindle in 2015, I would revisit the characters and themes to (as objectively as I could) reflect on whether I still deemed them to be meaningful.

In 2019, I decided to cement the content in a printed paperback.

Having studied Philosophy at University of London, my curiosity is peaked by ideas and belief structures. Their manifestation in our behaviour and treatment of one another is of particular interest to me, especially when engaging in amorous relationships.

There are multiple questions to rationally ask ourselves about commitment to another person.

How much of ourselves should we appropriately compromise for a prospective partner?

What psychological needs are we hoping to fulfil through another person which we can't achieve ourselves?

Knowing the disastrous potential to our being if/when things sour, why even enter a relationship?

Can we be truly happy alone?

These are by no means simple questions, and exploring them through the characters you will be introduced to will only raise more dilemmas – many of which are harder to contend with as they call to question sexual ethics and co-dependency.

One thing that has struck me is the emotional maturity it takes to deeply think about these issues, while remaining pragmatically faithful to that maturity as real life unfolds catastrophically in front of us; because, of course, plans of how we intend to act – in our glorified view of our infallible selves – seldom come to fruition. Pair this with our general yearning to engage in these relationships (when we are, frankly, not ready to commit to them), and we have a mutually-assured ball of tempestuous emotions which we call *love*.
For love itself is rational; it's the people in love who are irrational.

I tried to explore this vulnerability through a teenage relationship during the regeneration projects of East London in 2011. You will witness the interplay between the openness and naivety of one person – her romanticising the idea of a relationship and forsaking herself in the process; coupled with the aloofness and detachment of another – him being the victim of a previous emotional scorn, harbouring resentment and distrust.

In (sometimes, blindly) committing to another person, there can become an unwillingness of people to look after themselves as well as they are inclined to look after their partner. This can even be a prerequisite of some relationships, with the expectation that one partner is ultimately responsible for the wellbeing of the other. And what's the result of looking after someone else's interests more so than your own?
This was a motivating question that drove me as the story between the characters unfolded.

Such blind commitment to someone else can lead to normalising certain patterns of behaviour, particularly when we conflate 'normal' and 'common' – two terms often mistaken for being synonymous.

Behaviours that we consider to be normal in a relationship, merely because they are commonplace, can often be symptomatic of a much more insidious element of co-dependency. There can arise a tendency to make a partner responsible for our own wellbeing and happiness. And if we neglect ourselves in this way, we remove responsibility for our own actions and leave ourselves ill-equipped in the ever-present face of looming solitude.
Cyclically, we will want to avoid being alone and continue this pernicious path of self-destruction. And why would this change? What conscious desire is more innate than to love and be loved? This is something that has the potential to fester beneath the surface of a relationship, slowly eroding it from nurturing to habitual. Being with someone simply through habit can lead us to treat them the way we treat ourselves. And who genuinely cares for themselves as well as they should?
Self-contemptuousness can be a motivator in not wanting to be alone, and being with someone habitually makes them an extension of ourselves – weaving them into a tapestry of self-loathing and neglect. In doing this, there is the proclivity to not evaluate whether the partner is still a meaningful part of our lives – or even a healthy one.

The antidote to this would seem to be remedying the relationship with oneself – the highest order of long-term relationship – before dragging others down into the emotional abyss with us. Who else will we ultimately share our life with, if not ourselves? Of course, there is utility in companionship, but it seems preferable to build and maintain that sacred connection with the self, before arbitrarily filling that void with a partner – them having their own unique set of idiosyncrasies, which would need equal consideration if an organic relationship is to flourish.

The end of a modern relationship is plagued by doubt and fear. The horizon of future events, which once seemed so orderly (structured with certainty, whether it was positive or not), slips into chaos. Despite the worry and anxiousness necessitated in any major lifestyle change, a newer phenomenon hangs over like the Sword of Damocles after the end of a tumultuous relationship. Intimacy in the digital age can include the consensual sharing of explicit photographs between one another. Once the trust has parted, the photographs remain – as does the danger of revenge porn; the threat of circulating the images (sent in confidence) as a means of vengeance or humiliation, at little more than the click of a button. Severance of ties becomes all the more difficult, even coercing the victim into certain actions to appease the wrathful resentment of the former partner. It is difficult to think how one could ever be truly rid of a partner while such bonds exist, shackling them to a past they would feel is better left forgotten.

After a difficult breakup, it seems clear that we are still committed to the ex-partner, for one reason or another. This can be true both physically and metaphysically. They come to represent facets of ourselves that we cannot overcome. They embody our insecurities and sit as this unspeakable (because we don't dare mention them) blip of our past, which we hate to admit has shaped us.

Not acknowledging the underlying problems and refusing to talk about them could seem to be a valid form of coping, albeit temporary. But choosing not to speak about a problem or trauma doesn't make it not exist. It is still just as real, but lingers in the landscape of our daily lives – hiding in plain sight, silently puppeteering our choices and decisions. Not speaking of a problem only removes the means by which we can face it and overcome it, which is why we value speech so highly – the signifiers of the abstract, making sense of the non-sensical.

To allow the existential threat of the ex-partner to occupy the domain of the unspeakable is harmful to our emotional development and stagnates over time. That which is so terrifying as to be unspeakable truly has the greatest hold on us, interfering with the very means by which we articulate sense of the world. It perpetually gives us something to avoid and fear, with the unease of never being in control of when we are forced to confront it. To bring that experience/person into being (by speaking of it/them) is half the battle fought and won.

This is a struggle that you will see unfold in reality throughout the story – the silent battle between what should be said or done in a situation, against what we allow to transpire when we refuse to acknowledge the situation even exists.

As gregarious and communal creatures, we base our intrinsic value on how we are perceived by others. We pair at the earliest given opportunity and rarely stray from our social herd. For better or worse, we judge ourselves on our social appeal. Detrimental to this psychological disposition is a way in which we can be given a false representation of our place in the social hierarchy.

Enter social media… Because you're never alone with a phone. The integration of social media into our lives has presented us with a live feed from which we can determine our superficial (quasi-) 'value' in society. Constantly chasing the proverbial bunny around the dog track in the form of *likes* and *reposts*, Big Tech has found a way to mobilise and monetise our primordial desire for social acceptance, reducing users to little more than data-collecting agents. The nihilistic, short-term gratification of the '*thumbs-up*' pits users as slaves to algorithms, advertising and selling their ideas back to them in an automated echo-chamber. Consequently, users of social media can find themselves doing what is popular rather than doing what is meaningful – or even right. And why wouldn't they? Abstract as they may be, the rewards are tangible and easily quantifiable, encouraging imitation of that behaviour by the '*followers*' – a term itself with grossly messianic and dangerously deified connotations.

Generally, users will advertise only the hyper-positive aspects of their lives and – for good reason – avoid truthful depictions of their daily reality. The ambition of some to become an '*influencer*' is arguably a product of this; a professional trader of the twenty-

first-century currency – *likes* and *followers*.
But there does seem to be something harmful about objectifying
ourselves in this way – narcissistically counterfeiting ourselves
for the superficial approval of others (sometimes, people we
haven't even met) in what is little more than a digital popularity-
contest. Infinite access to perpetual feedback isn't something we
are used to as flawed creatures. At best, it is the shallow feeding
of an insatiable appetite for acceptance. At worst, it is the pseudo-
reality by which people gauge their existential worth. Worryingly,
this is a technology that is being introduced to generations at an
increasingly younger age, even less prepared for the ramifications
of it on society and individual mental wellbeing. Couple this with
the relationship between use of social media and depression, and
the results are unlike anything humankind has ever encountered.

Able to dictate what they are exposed to, users can shield
themselves from what they do not agree with and simply block
what they do not wish to see. This idealistic bubble is thickened
further with automated '*suggestions*' based on shared keywords
and algorithms – an attempt to expose the user to additional
content which may be of interest.
Helpful as this all may seem, it does come at a price.
It creates an inevitable intolerance towards differing opinions and
intellectual diversity; it explains and justifies the shutting down of
what we do not agree with, as opposed to discussing it on
intellectual merit through civil discourse. It enables users to live
digitally in an idealistic vacuum – impermeable, seldom
challenged, and devoid of differing opinions or ideas. Simply put,
this isn't an accurate reflection of a diverse and varied humankind,
and time spent in this environment is time spent out of reality.
There is an epistemic distance between the post and the viewer,
making it impersonal for obvious reasons. Yet, when we
encounter something we do not agree with, we are inclined to
receive it as a personal attack – regardless of whether the original
post was even intended that way. Intent is deemed irrelevant and

secondary if content invades our digital space. Consequently, it is kept at arm's length, often with the expectation that it is removed altogether. This totalised shielding of what users allow themselves to experience has visible societal ramifications. Given the reach and influence of the technology, this extrapolates into a widespread culture of censorship and cancellation.

Psychologically, voluntary exposure is arguably most effective in equipping us with the resources to deal with what we are uncomfortable with and can't control. The intrinsic nature of social media seems to be doing the exact opposite of this – addictively antithetical to psychological wellness and spilling out into the broader workings of society. Users are almost (perhaps, unknowingly) self-indoctrinating; at risk of falling into the grips of ideology and polarised tribalism in keeping differing ideas and opinions distant – favouring presupposition over dialogue. It seems the rate of advancement of technological prowess is outrunning the human ability to properly understand the ethical implications of it. Being so intimately entwined and connected with the rest of humanity, there lacks an understanding of the responsibility and gravity of the content put out (as well as how it should be appropriately received) – a responsibility that is seldom taught or learned. For the first time in human history, the archaic 'Town Square' as a forum of discussion for ideas is portable and (generally) universally accessible, disproportionately amplifying the views and beliefs of any user willing to post them – whether genuine or baiting.
This is a phenomenon very new to us all, so it is unsurprising that we don't know how to manage it. We are still in the relatively early stages of the technological revolution, feeling our way through the dark in how best to harness it.

To this end, it seems social media is a breeding ground for anxiety in shielding us from that which we ought to face (leaving users vulnerable to inevitable 'keyboard warriors'), as well as encouraging the artifice of how we want to be perceived by

society (often, by any means necessary).
Inflict this on young, impressionable minds who don't know a life
(or childhood) outside of this – drop them back into a society of
chasing celebrity – and we have a generational epidemic of
nihilism, anxiety/depression, and self-identifying victimhood;
with people constantly (whether knowingly or unknowingly)
comparing themselves to the artificial, digital personas of others.
I have attempted to explore how all of this plays out in the life of
a modern teenager, being particularly susceptible to the negative
implications of this lifestyle.

There are a variety of views and opinions expressed in the
following manuscript, and they aren't necessarily ones that I hold.
I have tried to empathetically engage with the characters and
present them in as realistic a manner as possible.
Among the study of literature, particularly in schools, there is an
insistence on critiquing from political and ideological
perspectives, namely: Marxist, analysing the representation of
socio-economic hierarchal structures; and Feminist, analysing the
representation of women (or lack thereof) in positions of power.
For universality of themes, I have attempted to present characters
in their sovereign individual states. I would urge readers to
dispense with viewing characters through an ideological lens and
avoid politicising this story. Some details about characters have
been deliberately omitted to avoid the tendency to do this. The
characters are intended as a collection of paramount individuals
(not deliberately representative of collective social groups),
idiosyncratically placed in society and doing their best to navigate
their way through the turmoil of human existence.

One aphorism that I would advise you to keep mindful throughout
reading…

The consequences we fear enslave us with inaction.

Liam Gammalliere

LIPGLOSS

LIAM GAMMALLIERE

If you're anything like me, you'll have an urge to read the last line of a book when you get so far in.

Don't.

1. JAMES'

'Who's that?'

'Huh?'

'Who you texting?'

'…No one.' I make sure I don't shield the phone from him. The screen is in sight, so he knows I've got nothing to hide.

'Well, it's not *'no one'*, is it? You're not texting *'no one'*. It's gotta be someone because it's just gone off. Phones don't go off for no reason, do they?'

Here we go. He'll start, now. I haven't done anything wrong, but he'll still find a reason to start over this. Guaranteed. It's best to be honest with him. 'It's just Nancy. She wants to know if I can go out tonight.'

'And can you?' He asks it as a question, but I don't know if he expects an answer.

'Well, I dunno…' I really don't know what to say.

'Why d'you even hang around with that girl? She's such a little slut.'

There's no point in responding to that. It's just going to turn into an argument. 'She's not a *slut*, she's my friend.' I couldn't help myself.

'Which means she can't be a slut, no? Because she's your friend, she can't be a slut? – Makes sense. I proper don't trust that girl, y'know. Dirty little slag.'

'Well, you're not going out with her, are you?' That came out wrong – way too harsh. His eyes dart towards me with a scowl. I hesitate to measure my words. '…Sorry – I mean – you're going

1

out with me. So… It doesn't matter what she's like, does it?' I try to break a little smile and diffuse the atmosphere.

'So – you gonna go out with her, then?' He acts like he doesn't care about the answer, as his eyes slump back up to the ceiling above the bed.

'Dunno yet. Not sure where she wants to go.'

'Oh, you going *out* out? Like, to a club?' His eyes come back down to me, lying next to him.

He's got a problem with me going out, like I'm going to cheat on him at the first opportunity of speaking to another boy. As if I ever go out, anyway. 'Nah, probably not. I'd rather stay in, I'm kinda tired.' I cuddle up to him and put my head on his chest.

'Well, don't let me stop you. If you wanna go out, then go.' He picks up his phone from the side, angling his body away from me. I'm sure he's not texting anyone. I haven't seen it go off.

'Who you texting?' I try to ask in a shy, non-accusing tone – more like curiosity.

He tosses his phone – face down – on his chest of drawers, by his side of the bed. 'Who's going tonight, then? Just the two of you?' He finally brings his attention back to me.

'Yeah, probably. I might just go to hers… *If* I go out at all.' My phone has started vibrating under me. Please don't let it be her. I dig it out. *Nancy* flashes hysterically through my phone. Of course, it had to be her. I tuck it back under my leg.

'Why ain't you answering?'

'Nah, it's fine. She'll just want a general chat, and I don't like being anti-social. She could be talking for hours. I'll ring her on my way home.' It's best to just brush off any conversation about Nance at this point.

'So – you're not staying here tonight, no?'

My phone is still humming under my leg, rattling the entire bed. 'Yeah, I can do – if you want…?' I speak through the purring of the mattress.

One missed call.

'Nah, it's cool. Forget it.' He shuts down the conversation as quickly as it started. I can tell he's annoyed. He's turned his body away from me, lying on his side. I've got a wall to my right and his back to my left – less room than I had a minute ago, which wasn't a lot. It's only a single bed.

'James!' His mum calls from downstairs.
'What?'
'Are you two in for dinner?' Her voice is muffled through the door and thick beige carpet. He looks at me, waiting for me to shout down my answer.
'I better not. D'you mind?' I whisper gently for approval.
He doesn't answer me. Just looks to the Scarface poster on his door and shouts through it. 'Nah!' His voice rattles the room. 'Why say you're gonna stay, then? You obviously weren't gonna in the first place. Don't say you will, when you've blatantly got no intentions of staying here.' He talks with his hands, flapping them around with each word.
Two missed calls.

I didn't say anything about staying at his tonight. I've been here for the last few days already, so I should leave at some point. I want to go home and check on mum. 'I never said I was going out. I wanna stay in with you, but – ' My phone is still vibrating.
Four missed calls.

'Nah, go on. Go out with your little *hoe* friend. Both of you go out and suck some dick together.'
'I wasn't even gonna meet – ' I react too late. He's already standing up, leaving me lying on the bed. He grabs his laptop and – before it's even open – he puts his headphones in. I shuffle down to sit at the bottom end of the bed, looking up at him. He throws himself down next to me and opens his laptop – supporting it on his knees, so I'm left sitting at his feet. I stay looking at him, waiting and trying to catch his eye. He lights up his phone and looks back at the laptop. His eyes haven't lifted to me yet.
I take the hint.

3

I get up and slip my UGGs on, tucking my grey tracksuit bottoms inside. I sigh over him, loud enough so he can hear that I actually do want to stay.

Well – I *did* want to stay.

I grab my puffer jacket body-warmer from the floor and slip it on over my hoodie, digging my hood from under my hair.

'Bye, then?'

No reply.

'Text me later?'

Nothing.

I turn around and follow the carpet to the stairs. I can feel his eyes digging into me as I walk away, as if he's finally pulled them away from the screen.

I pass his mum at the bottom of the stairs and swallow hard, making my voice as normal as I can. 'Bye, Sue. I'm gonna head off.' I try not to look straight at her, as she walks from the living room into the kitchen. Hopefully, she hasn't heard him saying all that. I don't want her to think I'm a slut or that I'd ever cheat on him. I just go straight for the door.

'Oh, you off? Bye, love.' She didn't notice my voice shaking. I can hear the concrete patting of the rain before I even open the front door – over Sue knocking cutlery in the kitchen.

Dinner smells nice. The Hollyoaks theme song is playing from the darkened living room next to me, and the flashes of the telly are lighting up the entire room. If it's just starting, I know it has to be about half past six. I missed it again this week. James doesn't watch it, so I can't watch it here. Sometimes, I'll sit downstairs with his mum and we'll watch all the soaps together, while James is upstairs playing some football game on Xbox. No idea which one, but it gets him worked up. I might try to catch a few episodes online, but I'm really far behind.

It's so warm in here. It's not a big flat, so the cooking seems to heat up the whole place. It's so annoying that I have to walk home through this rain. I didn't even do anything wrong. As soon as she texted me, I knew it would cause an argument.

I was replying to my friend. I didn't message her first – I make an effort not to when I'm around him. It's not my fault she texted me. And I can't exactly blank her.

Luckily, I don't live that far away; only a ten-minute walk down Woolwich Church Street. It's a really miserable walk in this weather, so sometimes I'll go along the river at the top end. It's not that far, just at the bottom of Woolwich High Street. It takes a bit longer to go that way, but it beats walking through his estate. It's safer – and, generally, nicer of a walk. It means going onto the main road and over the roundabout. There's a staircase at the top of the road you can climb, with a few benches at the top. I've always liked the way you can see the other side of London from there. It seems so far away, but you can see Canary Wharf and the City across the Thames.

You have to look over hundreds, maybe thousands of people – all crammed into tower blocks. Grey filing cabinets of people, piercing through the clouds. You have to look past all their lives to see the bright lights of the City.

There's more money in one of those offices than in an entire neglected tower block on the way.

And each one of those office-types has more space at their desk than a whole family has to live in – more space in the office lift than a family has to eat their dinner.

It's a different lifestyle over there compared to south-of-the-river. I prefer it here. People are genuine. No snobs on this side. Not yet, anyway.

They'll probably make their way over here at some point – from their poncey new-builds in the City; as soon as they realise they can't afford the rent in their luxury studios. They'll come over, the first independent coffee shop will open up, and they'll all suddenly think it's cool to live in a tower block with no working lift.

It is cool. Especially when mummy and daddy can move you back to your four-bedroom, semi-detached in Surrey at any point.
'Now, remember Oscar – if you see any unsavoury characters – your father and I will drive straight down and collect you.'
Lucky you.

I tend to stick to what I know around here. I only really go over the river for the West End and shops. Maybe the very occasional girls' night out, but that hasn't happened for months. I usually only go out for a birthday or an event, just so I can say I showed my face. It's better now we've got Westfield in Stratford that opened this year. I don't need to go far for shopping. Just get the DLR to Canning Town and change for the Jubilee Line.
The only annoying thing is – there's always the chance I might bump into someone from college. Everyone usually goes to the Food Court down there because Westfield is the only thing in the area.
I'm sure they only built that for the London 2012 Olympics next year. Very convenient timing to open it. It wasn't built for us. The whole world is coming to East London – need to make sure they have something to see.

Even though it's massive, I still manage to bump into someone I'd spoken to once or twice in my life.
Usually a boy.
Usually when I'm with James.
Not ideal.
At least, down the West End, I don't have to worry about that. You couldn't walk past the same person twice. Everyone's just another face down there, you forget them straight away. And they're so wrapped up in themselves, they don't notice you either. Until they barge into you without apologising and turn around to see Nancy giving them an earful of abuse. They'll quickly notice that.

Everyone gets lost in a sea of clones; thinking they're individual while wearing the same clothes, with the same hair, and the same make-up. The worst is around Oxford Circus. They've got some decent stuff around there – overpriced, but nice. I avoid it. The girls down there love themselves. They're the kind of girls who scream when they meet each other at Oxford Circus Station because they haven't seen each other *'since, like… Forever!'*. Then, they'll talk at each other – about themselves – in their own reflection of each other's oversized sunglasses. None of them listening; just hearing and waiting for their turn to talk.

I'd like to get over to Winter Wonderland down there at some point – I'll go with James a bit nearer to Christmas. I still have to decide what I'm going to get him. He's so hard to buy for. I don't like to ask people what they want for Christmas. It ruins the mystery of it. What's the point in wrapping something, if the person knows what it is? There's nothing better than a big box, nicely wrapped, having no idea what's inside. If you have to ask someone what they want, you don't know them well enough. You should know exactly what they would like. Be able to walk into a shop and know what they would choose. If you have to ask them what they want – or tell them to get it themselves and give them the money for it – what's the point?
No thought.
No mystery.
It's not a gift.
It's just a thing – bought because they felt they had to.
This will be our first Christmas together, so I want to make an effort for him. Even with the little money I'll have.

My hair is going to get ridiculously curly in this rain. I'm going to look like a court judge by the time I get home. And my straighteners are going to pack up soon. They don't heat up as much as they should, so it's basically no different to brushing the curls out.

I look like such a tramp. Hopefully, I won't see anyone I know.
I pull my fur hood over my pony tail and go across the park. Can't
really call it a *'park'*. Parks are meant to be green. This one is
grey. Now it's raining and it gets dark so early, it's trapped in an
orange glow from the streetlights. I never understood why some
streetlights are yellow and some are orange; orange ones are
scarier – the dark light feels like a Crimewatch Reconstruction.

My toes wriggle in the cold as my UGGs start to soak through.
Luckily, I'm wearing my thick, fluffy socks. My feet are slapping
on wet paving stones and the echo is bouncing from James' place
behind me.
Wonder what he's doing now... He'll probably go and sort himself
out – I've seen his internet search history. Plus, he gets those pop-
ups that he always denies. I don't like the idea of him going on
those websites, but it's better than him going out and looking for
sex with another girl.
Or he'll probably be messaging that bitch ex-girlfriend of his. I
don't know how he can call Nancy a slut, when his ex gave him
head in the park... Before they were even going out.
But Nancy's the slut?
Sure.
I wouldn't say that to him, though. He gets annoyed when she's
brought up in conversation, even though I'm sure he still speaks to
her. I tried to stalk her on Facebook, but it looks like she's already
blocked me.
Clearly, she knows about me.
Nancy stalked her for me through her profile, but she's got it set to
'private'.
Selfish bitch.
Why can't you have a public profile and let me obsess over you
and compare myself to you and get annoyed that you exist?

My eyes are drawn to the glow of my phone through my grey tracksuit bottoms. I live in these at the moment – they're so comfortable.

I'd better ring Nance back. Six missed calls and two texts.

My read receipts are on – so she'll know I haven't seen them yet, and I'm not just ignoring her. I'd love to turn them off, but I can't deal with having to explain why to James and the headache it would cause.

The phone lights up my whole face under my hood. The wallpaper is a picture of me and James after our first proper date. It's so bright, I can't see anything but the screen in the dark. Feels like I'm blinded to everything but the old picture of me and him.

I dial Nancy, and she answers after barely one ring. 'Alright, babes? One sec – let me ring you back. I got minutes…' She hangs up straight away.

Couldn't have been that important.

Think I'll go straight to hers.

2. NANCY'S

Nancy's is identical to mine.
And James'.
And every other place around here.
Even our rooms are similar.
Hers is a dark purple – same as mine.
Chest of drawers by the bed – broken top drawer, doesn't close fully.
Mirrored wardrobe with sliding doors – I had mine before her.
Single bed – pushed right into the corner, just under the window; a load of fluffy toys at the foot of it.

By her bed, she's got a load of photos on the wall from her seventeenth birthday and some of the other girls' birthdays. There are only a few photos from mine because I had to leave early. It was only a couple of months ago, so I remember it well.
I was staying at James' that night. He was leaving his mates after half past twelve, so I met him at the bus stop on the way home.
Me and the girls decided to go to a club in Plumstead. Obviously, we would have trouble getting in because we're all underage.
I got away with borrowing someone's ID from the year above.
Nance just changed the date on hers with a biro. So blatant. I doubt she would get asked for ID, anyway. She looks a lot older.
Plus, the bouncers would probably be too busy looking down her top to notice her ID.
The rest of the girls usually borrow their other friends' IDs and swap around with each other, so they had no problems.

We must've looked ridiculous when we gave them our little collection of passports and green provisional driving licences. It was a tense moment as we all looked up at the security guys, with our completely mismatched faces. Luckily, we got away with it. No idea how.

Nance was saying we should go to some club in Dagenham, but it would've been the same one she went to for her birthday. Plus, I had to get back early for James – so I wanted to stay local. And it's a mission to get back from Dagenham. A cab back from there would be well expensive – probably more than the whole night out. I wouldn't want any of us to be the last one in the cab with some random driver, so better to keep it local.

It was a good night. I wore this beautiful dress – white, with subtle diamantes flowing up the side of it. I saw it about four months before, on a stick-thin mannequin in Westfield. Every time I went in, I tried it on. I had to.

I was so happy when I got it. It was seventy pounds. A lot of my money went on it. It was worth it because it could be my *'going out'* dress. I don't usually wear things that flashy; I prefer dressing in dark colours and slipping into the background, so it was a big change for me.

The girls loved it. Still... Seventy quid is so dear. They didn't do student discount either, which was annoying. I was really scared because I put fake tan on the day before, and I was worried it'd go all over the dress. It had one strap on the right shoulder; the diamantes started from there and wrapped around the whole body, going down the front to my left thigh. Nicely covered my little pot-belly, but it did make my legs look pretty big. It was such a nice dress – so who cares?

Managed to get the last size ten... And fit in it. I thought I'd be at least a size twelve because it was proper fitted.

James was acting funny with me when I met him. I did make an effort that night – only because it was *my* seventeenth. I wanted to look nice, so I could feel good and comfortable in myself. That was the only reason for it. It wasn't for anyone else.

I straightened my hair and side-parted it – just dyed it back to chocolate brown.

I got my nails done with mum – went for a blood red to match my lipstick.

I took a bit of time to do my eyes – they're light blue, and James likes it when I've got heavy eye shadow around them with mascara, looking smoky and dark.

I was a nice, healthy colour – the fake tan was a couple of days old, so I didn't look like a bright orange podge running around London, and it wasn't all streaky or blotchy on my hands.

I had my Links of London bracelet that the girls got me, with a cute bear charm attached to it.

I felt good.

On the way home, out of the blue, he went mad – literally, from nowhere. It was all over one stupid photo, completely out of context. Nance tagged me in a picture while we were out. I was barely even tipsy. I'd had about three vodka lemonades, maybe one was a double. She got someone to take a photo of us on the dance floor. I was leaning in to get into the picture, and Nance had her hand on her hip, pouting at the camera. She had her bum pushed out one way and her boobs out the other. She knows exactly how to take a photo. She loves the camera and the camera loves her. And she knows it. Bitch.

There was a guy standing behind me, who I hadn't even noticed. I'm not a hypocrite. I know, if I saw a picture of James on Facebook – dancing with another girl on a night out – I'd be annoyed. But this guy, who I wouldn't go for even if I was single, was dancing with the girl behind me. I had heels on, so you couldn't really see her in the photo because I was eclipsing half of the club with my big head. You could just see a bit of her hand and the top of her beehive hairstyle. I think she was his girlfriend, actually. I thought he was gay, so who knows?

12

They were definitely together. I knew that much.

Still, I wasn't even facing this guy. It didn't look like I was grinding on him either, which James might've thought. He doesn't let me speak to boys when I'm out, which is fair enough. But I didn't even notice this guy all night. He wasn't even that nice looking. He was too much of a pretty-boy; clean-shaven, had his hair short at the back and sides, the top was combed over. Everyone seems to look like that, nowadays. Looked like he'd spent more time getting ready than I did. Instant turn-off.

James was acting strange when we met at the bus stop, before he even mentioned the photo. He didn't ask how my night was or anything, so I knew something was wrong.

We'd been messaging each other all night and Nance tagged me at the event on Facebook, so he knew I wasn't lying about where I was. I don't know what else I could've done. I didn't see what the issue was. I might've been a bit blunt when I asked him what was wrong, just because I'd had a good time and left my own night early to go and stay at his.

Then, he started going mad at me in the middle of the street.

'Fucking little whore.'

'Dirty, cheating slag.'

'This is why I don't trust you.'

I was trying to get through to him – *'why would I need to speak to other boys when I'm with you?'* and *'I only wanna be with you'* – but he wasn't having any of it.

He was having a go at me in the street for over an hour. I'd told Nance I'd let her know when I was home safe, so she kept ringing me to see if I was alright. That was making him more suspicious, as if the two of us were hiding something and she was ringing me to get a story straight.

We made up afterwards and I said I was sorry; that he knows I would never cheat on him and I'm not like his ex – I wouldn't do that to him.

I must've looked a complete mess after. All my eye make-up was smudged and had run down my face. Some of it got on the strap of my dress, which didn't come out in the wash.

Won't be wearing that again.

To be fair, it wasn't his fault. I shouldn't have been so dramatic.

Nancy's sitting on the bed, smiling into her phone. She's not dressed to go out, which is a big relief because I look so trampy. And I'm not in the mood to go out and justify myself for a whole night. The worst is when we've had an argument, then I go for a night out. That's when he'll start wondering if I've done anything to get back at him… Like that would even occur to me. Then, that obviously leads to another argument.

At least I've avoided that tonight.

'Alright? What you been up to? Oh my God – did I tell you about your mate, Shaun? This boy's proper on me. You remember? The one we met in Westfields that time…? From your college? He keeps asking me if I wanna come his tonight and *'watch a film'*. I knocked him back, though – for my *guuurl*.' She shoves her phone into her bra. You can see the bright pink lace poking over her white top. It's not that low cut, but I wouldn't wear it. I like her jeans, though.

'No, don't be silly. Go see him if you want.' I'm not sure they're a good match, but that's none of my business. He's a bit of a drip. And she's, well… Nancy.

'Nah, forget him. Do you wanna go out tomorrow, by the way? The girls was talking about meeting down Central and going for a meal.' She pulls her phone out, taps it quickly with an abrupt reply, then throws it on the side – face up.

'I've got no money.' That's a bit of a lie. I just can't afford to be spending money on rubbish this close to Christmas.

'We ain't gotta order a full-blown steak dinner. Just come. It'll be a nice day out.' She takes a break for air. 'Actually, let's go

14

Stratford. Just me and you. Central is a mission to get back from, and I haven't seen you in ages. We can knit off the others.'

'Yeah, go on then.' I guess I could. Stratford is much easier to get to. And it beats sitting in all day watching daytime telly.

Nancy's mum has ordered a Chinese takeaway for us. She's so lovely. She's started seeing a guy who she met at the Job Centre. She seems to really like him. And she's always talking about him when I come over. Good for her. I think they're starting to get serious, now.

Even though she met him at the Job Centre, she's not a scrounger. She's worked for her whole life, even after Nancy's dad left; basically raised Nance – and me – on her own. She used to be a hairdresser, but the shop she worked at had to let her go. They got rid of a few people there because of that recession stuff a few years back. She still does my hair and she's really good.

Good luck to her. She deserves a nice guy.

When we finish our dinner, the two of us get ready for bed. I get changed into a pair of Nancy's pyjamas and settle in for the night. The two of us squeeze into the single bed, barely able to fit after we finish the takeaway.

Nursing my chow mein food-baby, I plan my day in my head. If I leave here tomorrow before eleven o'clock, that'll give me time to go home, wash my hair, get changed, and come back to hers.

There's a tiny draught coming from just under the blinds and it's catching me right on the nose. Nance is spooning me tightly, warming my whole body. The occasional car at the window is making the shadows in the room swing from left to right.

As the gnarled shapes claw up around me in the orange glow, my phone vibrates on the side.

A text from James.

3. FOOD COURT - WESTFIELD, STRATFORD CITY

'When do you come on?'

'Huh?' I'm sure I heard her right.

'When do you come on this month? The third or fourth?' We both start our periods at roughly the same time of the month, so she uses me as a measure of when she should start. She's reminded me that I was due on last week.

I'm a few days late, then.

Four.

Five.

Six.

A week?

Fuck.

'Erm, I came on last week… The fourth.' I will have to check this when I get home. I don't want to panic myself if I don't have to.

I light up my phone.

No texts.

'Ah, that's good. We got lucky. I was worried we'd be on for New Year's. *Hello 2012! – Year of the Bloodhound!*' She raises her voice with each word. This isn't the kind of conversation a lot of people would have in the Food Court.

That's Nancy.

I count the dates in my head.
Third.
Fourth.
Fifth.
What's the date today? Eleventh of December. So, I'm about a week late. More than that, actually. Fuck. How did I miss this?

'Imagine that – New Year's Eve with a fucking tampon in. Running round London with a string hanging out of me. Someone might try and ring my vag at midnight, like it's Big Ben.' She lifts her legs above the table, spreads her knees as far as they stretch in her skinny jeans, then pulls an imaginary string hanging between her legs. 'Ding! Dong!'

'You're *so* grim!' I can't help laughing out loud and spit my KFC into a tissue. My head swells up over my body.
This is why James doesn't like her – because she says things like that. She's funny, though. I don't see how this makes her a slag. She's only slept with one boy, and she was in a relationship with him for a year and a half. They met in Year Ten, so she was about fifteen. That's quite late for a first boyfriend, compared to a lot of other girls. And it was *him* who cheated on *her* – so she got rid of him. I think he's moved out of the area now because we haven't seen him for ages. He was a prick. He was James' friend, which put me in a really awkward position with James and Nancy. That's what annoys me, though. James' ex cheats on him and she's a *'fucking slag'*, *'hope she dies'*, *'ugly whore'*, and all that. But when Nancy's ex cheated on her, it was alright. Because apparently, he *'wasn't getting sex off her, so obviously he's gonna get it somewhere else'*.
Really? That's an excuse to cheat? And he told James *'if Nance wasn't getting it off him, she must've been getting fucked by someone else'*. Not sure how you reach that conclusion, but at least he's out of her life now.
She seems happier, and that's all I care about.

That mentality sums it up. It's ridiculous because a boy wouldn't think twice about sleeping with a *'slag'*, would he? James went out with one for two months before me. She wasn't a slag when he was buying her Me to You Bears and jewellery from Argos, was she?
Bitch.

I check my phone.
No texts.

I count more days in my head.
Five.
Six.
Seven.
Definitely over a week late.
It should be alright. I'll wait for a few more days and see. I don't want to think about it now. We're being careful, anyway. I was thinking of going on the pill, but I've heard it makes you put on a lot of weight. And it's not good to stay on it for too long because of the hormones.
I can't afford to start putting on weight.
Apparently, there's a coil you can put up there as contraception. No way. Not for me, thanks. I don't even like putting tampons up there, never mind a whole Slinky. We tried to use condoms at the beginning, but James said they weren't comfortable and you can't really feel anything when they're on. He always said they were too tight and he would never stay up if he had one on.
Now, he just pulls out and finishes on the sheet or my stomach. We make sure nothing goes in, though. And I'll usually run to the toilet after and rub myself with a tissue, just to make sure nothing goes in.
So, we *should* be alright.
I'll try not to think about it until I have to.

I check my phone, again.

Lipgloss

No texts.

'Oh, yeah…' Her mouth is full of chicken salsa. 'Remind me…'
She chews through her words. 'Before we go, I wanna get more
foundation.' She swallows and wipes her greasy hands on her
jeans; still talking with a lump of mayonnaise on her lip, right in
the corner of her mouth. I tell her about it and she asks me to take
a photo of her licking at it. We both collapse over the table with
laughter. Her eyes are looking at the camera – trying to be
seductive – and her tongue is reaching for the mayonnaise. 'Does
it look like I just gave head?'

'You dirty bitch!' I go to wipe my hands on a sanitary wipe, but
it's hardened and dry from where I've been tearing at it. The
disinfectant smell of lemon has seeped into my fingers. I didn't
even realise I'd been fiddling with it. 'Is that from Shaun, yeah?' I
try to occupy my mind.

'Don't be stupid! I wouldn't go for that! What time's James
meant to be meeting you, by the way?' She starts brushing the last
minerals of foundation all over her face. She twists her mouth
from left to right, covering every patch of natural skin. It's caked
on heavily and chalky. It's still powdery from where she's applied
it so thick and not blended properly. She pouts at me through it,
and it crumbles in a tiny, orange avalanche off her chin. 'Do I look
like I'm from *Essiiix*?'

'I dunno. He said three, but he ain't text me yet.' My eyes go
towards my lock screen photo of me and James. My sanitary wipe
is in pieces under my fingers, my hands still nervously fiddling
with each section.

'Serious? You know it's half four now? Fuck him. Come, let's
go Boots.' She picks up her bag and leaves her tray on the table,
all her rubbish chaotically scattered around it. I go to pick mine up
and throw it in the bin, but she takes it off me. 'Eurgh, babes!
Leave that, let them clear it up. It ain't your job.' She takes my
hand.
Fair enough.

I love her bag. It's from Ted Baker – red, with gold trim. She's wearing a thick, dark purple, knitted jumper that hangs off one shoulder, exposing her red bra strap.

She looks really nice. I wish I had the confidence to wear that kind of stuff, but she's got a much nicer figure than me. She's curvy – with big hips, a big bum, and big boobs.

I'm *that* girl; the girl with small boobs who still manages to get rolls of fat.

I've got a big bum, but it's not a *nice* big.

Just a *fat* big.

I've got an average body.

Not small enough to be petite. Not big enough to be curvy.

I'm like a piece of lard wrapped in a lettuce leaf.

Don't quite fit anywhere on the shelf.

I bet I'm warmer than her, though. I'm wearing a pair of old skinny jeans and one of James' hoodies. I've only got a bit of lip gloss on and some eyeliner. Got a couple of spots coming through, so I had to smother them in concealer – which I need to get more of.

If I've got the money.

Which I don't.

I check my phone as we get up.

No texts.

We make our way past thousands of mindless, robotic shoppers – who walk way too slow for my liking. I dodge past them as I hold my phone up, shouting after Nancy. 'Have you got signal in here?' He should've texted me by now. It's after half past four. I hope he's alright. I tried to ring him earlier, but there was no answer. Then, when I rang back, it went straight to voicemail. I thought it might have been him returning my call and we both rang at the same time. That does happen, sometimes. But when I tried again a few minutes later, it went to voicemail – as if it was turned off.

His phone probably died.

Hope he'll know where to find me.

'Yeah, I think so. Come, I need more foundation.' She links my arm and we walk together past all the shops.

It's packed in here. Everyone's doing their Christmas shopping. I've left it really late this year. I haven't got anything for anyone, mainly because I haven't had the money. They reckon there'll be loads of new jobs next year with the Olympics coming in, so I'll hand out some CVs around here after Christmas – maybe apply to some clothes shops and I can get staff discount… Not that I've had any luck with that in the past.

No doubt they'll all want ten years' experience and a degree in folding jumpers from Oxford University.

'And why would you like to work here?'

'Because I'm friendly and enthusiastic and I have a passion for clothes and I'm a hard worker and I'd like to build on my current skills set and I'm a good team player and I can work independently. Oh… And I need money.'

'And do you have experience?'

'Yeah, I don't have experience because I'm seventeen. I was kinda hoping you could help give me experience…'

'Nah, sorry. You need experience to get the experience.'

'And how do I get that?'

'Sorry. Due to the high number of applicants, we cannot provide individual feedback. In fact, you'll be lucky if you even get a rejection email after you spent two hours applying online.'

I hate everyone.

A voice sneaks over my shoulder. 'Don't you answer your phone, no?' James appears silently from behind us.

I turn around quickly and unlink Nancy's arm. 'Oh, hiya! I didn't get anything?' I pull out my phone and hit the code to unlock it.

8524.
I don't bother to shield it from him. He knows it, anyway. We know each other's lock codes and social media passwords.

Open WhatsApp.
No texts.

'Here, look. Nothing's come through. Did you text me?' I hold the phone out to him. 'I was just saying to Nancy that I don't have signal in here.'

'Where you going now?' He doesn't acknowledge what I say. Nancy's standing next to me with her phone out, gazing blankly into it. They haven't acknowledged each other yet. She makes no secret of it – she doesn't like him.
And he definitely doesn't like her.

'We were just gonna pop into Boots and get make-up.' I smile at Nancy, trying to bring her into the conversation.
She keeps her distance.

'Yeah – I was about to say – you're a bit dolled-up for Westfields.' He studies over me.

'Am I? I feel trampy. I'm having an ugly day.' Dolled up? Is he serious? I look like a tramp. The only nice thing I'm wearing is a pair of white Converse. Nancy is matching. Hers are cleaner than mine, but I quite like them being a bit grubby.

'Why you got so much make-up on?'

'Do I? I've only got a bit of concealer because I'm proper spotty today.' He can't have anything against that... I keep looking to Nancy to interrupt us. She's getting impatient, staring up at the floors above us and sighing – loudly.

James' eyes scan the rest of my face. 'And eye liner. And lipstick. And – '

'Come, babes. Let's go.' Nance shoves her phone into her bra, grabs my elbow, and marches me away. 'Is he fucking serious? He don't even say *'hello'* to you? And he's two hours late? Fucking waste of space.' Her voice is agitated and eats itself as the words come out too fast for her mouth.

I look behind as she drags me away. James is trailing with his head buried in his phone.
Who is he talking to?
I unlink Nancy and wait for him to catch up, still holding Nancy's hand tight.
I put my hand out for him to take it.

Nancy walks off.

4. LOBBY - WESTFIELD, STRATFORD CITY

This is awkward.

We're walking towards Boots. James has got his right arm over me, wrapped tightly around my neck. I'm tucked under his armpit, with my left arm around his waist. He's walking me into Boots. Nancy's strutting a couple of feet next to me. I peer over James' arm and call to her. 'You just getting foundation, Nance?'

'Yeah.' She answers quickly, barely acknowledging what I've asked her. She doesn't even look at me.

'I'm gonna wait out here. Don't be all day.' James has finally loosened his hold on me.

Nance looks over straight away and gets ready to unload on him. 'Are you fucking ser – ?'

'Come, Nance.' I grab her quickly and link her arm, pushing her through the next wave of shoppers. I could tell she was ready to go mad at him, but I don't need this. Not today.

James shout after me. 'Get yourself something in there for Christmas and I'll get mum to give you the money for it.' His voice chases me through a thick forest of legs and shopping bags, sitting on the floor and slumped against the wall of the escalator. His elbows are resting on his bent knees and his head is buried in his phone.

First Christmas together – I thought he would've made an effort.

24

Unless he hasn't got the money or he's already got me something else. I'll give him the benefit of the doubt. Nancy is a few paces in front of me. It's good she didn't hear him say that – or she'd give me another lecture about him.

I catch up with her at the entrance to Boots. She leads me straight to the perfumes and we try some of the testers.
Tommy.
Daisy.
Jean Paul Gaultier.
They smell beautiful and we smother ourselves in them. You're supposed to spray them onto a little stick and smell them, but where's the fun in that?
No harm in getting a free dose while we're here.
'What foundation you gonna get?' I'm not really asking, just trying to rush her out.
'I dunno. I wanna try a new one and go a bit darker.' She examines herself in the cold, metal reflection of the display case. She's always a really nice colour and it blends well with her hair. It's a similar colour to mine – the chocolate brown shade. It's not much different from her natural colour, but she just dyed it back from red.
We straightened each other's hair before we came out today. My straighteners officially packed up today and she's got GHDs, so I'll be living at hers for the rest of my life.

'Nance, I'm gonna check out the Meal Deal.' I prepare to walk away, out of her sight.
'Fat bitch! We just ate!' She shoves her hands under her top and puffs it out. 'You're gonna have a little *food-baby*.'
Good choice of words, Nancy.
I cough out a little, unconvincing laugh.
She seems to have cheered up, now James isn't around.
'Nah, I might just get chewing gum. My breath stinks of chicken.' Quick comeback – considering I haven't rehearsed this.

'Wait a sec…' She rummages through her bag, clanking through glass and metal products as she digs to the bottom. 'I've got some here.' She holds a small packet out to me. The foil is scrunched and rips as she eases a chewing gum out.

'Nah – honestly, it's fine. I'll go buy some.' I turn away before she has the chance to say anything else.

I walk along the middle of the shop and head for the Pharmacy. My eyes dart around me, making sure I don't recognise any of the flushed, worn-out, winter faces.
I walk past the counter, trying to psych myself up to speak to the pharmacist.
What do I even say?
I pace.
Do I have to speak to someone?
I pass, again.
Can't I get something over-the-counter?
I walk by again, picking up a bottle of water.
Why did I do that?
I fiddle with a promotional display by the counter, sticking my finger under the card.
The price falls off the display shelf.

As I bend to pick it up, I see the shoes of a sales assistant coming towards me. 'Can I help you, miss?' An unfamiliar voice from above me.

'No, I'm okay. Thank you.' I don't look up – scrambling on the floor, trying not to make a scene.
Fuck it. Let's just do it quickly.
I wait for the sales assistant to turn around before I head back into the aisles, constantly dipping and diving from wherever I guess Nancy is. I pick up the first pregnancy test I see and bring it to the till.
All the self-checkout stands are in use.
My eyes draw a line to the first available cashier and I don't dare stray from it.

I take the box – and the bottle of water I don't need – down my imaginary line; while the eyes of a thousand strangers judge me. They all know I'm not thirsty and they all know what I'm buying.

Hi.
Hi.
Anything else?
No.
Loyalty card?
No.
Want a bag?
No.
Insert card.
Enter PIN.
8524.
Accepted.
Remove card.
Receipt?
Definitely not.

5. DLR, WOOLWICH ARSENAL via CANNING TOWN

We were lucky today – we were able to get the DLR quite quickly and didn't have to wait.

Stratford is looking so much better. I can see they're finally starting to make use of the space around there. It was a wasteland before Westfield got there. The name confuses me a bit. I don't know why they've called it '*West*-field' if it's in East London. They should've called it '*East*-field', so they could compete with the one in Shepherd's Bush.

I'm sitting between James and Nancy on the train. I feel like a referee between these two; either one of them could go mad at any point. The train is pretty empty. There's a million miles between the two of them and it's full of egg shells – which I get to tread on the whole way home. Not sure if I should make it more awkward by saying something or leave the uncomfortable silence as it is. They haven't said a word to each other the whole day.

We are sitting right at the front of the train, on the seats facing forward. Nancy sat down first, then I sat next to her. James gave me a look, as if I shouldn't have sat there because there was no space for him. He had to sit on the other side of the aisle. I've got a feeling I'll hear about this in an argument later.

The three of us are facing the front window. I like to sit at the front on the DLR. It's always strange sitting here because there's no driver – the front window looks right onto the tracks ahead, and the train is automatic and driverless. It feels like I'm in control when I sit here. I could take this train wherever I want to go. I still don't know how it actually drives. Not sure if I want to – I like the mystery of it.

The train is travelling towards our reflections in the window, never quite catching up with them. It's so dark outside and light in here, all we can see is ourselves ahead of the train. Every so often, I catch Nancy scowling at James in the window. I put my hand on her knee to try to calm her down, but she doesn't take her eyes off his reflection. She wants to say something to him – I can tell. I hope she doesn't. I don't need more drama. Not today.

I get my phone out to check the time. Across the aisle, James looks over my shoulder when he sees it light up.

Nearly six o'clock, so I should be home for about half past six. Should really stay at mine tonight – I haven't been home properly for a few days. And no matter whose house I go to after this, I'm going to upset someone. I'd rather avoid all that.

I'm using the reflection in the window opposite to keep an eye on both of them.

This is uncomfortable. No one has said a word since Stratford.

We're gliding over a lot of neglected parts of London in the darkness.

The London that no one wants to think about.

The London that isn't on the postcards in tourist shops.

The London that isn't on the adverts for the Olympics.

The London that nobody wants to go to.

The people who don't exist.

I sense I've suddenly got a lot more space around me. My eyes focus back on the reflection, noticing James has shifted to the empty window seat further from me, away from the aisle. Don't know why.

Nance is still sitting stiff on my right. Her hands are linked in front of her and her eyes are fixed on the window, staring right through the glass to James and trying to shatter his reflection. His reflection has taken his headphones out of his pocket and put them in. He's leaning away from me with his headphones in, staring out.

I'm confused. What's he so annoyed at?

I place my hand back on Nancy's leg. Her jeans are skin-tight on her thighs and I can feel them stiffening up, like she's ready to jump out of her seat and launch through the window to attack the fake image of James.

I twist my right arm up to Nancy's head and lean her on my shoulder. She rests herself on me and closes her eyes, taking a long breath out that she's been holding in since Stratford. She sounds exhausted.

'This stop is: London City Airport.'

The planes are so small. I always notice that when I pass here, but I haven't been down this way for a while.

Do people go on holiday from here? Where's the runway? I would've thought there'd be no space for the planes to take off. It seems to have changed a lot since I was last here – obviously the *'regeneration'* for the Olympics. Make sure when the world comes to East London, they don't see anything real.

The whole skyline has changed so much since I was little – and more so recently.

Buildings coming up from nowhere.

Cranes flying up and disappearing.

Seems to be a lot of wasteland around here and they've finally decided to make use of it.

Nancy twists her whole body and cuddles up to me. Her eyes close and she finally breathes out her tension. She seems indifferent to James' reflection now, which is barely visible. He still has his headphones in, staring into the darkness. He's seen Nance cuddled up to me in the reflection, so turns away more – almost facing the other end of the carriage. He breathes out, hard and angrily.
I really can't be bothered with this.
I hope he's not annoyed at me because of how she's sitting.

'This stop is: King George V.'

Next stop is ours. I cannot wait to get off this train.
I look at my phone again. Five minutes past six.
James' eyes swing back to me when he senses me getting my phone out. I take the time to notice the wallpaper on my phone. Nance must have changed the background picture when we were at the Food Court – from the picture of me and James, to the one of her licking the mayonnaise.

I look over at James.
He looks pissed off.

6. AT MINE

Feels like ages since I've been home. Now, I remember why –
it's colder in here than it is outside. I can't tell if mum is in. She
might be in bed. I should be quiet in case I wake her up. It's only
half past six, though. She shouldn't be in bed this early. I call
around the flat. 'Mum!'
No answer.
The sound of my voice gets lost in the dark.
All I can hear is the clock beating in the hall, broken by the
occasional car going over wet road through the front door behind
me.

I check the living room. It's dark. Just the orange streetlights
piercing through the net curtains. Another car slides past the
window. I tap my hand on the wall, fiddling for the light switch.
Nothing.
The bulb must have gone. It can't be the electricity because the
hall light worked fine.
I use the light from my phone and shine it over the sofa.
I see a bare foot.
Another foot – a slipper dangling from it.
A blanket – rising and falling, slowly.
An arm – the other one is under the blanket.
Mum's face. Her eyes are shut, eyelids loose and wrinkled. She's
breathing deep and slow.
That explains it. Beside her head, on the coffee table.
A bottle. Nearly empty.

I can't make out what's in it, but I can have a guess. There are another few mouthfuls in there, which means she would have been at it for the past few hours. She was still in bed when I came home earlier for a shower, so she's probably got up and started it straight away. We were meant to put the Christmas tree up tonight. She said we could do it together a few days ago. Thought she'd at least stay good for that. The tree is lying in the corner, with a couple of baubles and gold tinsel scattered around it. I'll probably do it later, before I go to bed. No chance of waking her. She'll usually be like this for hours.

The worst was a few months ago. I came home from college with Nance, no later than seven o'clock. It was just before the summer holidays this year, after our last exam. It fell on the same day as my seventeenth, so I had double reason to celebrate. I opened my cards and presents in the morning because I wanted to go straight from the exam to get my dress – the one for my night out. It was our last day of college and the weather was nice, so we went shopping, then to the park for a few drinks with the other girls.

I felt like the exam went well. It was the first part of Health and Social Care B-Tech, and I'd been stressing myself out because I want to work with kids. I'd already had an interview at a nursery in Eltham – they told me I needed to pass that course to get a placement as a nursery assistant with them.

A few weeks later, I heard I'd got it. They sent me a letter saying that I'd been accepted. They're giving me a work experience trial next year.

Absolutely cannot wait to start.

I can get the 161 bus the whole way there. It's a bit of a journey, but it'll be a nice area to work in and a good start to 2012.

We left the girls in the park, and Nance came back to mine with me. Mum said she was going to make a roast dinner for us to celebrate finishing the exams and for my birthday.

Because of that, I'd arranged to go to out for my birthday the day after. It worked out well because it meant we'd have dinner with mum on Thursday and go out on the Friday. No one goes out on a Thursday, anyway; it would've been dead – no matter where we went.

We got to my front door and I couldn't find my keys. There was no answer when I buzzed the doorbell, so I tried to ring mum's mobile. It rang out and went to voicemail.

Nancy could see that I was worried.

We had to go climb over a wall to get onto the concrete slabs of the patio garden. We jumped over the wall to come through the back door into the house. Luckily, it was quite hot that day, so the back door was open. I gave Nance a boost over the wall first. When her feet hit the floor on the other side, I heard her scream. I knew something was wrong straight away. I've never heard her scream like that, and I've known her my whole life. It wasn't a painful scream – it was something worse.

I came over the wall after her and she was standing by the back door. She came running towards me – away from a cloud of smoke coming out of the house behind her. It was starting to get darker and thicken.

God knows how none of the neighbours saw it.

Mum must have left the oven on, and our smoke detectors don't work for some reason. I ran past Nancy and through the open back door – switched the oven off straight away and went looking for mum through the smoke. I followed my feet down the hallway and found her. She was unconscious and slumped over the stairs. Obviously, because I was panicking, I thought she must have passed out from the smoke. I dragged her straight out the front door; it was only about six feet away, but I was running on pure adrenaline. I barely remembered going into the house, let alone how I managed to get her out by myself. It was as if I was watching someone else's life happening in slow motion, but it had all happened in one instant.

34

She was in her dressing gown and slippers – as always – and her hair was greasy and matted. When I got her outside, I was screaming and crying. Nance must have jumped back over the wall or ran through the house after me because she met me at the front door.

I was lifting mum's head up and shaking her body, trying to get a reaction from her. She was limp in my arms and her head flopped back without my support.

Smoke was escaping from the front door as it was beginning to air out.

She started to wake up as I pushed her hair back off her clammy forehead. She was slurring her words and laughing. She must have been drinking and fallen asleep on the stairs while she was cooking.

There was me – thinking she had died from the smoke.

No.

She was just pissed.

Nance started crying when she saw me going mad; walking around in concrete circles in the front garden, pulling my hair out, screaming and crying. She was trying to hug me and calm me down, but I was so pissed off when I saw mum on the floor, laughing at me.

She'd fallen back to sleep, still lying on the doormat.

Happy Birthday.

It's freezing in here. Mum doesn't like to put the heating on because of the high bills. I go over to her and kiss her forehead. It's cold and clammy, sticky with sweat. She shivers as my lips touch her. I pull the blanket just under her chin, tucking both of her arms under it. I turn her onto her side slightly, in case she gets sick during the night.

Her body reacts a little to my touch. She knows I'm here, letting out a deep breath of exhaustion. The smell of alcohol lingers in the air above her – creating a thick, invisible mist over her face and leaving her unrecognisable behind it.

I pull the door, leaving it slightly ajar. A thin strip of light snakes its way into the room, as the blanket rises and falls deeper. 'G'night, mum.'

7. AT MINE cont.

Without any expectation, I think of dinner. I follow the darkness into the kitchen and turn the light on. It flickers on and off, and the electricity surges through it until it finally stays on. It's a long, sterile light – constantly blinking. The kind you would find in a school or a hospital. There's nothing homely about it at all.

There's a sweet smell as if something has been spilt. My socks stick to the off-white tiles of the grimy floor; peeling off as I walk. Feels like the floor hasn't been cleaned since I was last here. I'll have to do that later on, too. Maybe put the tree up tomorrow. The oven is empty. I knew it was a long shot, but I thought something might have been prepared. I texted mum earlier to tell her I'd be in for dinner before seven o'clock.

She obviously hasn't eaten either, then.

I kneel down to the fridge, slotted between the wooden kitchen cabinets and tucked under the battered worktop. It's covered with colourful magnets from friends' holidays. There might be something to cook up in there. The door sticks as I try to open it. The anticipation is killing me.

Milk.

A few slices of wafer-thin ham.

One or two slices of bread – crusts don't count.

Two eggs – expired.

Butter – toast crumbs are dotted around the edges.

Tomatoes – furry.

Cucumber? Random.

I'm not that hungry, really. Might make a ham sandwich before bed. I'm sure there's pickle in the cupboard. I take a plate from the side of the sink – one that I washed a few days ago. Some last drops of water fall off it and rattle the metal draining board. I take one slice of bread and fold it over the ham, making half a sandwich. Mum might want the other slice in the morning. My eyes spot a cereal box by the sink. Breakfast always tastes better for dinner, so I pour myself out a bowl. Let's call it *'dessert'*. The pieces bounce around the bowl and float with the milk added; proper hungry watching the milk turn chocolatey. Need to get upstairs and eat before they go all soggy.
I grab my bag, shoes, plate, and bowl – before hobbling up the stairs. I'm careful not to drop anything and startle mum.
Feel like an old bag-lady going upstairs with all this.
I open my bedroom door with my foot and hold it open with my bum, backing inside and balancing everything carefully. My room is freezing. I cannot wait to get under those covers. My bed has been calling me all day.
I let my shoes drop onto the carpet, place my dinner on the bedside table, then throw my bag on top of the bed.

My bag.
I'd forgotten about that.
Or just tried not to remember.
I rummage quickly to the bottom, dropping receipts and rubbish in my way – then pull out the crushed, unfamiliar box.
I feel myself begin to breathe heavier.
Luckily, even though I picked it up in a blind panic, I got one that tells you early on.

Let's just do this and get it over with. I quickly get changed into my cosy, pink pyjamas and grab the box. I'm suddenly aware of all the childish, innocent, girly things lining my room. All my

fluffy toys are suddenly judging me. Dozens of beady, marble
eyes are fixed on me as I walk out into the hallway.
I feel like mum will wake up at any moment and come upstairs.
I hang over the banister and look down into the darkness.
Silence.
It feels way too quiet, as if someone else is trying to listen out for
me making noise.
Why am I holding my breath? I can hear my heartbeat.
My breathing starts again. It's louder than before. Louder than
breathing should be.

Let's do this as quickly as. I go along the carpet to the
bathroom and lock the door behind me. This suddenly feels like
the smallest room in the world. I'm in a fish bowl, pacing up and
down, constantly trying to chase my last step. Feels like the whole
world is watching me through the frosted glass.
I check the door is definitely locked.
The dull brass rattles loose against the bolt.
Locked.
I pull my pyjamas bottoms down.
Sit on the toilet. Freezing.
The bathroom fan is groaning monotonously above me – loudest
noise in the world right now.
I don't feel like I need to go.
My hands are linked in front of me and I'm leaning forward, ready
to jump up and go straight to bed; and never think about this ever
again. I feel myself picking at the last flakes of nail polish on both
my thumbs. My thighs are red from the imprint of my elbows that
have been leaning on them.

Okay. I think I'm ready.

I fiddle with the box, already broken and ripped at both ends –
battered and slightly damp. My umbrella must have soaked it in
my bag.

Do you just go straight on the end of it?
I skim through the instructions on the back. This one lets you know straight away and it's got the earliest result. It should be able to tell me immediately if I am. And how many weeks on I am.
If I am.
Which I'm probably not.
Hopefully.

I'm ready.

I tilt the box and the stick falls into my hand. The main instructions slide out after it. I don't think I need to read them. I got all the information from the back of the box.
I ease the stick between my legs, between my body and the toilet seat. My hand is crushed under my weight as I lean forward, trying to aim before I start. My hand is cold and soaks with beads of hot sweat, dripping down from below my belly button piercing.
I've started.
I don't know how long I can go for.
I'm going straight into the toilet and blindly try to direct my hand under me, listening out for when the flow inside the toilet is disrupted.
Left.
Back a bit.
I start to panic – not sure how much longer I can go for.
Too far back.
Fingers are wet.
Brilliant.

There.

The flow into the toilet has turned into a pat, bouncing off the stick and echoing around the bowl. How long do you have to go on it for an accurate test?

Is that door definitely locked? My eyes are fixed on the door handle – only a few feet away from me – looking for the slightest movement.
The flow gets weaker, until it's just a gentle trickle in the water.

My stomach is in knots and I'm doubled over with nerves. My head falls between my knees. My wet hand is lifelessly squeezed between my legs and the weight of my limp upper-body. The tip of the stick is trembling and dripping under me.
I don't want to look.
I rest my head on my free hand and stare at the tiles on the floor; noticing patterns I'd never seen, making shapes out of nothing.
The murmur of the fan gets louder, distorting to a growl. It wakes me up from my daydream as quickly as it started.
I've lived my whole life in less than a moment, realising the reality of what this result could mean.
What it could mean for me.
For James.
For mum.
For everyone.
What I'm about to see could change everything.

I suppose I'd better look.

My toes are curling into the damp bath mat beneath my feet.
I shake the test between my legs – feeling my coarse shaved hairs grate against my hand.
I pull the test out and hold it in front of me.

I feel sick. I don't want to look.

8. JAMES'

Mum wasn't in when I left this morning. There was a note on the coffee table in the living room, saying she'd gone to the shop. I don't know if she's gone there to get food or another bottle of drink. I doubt I'll be home tonight, so it doesn't bother me either way. At least at James', I've got a bit of company. He hasn't mentioned my wallpaper of Nancy. I changed it back to the one of me and him before I got here, and I made sure he saw it.
I think everything's alright, now.
Hopefully.
Seems like a nice atmosphere at the moment. I should enjoy it.

'Don't you think it's mad how it gets dark so early?' I'm standing just next to him, leaning on the window ledge, trying to see the sky through the broken metal slits of the blinds.
'What?' He's lying on the bed and his eyes are glazed over, staring through the ceiling.
'Like, remember in summer – five o'clock would be baking hot and proper bright. And now, it's already getting dark.' I lean through the blinds and press my forehead against the cold steam on the window.
The sun sets in the west, so this side of London is the first to be left in the dark.
The sky looks beautiful. Oranges and purples are splashed around the last few clouds of the day. They're leaving a trail of fire – burning across the sky and engulfing the whole of London from

above. The sun is disappearing behind a canvas of tower blocks and cranes, dragging the clouds behind it.
They're all escaping to brighten up another side of the world.

I can barely make out the sunset from his window.
I have to strain my neck to see any kind of light from James'.
Can't see any from my window.
Nancy has the best view of the sun.

'Well, it's obviously because it's winter.' He doesn't look at me.
'Yeah, but it's just crazy how a few months can make so much difference. Like, to the weather, the sky, people's moods...' I push myself away from the window.
'What d'you mean by that?' His eyes shift to me.
'Nah, nothing to do with you.' I scratch the top of his head, running my fingers behind his ear. 'Apparently, people get more depressed in the winter because it's always dark. I heard it's called *SAD... Seasonal – something – Depression*, I think. I saw it online the other day. That name alone is gonna depress you. Imagine a doctor telling you – *'you've got SAD'*.' I throw myself on the bed next to him. I'm in a weirdly good mood, feeling affectionate... And a bit needy. 'What you thinking?' I slump my body on top of him, resting my chin on his chest and rubbing his head.
He brings his eyes down to me.
'I was thinking – nah, don't worry.' He's started smiling. He looks like a little boy, all embarrassed and shy.
'Go *on*, tell me...' I'm genuinely intrigued. He's rarely like this.
'Nah, you'll say no...'
Interesting...
'To what?' My eyes squint.
'We should film ourselves.'
Confused.
'How d'you mean?' I sit up, still on top of him.
'Like... We should film it.' His expression doesn't change.

43

Again.

He kept bringing this up throughout the summer, asking me to send him photos.

I must be so naive. He randomly texted me one night and asked me to send him a picture of myself. I was at home in my pyjamas, so sent him a picture of me sticking my tongue out. I was trying to be playful and cute.

He texted me back, saying *'of your clit'*.

I didn't know what to say. At first, I thought he was joking or that one of his mates had his phone. I just laughed it off.

But he kept saying it; texting me and asking for a picture, and asking why I wouldn't send one. I really didn't want to do it, but I thought – at least if *I* do it – he won't have to text some other slag around here.

In the end, I just sent him one of me in my underwear. I made sure I didn't put my face in it, though. This wasn't even that far into the relationship. God knows what his ex used to do. But if she was the type to send him photos and I didn't, he'd think I was frigid. I thought – at least if he had a picture – it'd keep him happy for a bit. Plus, he said he'd delete it straight away and promised he wouldn't show it to anyone. I would always get nervous when I'd see his phone downstairs when he wasn't with it – even though it's usually glued to his hand and he'll go mad if I even press it to check the time.

But someone could *easily* look through his phone… Or he could lose it. Anything could happen – with a picture of me on there. Imagine if his mum saw it. She would think I'm such a slut. I don't think it's a slutty thing to do. It'd be different if it was just sent to some random guy – but if it's to your boyfriend, surely it doesn't matter… Anything that goes on in your own relationship is no one else's business.

Plus, every girl I know has done it *at least* once. It's just good for when he's in the mood and I'm with Nance or something. He can do what he has to do and get it out of his system. Saves him looking for it somewhere else. I want him to find me sexy. And if that means sending the odd photo, then I guess I've got to. Maybe it'd stop him from looking at porn for a while.

But because I'd sent him a picture in my underwear – matching set; I made an effort – he wanted more… Explicit ones.

'I thought you had them photos from before?' I'd say anything to end this conversation and get this idea out of his head.

'Well, yeah. But it's better to have a video, ain't it?' He grabs my bum and squeezes it. Tight.

'Nah… I look all horrible and fat.' I feel really self-conscious, now. Surely, the reality that it will be *me* on top of him – not some double-D-cup blonde from one of his sites – will put him off…

'Well, just do one of you giving me head.' He doesn't even flinch with his words.

Fucking hell. Is he serious? I can't avoid letting out a gasping, shocked laugh. I don't know whether to be insulted or not.

He stays looking at me – one hand is fiddling with his phone and the other is playing with my hair, tickling the back of my head. As if that will make me change my mind.

His hand is stiff behind my head. It seems relaxed when he's playing with my hair, but I can tell his arm is locked behind it – tensed and stopping me from moving away.

I *really* don't like the idea of doing this. '*No*… It's embarrassing.' I try to say it playfully, so I don't make him feel self-conscious about suggesting it. 'What if someone sees it?'

'Well, how would they?' He answers quickly.

'They could go through your phone?' I answer just as fast.

'…Which is locked.' He looks smug now and his hand has got a bit more forceful, subtly hinting where he wants it to go. His fingers start to wrap in my hair.

45

He puts his phone on his chest – face down. With his free hand, he starts unbuttoning his jeans while he looks down at me. He grabs a handful of my hair and pulls it tight, pushing my head down.

9. CHICKEN SHOP

'Y'know, that's basically rape?'

'Course it's *not*!' I think she's overreacting a bit – probably because she doesn't like him, anyway. She's looking for another reason to hate him.

We're sitting in a chicken shop at the top of the road, waiting for our food.

I stayed at Nancy's last night. I wasn't happy about staying at James' after that. I felt really uncomfortable with it all. He didn't get annoyed that I'd left, he'd got what he wanted by then.

We're both in pyjama bottoms, hoodies, and UGGs. The chicken shop isn't too far away from her house, so there's no point in getting dressed up. She straightens herself in her seat. 'Well, think about it. What's rape?' …Here comes Detective Nancy.

'Like – sexual assault.' I go on quickly. 'When you don't *know* the person, though. Not when you're going out with them. And please, keep your voice down. I don't want the whole world knowing my business.'

'Nah, see! That's wrong. We did it in General Studies, d'you remember? Rape is when the sex ain't… Argh, what's that word? Begins with a *'C'*. It's on the tip of my tongue. *Con* – something?' Her face goes into her hands as she thinks.

'Consensual?' Why did I answer that?

'Yeah, that's it! So, yeah – think about it. If you didn't wanna do it, then it weren't *con-sen-chall*. So, he basically raped you.' She sips her Coke. 'In the mouth.'

I can't help but laugh a bit. *Raped me in the mouth?* Really, Nance? This is all a bit drastic. How can you be raped by your own boyfriend after you choose to have sex with him? God. I wish I'd never told her, now. I just wanted to find out it if she ever did anything like that with her ex – a video or anything.
I know she took photos and sent them to him, but I'm not sure about videos. She still hasn't told me, so it was a waste of time bringing this up.

I feel like I need to defend him. 'Hold on. Firstly, he's my boyfriend. He can't rape me if I went down on him and chose to do it. The fact that I'm going out with him and chose to do it means I'm consenting, doesn't it? It's not rape if I just went down on him and I *chose* to do it.' I emphasise the words.

'Nah – see. That's not true. Imagine he wanted to have sex with you and you didn't wanna, then he started forcing you and being aggressive. That'd be rape. That's basically what happened, but without the aggression. Fact is – you didn't wanna do it. He made you. Plus… It's called oral *sex*, babes. Even if you just gave him head, it's still a *kind* of sex, ain't it?'

That I *chose* to do. Fucking hell. Where'd the lawyer come from? When did she become such an expert?
She's going over-the-top.

Our food comes over the counter and the guy calls us over to collect it. I don't remember what I ordered. I'm not even that hungry, now. The guy made a comment about how we both look lovely and all that rubbish.
Creep. He's about forty. Nancy loved it, but I'm really not in the mood for it.

'I'm gonna go home now, anyway.' I start to gather my stuff around the table.

'What you got the hump for?' She's getting defensive.

'How have I?' I really haven't. I'm fine.

'You do. You're getting a bit snappy. And we said we was gonna eat here.' She sits down and rips open the greasy, brown bag. An avalanche of soggy chips spills out.

'Well, you did just call my boyfriend a rapist in front of the whole shop, so I'm bound to be a bit pissed off. Can we just not have this conversation here, d'you think?' My voice makes itself louder. I'm not being out of order. She's just being a little know-it-all.

'To be fair… You brought it up. I ain't trying to be horrible. I don't like the boy – you know that. But I ain't interested in having a dig at him. I'm just looking out for you.' Her voice eases and calms itself.

'Alright. Well, thanks. But it's fine. Can we just not talk about this now?' I feel bad, but I don't want to talk about this anymore.

'Alright, babes. If you don't wanna.' She breaks a little smile, taking a mouthful of limp chips. 'Oh – by the way – mum is in with her boyfriend tonight. So, d'you wanna go out later? Down Piccadilly?'

10. CHICKEN SHOP cont.

Nance kissed me goodbye before we separated at the bottom of the road. We've both got to go home and get ready, and she takes hours. She said she would sort out an ID for me – another obstacle I tried to create to stop us going out tonight.
It was one of many.
All unsuccessful.

I'm going to have to tell James if I end up going out tonight. I'll test the water and see what he says. The worst part of going out is thinking how I can justify it. I basically have to ask if I can go. I always take ages to say it – trying to avoid the words *'bar'*, *'club'*, or *'night'*; because that translates to James as *'boys'*, *'drunk'*, and *'cheating'*. It really isn't worth the hassle.
On the way home, I tried to subtly put her off the idea of going out, but she didn't notice. Plus, after that little discussion, it wasn't worth falling out with her. It wasn't necessarily an argument. It was just a difference in opinion. There's no point turning it into an argument by telling her that James isn't happy about me going out. That will make her kick off.

We haven't had a night out with each other for months. Every time we go out during the day, even to go shopping, James makes sure he meets me at some point. It's mainly because of the time in Westfield, just before my seventeenth birthday.
Nance came with me to keep an eye on my gorgeous dress, so I could try it on for the hundredth time – and make sure no rough

girls were going in and buying it. I told James where I was going and who I was going with, as normal.

He knew that I had nothing to hide.

We went to check my dress, then Nance wanted to get some underwear. She got a nice, dark purple, lacy set. On our way out, I heard someone calling me. I don't know him that well. He was in my Hospitality B-Tech class in college. I only spoke to him a few times – Shaun – the same guy who is now trying it on with Nancy. It's all very incestual.

He came over and gave me a hug, to say *'hello'*. It wasn't in a flirty way or anything. I didn't really hug him back. I just kind of stood there. We spoke for about five minutes, mainly about the exam. He didn't think he did well and neither did I.

He was dressed quite nicely. Denim shirt, with the sleeves rolled up; light chinos, turned up at the bottom; espadrilles; short beard… The uniform all guys wear.

All dressed up, but no socks. I'll never understand that. I could never trust a man who doesn't wear socks. Something about seeing a man's ankles – all skinny and bony… Not for me, thanks. Turn-ups equal turn-offs.

I don't like him in that way. At all. Even if I was single, I probably wouldn't go for him.

I thought that was the end of it. He walked off, with his sweaty feet blistering down the aisles, and we went to do some more shopping. I asked Nance not to mention it because James gets funny about other boys, and we hadn't been seeing each other for that long. I didn't want to ruin things for no reason. I trust her not to say anything. It's not like I fancy this guy. *He* hugged *me*. Plus, I think he was looking at Nancy more. She thought he was lovely and started following him on Instagram that day, apparently. A bit keen.

As soon as we started walking away from Shaun, James had come from behind me. Straight away, he was fuming – calling me a liar; saying that I came here with Shaun and separated when I knew James was coming. He was shouting loud enough for people to stop and stare. Obviously, no one risked getting involved and I was standing there, embarrassed – waiting for the situation to end. When he was done, he started walking around Westfield with his nose in the air and his chest puffed out, looking for Shaun.

I was trying to calm him down because I didn't want him confronting Shaun and making a scene over literally nothing. It would've been really embarrassing for him to start a fight over a guy saying *'hello'* to me. I don't want to be known as the girl everyone has to stay away from, in case her boyfriend beats them up.

Plus, Shaun knows that I've got a boyfriend. Everyone knows me as *James' girlfriend* in college. A lot of people from college know James because we all went to the same secondary school.

So, surely if everyone knows that I'm his girlfriend, then he's got nothing to worry about…

He wouldn't see it like that, though. He gets really paranoid about other boys. It's fair enough… I wouldn't be happy about him talking to other girls. He just takes it to another level at times. I can't help it if someone comes and talks to me. I can't be rude and ignore the boy. I make an effort not to get into a proper conversation if a boy talks to me, but he doesn't believe that.

It was a complete non-event and it got blown out of proportion.

God knows how he'll react to me going out tonight. I'm meant to be seeing him during the day. I'll probably get ready at his. I'm dreading telling him, mainly because we've got no reason to go out. If there was a reason – one of the girls' birthdays or something – I could say *'I should show my face'*, or *'she really wants me to go and I'll feel bad if I don't'*, or something like that. Either way, I'd have a reason to go out.

On the rare occasion I do go out, I make it clear that I don't want to go – or I'm not really that bothered about going.

That usually leads to me either bailing on everyone at the last minute or leaving super early.
If I show that I'm looking forward to it, I can see his mind start ticking over and he'll ask me loads of questions about it.
He looks like he's just being curious and taking an interest, but he's always got another motive.
He's not stupid when it comes to things like that.

I have to always be on my guard when I'm answering him. When he interrogates me about going out, I want to be careful with my answers so I don't make him annoyed. I'll be hesitating to get my words exactly as I mean them, and I usually start stalling and getting things wrong out of nerves. I'll end up digging a massive hole for myself over one question, just because I want to avoid an argument. That obviously makes it look like I'm trying to get a story straight. Either that or the answers sound so rehearsed. That's only because I know exactly what he'll ask.
'Where you off to?'
'Why you going there? I heard it's shit there.'
'What's the big occasion?'
'Who's going?'
'Is it just them?'
'Are you meeting anyone else there?'
'D'you wanna stay at mine after?'
The last one used to seem quite nice and caring, but I realised – in his head – if I stay at his, he knows where I am.
If I stay at his, I'm not staying at anyone else's.

Fucking Nancy. Why do we have to go out?

11. AT MINE

I don't want to stay indoors for too long. Being at home the other day made me remember why I'm always somewhere else.
When I'm away for a few days, I miss home.
When I'm indoors for a few minutes, I want to leave.
I arrive at the front door – carrying the familiar, knotted cramp of anxiety in the pit of my stomach.
I get nervous coming home since the summer. That was the worst she's been. Now, I never really know what to expect. And I can only ever relax when I see mum is actually alive.
It's only six o'clock and it's already dark. I used to love going out in the evening when it got this dark. It would feel like I was out really late, and I'd feel all rebellious and older. I was only eleven or twelve, but I remember going over to Nancy's at about seven o'clock and it'd feel really late. Then, mum would make me ring her – so she'd know I'd got there safe.
She was good… When I was younger, anyway.

I get to the front door and open my bag, resting it between my body and the rough, damp surface of the brick wall. My keys are floating around in here somewhere. It's full of all the rubbish I brought to James'.
The change of clothes I didn't need.
The umbrella I didn't use.
The scarf I didn't wear.
My phone charger.

Lipgloss

I should tell him that I had to do the test.
Don't think about that right now.

I hear the metal rattle of my chunky keys in the corner of the
bag, working them out using the inner wall. It's so hard to see
what I'm doing, so use the light on my phone to find the lock on
the door. I let myself in, calling to the dark. 'Mum?'
No surprises, hopefully.
All the lights are off and the curtains are drawn. The carpet is soft
under my feet as I go up the stairs.
My stomach cramps the higher up I go.
I stare at her room through the banister. The door is slightly open
and the telly is whispering through the gap. The light from the
telly flickers around the room, flashing bright to pitch black on
the other side.
I cling to the door, slowly easing it open. Nervously, I hang my
head around it.
My eyes focus through the dark and etch mum's outline against
the wall; sitting up on the bed and reading a magazine, she smiles
at me over it. Her face glows in the white of the telly.
We don't say anything to each other, but everything is alright.
I smile back at her.
She seems happy at the moment.
After another flicker of light, her face disappears into the
darkness.

With a bit more certainty than I had earlier, the carpet takes me
down the hall to my room.
No idea what I'm going to wear tonight.
I catch a glimpse of myself in the mirror. I look awful. The
mirrored wardrobes aren't flattering at all. I'm sure someone at the
factory installed the circus mirrors on here for a laugh – the ones
that make you look all stumpy and round.
The dress I wore to my seventeenth is still hanging up. I pull it out
and glance over it. Could I still get away with that?

I hold it up against myself and push the creases out.

Look from the front.

Left.

Right.

I can't. My eyes keep floating towards the stain on the strap. I can't even scrub it out – in case the diamantes come off. I should throw it away, really.

I place it back on the hanger and rest it inside the wardrobe.

None of my clothes look good on me. Every time I get an outfit out and try it on, the fat under my armpits wobbles and kills the whole look.

Fat under my armpits… No idea. It's like another pair of boobs, but smaller – between my normal boobs and my arms. Two disgusting rolls of armpit fat that dangle down for no reason. They can make the nicest outfit look horrible. It's why I don't own a single strapless bra or dress. I look like I'm giving a headlock to two gammon joints. I'm sure I was born with them. I've had them for as long as I can remember – and I can't get rid of them, no matter what I do. I wish I could just snip them off with a pair of scissors. It looks like the fat you would have as a baby, from drinking nothing but milk all day. I try to wear dresses and tops that hug my arms to keep it all hidden from public view.

It's the first thing I notice in any photo I get tagged in.

Instantly delete… If I didn't take the photo myself, it's not going up.

It's just a weird place to hold fat, and no one else seems to have it. I follow a lot of different pages on Instagram and Facebook, and none of the girls on there have anything like that.

They're either *catwalk skinny* – zero fat, abs, and a thigh gap you could drive a bus through; or *model curvy* – all hips, no waist, and boobs permanently pushed up and in.

I don't know how so many girls manage to get curves only in certain places, without carrying fat all over. I know Nancy doesn't have the same problem as me. Even though she's a little bit bigger than me, she's got a much nicer body. I'm not curvy enough to pull off the clothes she wears.

It must just be me. I've got the body of a small boy; with some doughy, dangling bits of baby fat.

What else is in here? Is a dress too dressy? I've only really got casual clothes, and they're all black. I'll wear black until they invent something darker.

Wonder what Nancy's wearing.

I text her.

I hope she's not wearing heels. They're alright for the first hour or two, but then they start aching and give me blisters. And I can't walk home barefoot in this weather, so I might as well just bring flats with me. James doesn't like me in heels and I'm not the biggest fan of wearing them. There's nothing more embarrassing than walking past a group of boys and being taller than every single one of them. And when I see girls in heels that are shorter than me, they automatically look more feminine.

I'm not even that tall – I just can't do heels. They can look quite nice when they're on and they seem to make my legs look a bit skinnier, but as soon as I stand next to a normal human being, I feel butch. I just look like a big giant, hammering my way across the dance floor.

Real attractive.

Maybe that's why James doesn't like them? Because I look too butch and it looks weird for the girl to be taller than the boy. My heels usually give me about an inch or two on him.

I guess that's a lot – an inch is a lot to most boys.

Black pumps will be alright, I reckon. They go with everything.

My eye catches something unfamiliar. I forgot about this; a nice, minimal, black dress. I bought it for my interview for the school placement. I got it in the sale. Forty pounds, reduced to twenty-five. Not bad.

Don't know if it'll still fit.

That's how long I haven't been out for – I've forgotten what clothes I've got.

That's the dress sorted.

Tights… Black or clear? Black tights with a black dress is too much. I'll look like I'm going to a funeral. I'll bring both pairs and try them on. They'll probably look like a building site with all the ladders I've got.

I grab my make-up bag.

Purse.

Keys.

Phone.

I'll bring a big bag to James' for my coat and shoes, then just take a small bag out with me.

I throw in a pair of jeans and a T-shirt to wear for the morning. I'll probably stay at James' tonight.

Is that everything? I think so.

'Bye, mum. I'm off out.' I don't go in, just shout from the top of the stairs.

'You out for the night?' She sounds preoccupied.

'Yeah – I'll be back in the morning, though. Love you.'

I'll go straight to James' and get ready, meet Nance at the station, then we can go to the West End together from there.

12. JAMES'

'Hiya, love! James is upstairs. God, you must be freezing…
Get yourself in here!' James' mum ushers me inside, giving me a
warm hug and a kiss on the cheek. She's answered the door
wearing a fluffy dressing gown, hitting me with the warm smell of
pasta coming from behind her. My mouth waters straight away.
It's bitterly cold outside, catching me all the way to my bones.
How can it be this cold and not even have the decency to snow? I
wonder if it will snow before Christmas… I hope so.
I still need to get James something. I'll see how much money I've
got in my account when I go to the cash point tonight.

'D'you want anything to eat?' She tempts me in with my first
home-cooked meal for ages.
I really want to.
I can't.
If I do – I'll have a little pot-belly in my dress.
If I don't eat – I'll feel tipsy earlier, have an excuse to drink less,
spend less money, and leave earlier.
Everybody wins.
I'm not going to get drunk tonight – not if I'm coming back here.
'Ah, no thanks, Sue. I'm alright. God, it's freezing outside, ain't
it?' I rub my hands together and defrost, scraping my UGGs on the
doormat.
'Alright, love. Well, it's down here if you want any – there's
more than enough. James is in his usual place… Unsociable little
sod.' She disappears back into the steam of the kitchen.

I go upstairs looking for James. His door is shut. I'd better knock. 'James?' I speak quietly into the wood of the door, knocking and twisting the handle at the same time. I'm confronted with a massive canvas of The Godfather on the right, and a West Ham flag next to his bed on the left.

He doesn't have any photos up in his room. I guess that's more of a girly thing to do.

He's sat on his bed, laptop open on top of him and phone by his side. He flips his phone face down, then rolls his eyes up at me.

I go over to kiss him. 'You alright?'

He angles his head towards me, so I just get a connection with his lips. 'When'd you get here? I didn't hear you come in.' He types something abrupt into the laptop.

'Literally, just now. Your mum let me in. What you been up to?' I put my bag on the floor and nest myself at his feet.

'Nothing. Mum was telling me to look for an apprenticeship and all that, but I can't be listening to that same thing again.' His eyes are still on the laptop.

'Would you not like to do that? I swear plumbers get quite a bit of money? You could do a plumbing apprenticeship?' I kick my UGGs from my feet and stretch my legs off the side of the bed.

'I ain't working in shit for a living. Putting my hands down toilets and pulling condoms out of drain pipes.'

It'd be the first condom he's seen for a while…

We sit in silence for a minute. We don't really have much to talk about. He knows I'm going out tonight because I texted him earlier, so I should break the silence with that. I rummage through my bag, looking for the dress. Hopefully, it's not too creased. I pull it out and hold it up against me. 'Did I ever show you this dress? I'm gonna wear it tonight… Do you like it?'

I have to be a bit careful.

If I speak about my clothes too much and focus on how I'm dressed, he'll wonder why I'm making such an effort.
If I talk about the night too much, he'll think I'm rubbing his nose in it that I'm going out and he's not.
If I don't mention anything, he'll think I'm hiding something.

He doesn't answer.

I place the dress on the side of the bed, letting it hang off. Hopefully, any creases will just fall out. 'Can I have a quick shower, by the way? I ain't gotta wash my hair or nothing. I've got dry shampoo. Just wanna have a quick wash over because I didn't have time at mine. I wanted to get here early to come see you.' I rub his leg, trying to catch his eye. 'D'you mind?'
'Look at you making an effort. Go on then.' That took his eyes off the laptop.
I don't know how having a shower means I'm making an effort. Best not to argue, anyway. 'Thanks.' I give him a smile that he doesn't see.
I grab my bag, making sure my phone is in there. I've got nothing to hide, but I don't like the idea of my phone being in here with him.
I know he'll go through it.

I'll have a quick shower, dry shampoo my hair, tiny bit of make-up, then get ready to go.

13. JAMES' cont.

I come back into James' room, wrapped in a damp towel that was hanging over the bathroom door. I managed to keep my hair dry in a bun. The ends are slightly wet from taking it down and letting it rest on my shoulders. The body of my hair feels so greasy. He hasn't moved since I left. I shuffle over to the foot of bed. His carpet is rough under my feet. 'Have you got any deodorant? I left mine indoors.' He picks up a small bottle of roll-on from the side cabinet and tosses it on the end of the bed. His eyes don't leave the laptop at any point. I roll the deodorant across my armpits as I walk over to him. As I put it back on the side, I lean over next to him – letting the towel loosen under my boobs. 'Try to control yourself.' I look at him with a slight smile, trying to get his attention. I glide my hand over the crotch of his jeans, knocking the laptop on my way.
No movement underneath.
Rude.

'Can you stop?' He snaps, rolling his eyes over to me as I pathetically dangle beside him.
I tried to get a subtle look at the screen before I stood up. I wasn't able to get a proper look, but I saw a tab for Facebook Search was open.
I wonder who he's looking for… I might put his password in later – go through his recent activity and search history.
I don't like doing stuff like that, but that's a weird page to have open.

His eyes are still on the laptop. I slip my bra on and try to keep the towel up, pinning it under my chin. I put my knickers on in the bathroom already. I didn't realise they matched my bra. They're not part of a set, but they match… Generic black lace. Hopefully, he won't notice it.

'Matching, yeah?'

Knew it.

'Huh?' I play dumb.

'What you matching for?'

'Oh, it's not an actual set. I had to find the darkest stuff I had. I have to wear black underwear because I'm wearing a black dress, and it looks silly if I wear a different colour bra. And if I wear white knickers, you might be able to see them through my dress and that would look well rough.' He wouldn't believe me if I said it was a coincidence. It'd make him really suspicious.

It's not as if I'm lying to him. It would look silly if I had a rainbow bra on with a black dress. Plus, in bright light, you could probably see through this dress – especially when the fabric stretches on my bum.

I always need to be on my guard when I explain anything to him. He makes me lie about silly things because if I say the truth, it will start a totally unnecessary argument.

I put the dress on and pull it down, as low as it can go. 'Does this look alright?' I pull it down more and play with the bottom, running my fingers along the seam.

'You going like *that*?' His face twists.

'Erm, I dunno. Probably. Why?' I finger the hemline.

'Is it short enough?' His eyebrows frown.

I pull it down more, tweaking the bottom where it might have rolled under the seam. I flatten it down my bum and straighten out the creases, lengthening the dress to its limits. 'Is it too short? I wore it to my interview for the school placement I told you about.' It's about three inches from my knees.

'And did you get the job?' He glares through his eyebrows.

63

'Yeah, actually.'

'And was it a man who interviewed you?' A smug grin. Don't really know what to say to that. I just look at the floor and pull the dress down lower, pinching the bottom of it. His eyes go back to the laptop. 'Exactly.' Satisfied with himself.

'I can wear tights with it…' I quickly fall to the floor to get my bag.

'See! How short is that?' He points at me on the floor and his voice gets louder, travelling down his arm at me. The dress has ridden up slightly from where I've bent over to get my bag. It's tucked itself just under my bum.

'Yeah – but I'm not gonna be bending over like this when I'm out.' I bend my knees and crouch down to get my bag, showing him how I would bend when I'm out.

'Well, I wouldn't put it past you.' Eyes back to the laptop. I take my clear tights and roll them up my legs, keeping the dress hovering above my knees the entire time. I look at him before I look in the mirror. His eyes roll up from the screen. 'Looks exactly the same.' Eyes back down.

I don't bother to look in the mirror properly, just sit on the bed and roll them off. If he doesn't want me wearing them, then I won't be wearing them. No matter what I say.

The black ones are buried somewhere in my bag because I had no intention of going out in them tonight – they were my back-up in case the clear ones had ladders in. I ease them up my legs and stand up. I lift the bottom of my dress slightly and work them over my bum.

Ladder.

Brilliant.

'What about now?' I pull the dress back down, as low as it will go.

'Looks alright. Still too short, though.' Uninterested.

I catch a look at myself in the mirror at the foot of the bed. I look like I'm going to a funeral. It's barely above my knees. I'll have to wear it because it's the only thing I have with me.

And I can't wear my pyjamas to a club, no matter how much I want to.
Can't even be bothered to go out, now.

I kneel down in front of the mirror; the body-length mirror I've been using is next to his door. It's where he takes his scowling profile pictures.
I put my make-up bag in front of me and empty it out.
Foundation.
Lipstick.
Concealer.
Eyeliner.
Liquid eyeliner.
Eye shadow.
Mascara.
Lip gloss.

'Why you wearing so much make-up recently?' He speaks to my reflection, his voice rolling from behind me.
'Am I?'
I'm really not.
'Yeah. You was caked in make-up at Westfields when you was with that whore. And you're gonna put all that shit on your face again.' His words disappear into the screen.
I try not to react to the names he calls Nancy.
'I dunno. I just feel more comfortable when I've got make-up on. Otherwise, I feel ugly. It just gives me a bit more confidence.'
And I look about twelve when I've got no make-up on.
'To look more attractive – in other words.' His eyebrows lower with confusion. His words hover behind me, over the laptop and to my reflection.
'Well, yeah… In a way. But just for myself.' He doesn't understand that. If I make a bit of an effort, it doesn't mean I'm doing it to try to get with someone or get attention from other

boys. It just makes me feel more comfortable and confident in my own skin.

'That don't make sense.'

'Mmm… I know it sounds weird. It's silly, really. Hard to explain if you're not a girl.' I'm fiddling with my lipstick on the floor, rolling it between my hands and purposely stalling. I don't really want to put it on in front of him.

I click the lid between my nails.

I guess I don't really need to wear lipstick, do I?

I'm sat cross-legged, with all my make-up on the taut fabric of my dress. I catch him behind me in the reflection of the mirror. His face lights up from the laptop as he clicks on a new page.

Probably a different girl's profile he's stalking each time. I'll have to see if he's added or messaged anyone – get Nance to do a bit of stalking later on.

I'm happy he's not looking at me. He makes me feel embarrassed to wear make-up, without even saying anything.

I get nervous putting it on, like I shouldn't be doing it.

Liquid eyeliner looks a bit weird on me, anyway. Plus, it takes ages to put it on and get the flicks even. I won't wear that. I don't really need lipstick. I can get away with not wearing foundation. Do I need eye shadow? I'll just use a tiny bit of eyeliner and mascara instead. I'm sure he likes my eyes done heavily in make-up. That's only if I'm not going out, I guess.

There's a pile of unused make-up building up beside me – as I prepare to put anything remotely feminine back in the bag.

At least I can get ready quicker.

I've got a few spots coming through, so I smother concealer on them. I carefully draw identical lines under both eyes with eyeliner, then flick the lashes upwards with mascara. I brush the dry shampoo I've just sprayed through my hair and work it into a messy pony tail, hiding the greasy crime scene.

Lipgloss

My body lifts up. I pull the dress deeper into my shoulders and work out the creases to give it more precious length.
I hold my face close to the mirror, checking my eyes and the visibility of my spots.
Still there.
The mirror steams up as I breathe on it. I wipe the fog away and see James monitoring me over the screen.
Still there.
I catch his eye and look away quickly.
I feel so trampy. I look like a Goth. Or one of those emo kids; pasty-faced, dressed in black, shit make-up. I'll be slitting my wrists and devil-worshipping in a minute.
It'll have to do, now. It's a shame we're not going to Camden – I'd look half-decent if we were down there.

I give myself a quick touch of lip gloss and bite my lips together.
It's the only feminine thing I'm allowed to wear when I go out.
As soon as it goes on, it's invisible. But at least I know it's there, and it makes me feel like a normal girl.

My phone vibrates. I don't like to have the ringer loud because it brings attention to someone trying to contact me. It's only ever going to be Nance or one of the girls, but it still doesn't stop him from being suspicious.
Nancy replies.
She's wearing heels and asks me to wear them with her.
Right. Shoes.
As soon as I take the heels out of my bag, he'll say something. Guaranteed.

'Oh… I didn't know it was a proper dressy night out.' The voice over the laptop.
Knew it. Does he only take his eyes off the screen when he's checking up on me?

'Oh, no. It's only because Nancy's wearing heels. Otherwise, she'll be proper taller than me.' Answer was ready and prepared.

'Fucking slag. Bet she won't be too high up to give head in the toilets, though. Will she? Hoe.'
She's never actually given head in the toilets.

'Does this look alright? My hair doesn't look stupid, does it?' I'm really self-conscious, now that I'm all dressed up.

'Nah, it's fine. You coming back here tonight?' He barely looks.

'Yeah, I can do. I'll walk Nancy home first, then come straight here.' Even though it means walking through the park on my own from Nancy's, when I could just stay there.

'You got enough make-up on?' He's noticed my eyes.

'Is it too much, still? I thought you like my eyes done up all heavy?' I've barely got any on.

'Why you wearing any, at all? You never wear make-up when you're with me. But every time you go out, you cake it on.'
Why start this? Just before I go out, too.

'Well it's because we don't really go out that much? We stay in most of the time, don't we?' He looks right through me. His eyes are piercing. 'Nah, I'm not saying it like it's a bad thing. I like coming here – and I get on with your family and that. It's just… I can't get really dressed up if we ain't going out proper. Your mum would think I look slutty if I have loads of make-up on just to come over. And I don't wear that much make-up when I come here because I know you don't like me wearing a lot.'

'…When you're out.' He always has an answer prepared.

'Well, yeah. But I rarely go out, now. And when I do, I try not to wear that much make-up because I know you don't like it. And if me and you went out proper, then you know I'd make an effort, don't you?' This is a losing battle. His head is buried back into the laptop and his eyes are going from the screen to his phone – face down on the side.

My phone vibrates again. Nancy has got hold of an ID for me to use. I'd almost forgotten about that. That would have been embarrassing… Getting to the door of the club and being turned away, then having to walk back past the queue – looking like a kid.

I want to go as soon as I can.

I throw all my stuff into my bag and place it at the foot of his bed. I keep trying to make eye contact with him, but he's not looking at me. I don't want to leave with an atmosphere because that makes him more frustrated; thinking I'll be upset and – of course – confide in some random guy about our relationship.

Because that's *obviously* what I would do.

'I'll text you when I'm on my way back, yeah?' I tweak his foot through his grey socks.

'Nah, text me when you're there.' His foot recoils.

'Oh, okay.' I give him a little smile. 'Are you sure this looks alright? I don't look silly, do I?' I pull the dress down again, to a couple of inches from my knees; until the straps burn into my shoulders. I take my heels off and swap them for my black pumps. They slip on with ease. I'll wear these until I meet Nance.

'Well, it's a bit slutty, but…' He gets up to put his phone on charge, but stops and stands over me as he walks past. 'And don't talk to any boys when you're out. If you do, you know I'll find out, yeah?' He's taller than me now, so I have to look up at him.

'You know I won't.' My eyes fall away from him and drag down, noticing my heels inside my bag.

'And *don't* get drunk. It looks proper dirt when you're falling over everywhere.' He walks back to the bed and throws himself down.

'Okay, sorry.' I grab my bag, put my coat under my arm, and walk over to him on the bed. 'I'll see you in a bit.' I give him a kiss, but only get his cheek. 'Love you.'

14. PICCADILLY LINE, COCKFOSTERS via PICCADILLY CIRCUS

'Shall we stay on until *Cock*-fosters? We can both get off at *Cock*-fosters if you want?' We got the DLR to Canning Town, then the Jubilee Line to Green Park. As soon as we changed to the Piccadilly Line, Nancy pissed herself at the announcement saying *'this is a Piccadilly Line train to: Cockfosters'*. She carries on entertaining herself. 'No, no… Shall we go *drink* from the *Cock*-fosters?' She gets louder with every joke she thinks of.

'Eurgh, you dirty slag!' I go with her mood. She seems to be enjoying herself and we're not even there yet. It could end up being a good night.

'Me? You can talk! You'd probably film it!' She shoves her tongue inside her cheek and bulges it out.

'Oi!' I can feel myself going red. 'Shut up, you!' I give her a playful slap on her arm. She looks drunk already. I met her at her house and we've been pre-drinking since then. I haven't had much, really. Only one or two glasses. Her mum had a couple of drinks with us before her boyfriend came over. We had a few glasses of wine at hers, then got a little bottle of vodka from the shop and mixed it with a big bottle of cheap lemonade on the way to the station.

The actual definition of *'class'*.

Lipgloss

I got a bit nervous going into the station because it's against the law to drink on the Tube, now. As soon as we got on the train, I took the bottle off her and shoved it in my bag. Nance doesn't care. She was necking it when she swiped in at Woolwich Arsenal Station and had it out in plain sight; bowling through the barriers and all the way onto the platform. She's got a front. She doesn't care what people think of her.
I do admire her, really. Wish I had her confidence.

The train is full of little groups of people going out for the night. There's a buzz of an atmosphere. Everyone's excited to be out. Every time I go into Central London, the trains get louder. Everyone on the train is shouting over each other. The carriage lights flash on and off, bringing the train from pitch black to blindingly bright. I bet it'd be well scary to be a tourist on the Tube.
My eyes are counting the stops we have left and scan the adverts going along the length of the train.
Hair loss treatment.
Some vitamins for being tired.
Immune system supplements for pregnant women.
Don't really want to think about that one.

Now that we're in the tunnel, I can see the people on my side of the carriage in the reflection of the window. My bag is between my legs and I see Nancy reach down to it. 'Oi! Gimme a drop! Why you keeping the bottle between your legs for, anyway? Tryna put it up your vag!' She gets up and falls on top of me. 'Eurgh, everyone! This girl's bottling herself! She wants a bottle-job!'
There's a middle-aged man looking at us in the reflection of the window. He doesn't look impressed by us – probably because we're leaning all over him.
What's he doing out this late?

There's a group of snobby girls looking over from the right. Their faces are twisted in disgust, looking down their noses at us. I'm getting a bit embarrassed, now. They're eyeing us up, looking at what we're wearing from head to toe, judging everything about us.

I grab Nance and sit her on my lap. 'Calm down, you. Or they won't let us in the club.' Teacher training in progress.

'Yeah, they will! The bouncer will just look at me and think I'm fucking sexy and let me in for free.' She's admiring herself in the reflection of the window over my shoulder, pouting and fixing her side fringe.

'Shhh – come. Next stop's ours.' I lift her up by her bum to let her sit down on her own chair. She stands back up and tries to swing around the pole to do a dance. She falls straight onto the empty seat opposite me, laughing harder. The snobby group are still looking over at us, whispering to each other and shaking their heads. Nancy notices I'm looking at them and clocks them herself.

'Oi, fuck them slags. What they looking at? Fucking snobby cunts.' She straightens her body on the chair, composing herself, then faces them. 'Can I help you?'
All the girls look away at the same time, as the windows brighten and we pull into the station.
Good timing.

I lift myself up by the arm rests and grab her hand. 'Come, let's go. Try and sober up, otherwise we ain't gonna get in.'

We get off the train and she pushes past everyone on the platform, then throws herself onto the metal seat. 'I don't even care now. I'm tired.' Her eyes are half-closed and she's leaning her head back onto the gleaming tiles of the station wall. I'm standing opposite her, holding my bag, my coat, and all her stuff that she would've left on the train.
A guy walks between us. He's wearing red jeans, white Converse, and a blue checked-shirt. Got his hair styled in a messy look with a bit of matching stubble.

He's not my type, even if I was single. I only noticed him because he walked right in front of me.

'Alright, sexy? Where you going?' Nancy's suddenly perked up. 'Wait for us outside, yeah? We'll be there in a bit.' Her voice gets louder and chases him away. The guy hasn't taken any notice of us and continues further down the platform.

I start to gather all our stuff together. I try to put her long purse strap around my neck, but it starts wrestling with the back of my hair, tangling into my pony tail.

This is hard work.

'Come Nance, let's go McD's first and get some water – try and sober you up.' All our stuff is between my legs. I grab both of her hands and try to pull her up to her feet.

'Fuck him, then. He must've been gay. He's probably going Cockfosters.' She slumps over me with laughter.

This is going to be a long night.

It's worse to be sober and be with someone who's drunk. She's laughing at everything and I have to babysit her. Wish I could just have a bit more to drink. We could have a laugh and the night would just sort itself out. I hate having to be the sober, responsible one.

I don't even want to imagine if James was here, seeing this. He'd go mad. I've not done anything wrong. But just because I'm with her when she's like this, it would annoy him. He'd think it looks slutty – that all the guys would be looking and perving on us, trying to take advantage or something.

Or he'd think – because I've had a *tiny* bit to drink – I'd get talking to some random guy and take him back to Nancy's. And it'd be Nancy egging me on to do it because she doesn't like him and she's a *'dirty slut'* who wants me to be just like her.

I walk Nancy down the platform, towards the stairs and exit signs. She's chatting absolute bollocks to me and I've got no idea what she's on about.

I'm going to try not to drink too much when we get in there.
I shouldn't, really.
Because of James.

The pregnancy advert catches my eye as the train speeds past us,
disappearing back into the endless dark of the tunnel.

15. PICCADILLY CIRCUS

It's mobbed down here. There was even a massive queue to swipe out with our Oyster Cards. Nance made it clear she wasn't happy about that and barged through everyone to get out. I'm glad she did, with the state she's in. At least, if she was sick, we'd be out two minutes sooner and she wouldn't puke up in the station. She struts to the nearest exit and we fight through the wind to the street.

I'm sure there was a McDonald's around here somewhere... Near Leicester Square? Looks like they've changed it a lot since I was last here. Nancy's mum took us to Planet Hollywood a few years ago, so I roughly remember my way around.

Nance usually gets worse when she's out in the open after she's had a drink, but the fresh air seems to have done her some good. She's a bit quieter, now. At last. I take her by the hand. 'Alright, let's go find a McDonald's and get you some water, yeah?'

'Nah, I'm alright now, honestly. Let's just go straight in.' She stumbles about a bit which – in heels – doesn't look good. Her foot caves in under itself and she steadies her body on mine.

It's buzzing down here and looks so bright for this time of night. There are flashes coming from everywhere. The massive advert screen is lighting up the whole area, so you can't even see the sky. It brightens the buildings ahead of us, paving our way to Trocadero.

There are loads of people sitting down on the big statue behind us, and cameras are flashing from the fountain across the road. People

always expect you to go around them while they take up half the pavement; snapping photos of their posing girlfriends next to some old building that they look really interested in – but don't actually care about half as much as how their eyebrows look.
It's too crowded for that down here.
It can be really disorientating in Central at the best of times.

A strong breeze catches me right in the face from the direction we're walking in, taking my breath away. Nance is too busy falling all over the place to notice how ridiculously cold it is. All the boys we pass in the street are looking at us, tumbling down the road. A couple of boys have whistled – obviously at her. Nancy's got her arm around me and I'm supporting her dead bodyweight. So much for her feeling better.
We look like we're walking on stilts; wobbling and clinging to each other to stop from falling to the floor, straight out of our heels.
We go across the road and walk on towards Leicester Square. I can see McDonald's – that beautiful, red and yellow glow in the distance. Since we came out of the station, we've had about three or four people come up to us offering free entry, or drink coupons, or any other old shit to get us into some dead club for the night. They're so cringe-worthy; sleazy guys trying different lines and compliments to get us to stop.
'Ah, sexy girls. You want free drinks?'
'Pretty ladies! Half price. All night. Only for you.'
Do I look like I've got time to listen to your shit, with this girl falling all over the place?
She doesn't help because she loves the attention. She shouts back things like *'see you later, sexy'*, then they hassle us the whole way down the road.
Fucking nightmare. Give me Woolwich, any day.

'Oi – remind me I need to go cash point before we go in, yeah? Otherwise, I'll have to get my tits out and get people to buy me drinks all night.' She pulls her top down lower and exposes half of her bra.

That would probably work. Her boobs are massive and guys love her. She's in a long, dark coat; a tiny, black skirt with no tights; giant heels with metal studs on; and a tight, leopard print top that her boobs are popping out of.

Wish I could say it was a push up bra.

But it's not.

Bitch.

She looks nice. I wouldn't wear it, but she pulls it off.

We've just arrived in McDonald's and she slaps some random guy's bum as he walks out. He looks back – with his girlfriend. I just apologise for her. What else can I do?

The couple walk out.

'Dunno what he's doing with *that*!' She eyes up the guy's girlfriend before strutting in. 'State of it! See her eyebrows?' She stops to look around. 'Why'd you take us to Mc-fucking-Donald's? I don't want a Happy Meal! Can we just go in? The queue's gonna be well long.' She pulls her phone out of her bra. I've got no idea how it fits down there. She's a thirty-six double-E-cup and she looks like she's stuffed into one of my thirty-two C-cups. 'See… Look at the fucking time. Come!' She grabs my hand and falls onto the door to open it, then pulls me along the street back towards Piccadilly Circus.

She's reminded me that I haven't texted James. I take my phone out of my bag as she pulls me along.

Two texts.

One missed call. Private number.

That'll be him. The trick is, he's texted me and I haven't replied. I haven't purposely ignored it; I just forgot to reply because of Nancy. So, he wants to ring me from a private number and see if I pick up. Then, if I answer, he'll think I'm just blanking his texts.

Plus, if it rings, he'll know I'm not underground anymore, so I've got no excuse not to reply.

Better text him back.

'One minute, Nance.' I pull against her arm, trying to slow her down while I text him. I tell him that I didn't hear my phone because I was at the cashpoint. I had to say that – if I said Nance was in a state so I didn't check my phone, he would've started. It would've been either how we're *'both out getting drunk like slags'* or how I'm *'choosing her over him'*.

Either way, it's easier to say anything else.

I feel bad for lying, but it's only because he's made it so that I can't tell him the truth. Even if it's something minor like not replying for ten minutes.

I hope I won't have to text him all night while I'm out. I don't mean to be horrible, but I've come out to enjoy myself and I don't want to have to keep checking my phone. And Nancy will probably get annoyed with it eventually. I can get away with being on my phone if we're in a group, but if it's just the two of us out, she'll notice that I'm texting all the time.

I keep my phone in my hand as she pulls me along the street. This way, I'll feel it vibrate. I tried putting it in my bra like Nance before, but James said it looked slutty to keep getting it out of there. Guess he's right. And it's not even comfortable. Plus, my boobs aren't big enough to keep it secure. There's enough room for an old Nokia 3310 in my bra.

He replies almost straight away. Seems like he's been waiting for a text back. I usually try to reply within a few minutes when he texts me. If it gets too long, he'll ask about it the next day; questioning why I wasn't texting him back that much. If it gets to the half-an-hour mark, he'll be blunt in his reply and take longer texting me back.

'Oh… Look how busy I am… I didn't have time to reply either.'
If it gets past an hour, he'll send me another text or give me a missed call from a withheld number.

'Look at this hench queue! And you wanted to go McD's! We would've been halfway down by now if you hadn't taken us all the way down there. Fuck's sake.' She goes on a strop, flapping her arms to her sides. We've only just got to the back of the queue and she's sticking her head out to see how fast it's moving. She's got the hump, now.

'Yeah – to get *you* a drink and sober you up. Otherwise, we'd queue up for half hour and get turfed away because you're pissed.' I'm not having this. No way. Don't see how the length of the queue is my fault. I was trying to help her out.

She's doing my head in already and we're not even in there.

16. RANDOM CLUB

Finally. Forty-fucking-five minutes later and we've only just got in. Nance made a big scene because we got to the front of the queue and she remembered she needed to go to the cash point. Then, she had a go at *me* because I didn't remind her to go. And apparently, it's because I was *'too busy texting James'*.
I'm sorry that I've been preoccupied keeping you from falling flat on your fucking face. How can she blame *me* for that? – Her being too drunk to remind *herself* to get cash out?
I'm really not in the mood to be out now.
I feel ugly.
There's an atmosphere with me and her.
I'm dressed like I'm about to give a speech at a fucking funeral.
And now, James is being funny with me over text.
Why am I surrounded by fucking weirdoes in my life?

It's packed in here. Over the sea of people, I see they've done it up with Christmas decorations. It looks like there are a lot of people out for office parties. You can spot them from a mile away – group of snobby, office-looking lot; cheap, slim-fit suits; too much product in their hair; sitting around a table, nursing the second-cheapest bottle of prosecco; wearing their little Christmas-Cracker hats and rationing the fifty pounds their boss put behind the bar.
They all act drunker than they are and talk bollocks about their jobs that they think are really important because they've got a pretentious title.

'I'm Spencer. I've got a double-barrel surname, so you know I'm important… I work as a digital marketing executive at an e-commerce start-up in the City.'
I hate everyone.

I never usually look forward to Christmas. For as long as I can remember, it's just been me and mum sitting in, watching telly. I'll usually get up at about nine o'clock on Christmas morning; my inner-child wakes me up early with butterflies. Mum will wake up at about half past twelve, we'll exchange a couple of presents, watch telly, she'll do dinner at about four o'clock, then fall asleep before eating it – usually because of the wine she would've been swigging at all day.
Merry Christmas.
She'll send me out to buy all the food on Christmas Eve, with about thirty pounds and some change. Obviously, by then, everything's sold out and we end up with the shit that no one else wants. I tell her – at the beginning of December, every year – that I'll go out and buy the food. But she waits right until the last minute when there's nothing else left.
Nancy's mum orders the turkey a few weeks before Christmas and gets it delivered on Christmas Eve. I'll usually take a walk to hers on Christmas night and stay over. I used to feel like I was intruding or her mum would think I'm a ponce just turning up for Christmas dinner. Now, it's got to the stage where her mum would text me to ask what time I'll be there. I feel bad because I don't like leaving mum on her own, especially on Christmas. And I always imagine she'll wake up as soon as I've left and be on her own all night, wondering where I am.
She never does.
This will be my first Christmas with James, so he'll probably ask me to go there.

Me and Nance are leaning on the bar, waiting to be served by the barman in a Christmas hat. He looks cheerful – dressed completely in black, with short hair and stubble.

People will probably think I work here with the way I'm dressed. If anyone asks me for a refill, I'm going home.

My elbows are leaning into spilt drink on the bar and I keep wiping it onto my dress. There's no way the stains will show up on this. I'm a walking cocktail of about fifteen drinks from different people – half from the damp bar I'm leaning on and half from the drunk dickheads sloshing their drinks on me as we came in.

The barman is looking over at us as he pours someone else's drinks. There's a bit of distance between me and Nance, even though it's packed in here – that's probably why he's looking over. It's snowing over us; a frosty little atmosphere at this end of the bar, well in-tune with the time of year.

Down the bar, I see the smooth reflection of loads of hands waving notes and debit cards, waiting to pay stupidly high prices for their watered-down drinks. They must make so much money in these kinds of places, especially in this part of London where everything is twice as expensive.

In front of me, the two of us stand in a reflection behind the bar, looking miserable. That view is quickly interrupted by the barman stepping into us. My eyes drop away quickly and I rummage through my bag. He leans between us to hear what we want. I look at Nance to order while I get my money out. She's shouting in his ear and I can barely hear her. She motions with her hands.

Two tequila shots.

Two vodka lemonades.

Double or single?

Double.

Lipgloss

He looks at me while he's leaning in to hear her, smirking. I drop my eyes down again; fumbling quickly through my bag and feeling for my purse, trying not to catch his eye.

He walks off to make our drinks, as Nancy plumps up her hair in the reflection behind the bar.

She's blatantly going to try it on with him. I don't care. As long as she doesn't expect me to sit around third-wheeling while she tries to pull him, I'm not bothered. Let her do what she wants.

He dances back over to us, past another couple of barmen. He's got our drinks and comes back with an extra shot, sliding it over to me. He keeps another one for himself. I tell him that I didn't ask for it, pushing it back towards him. My hand follows it to give him twenty pounds.

That's over half my money gone.

He shakes his head, leaning in with a wave of sweet aftershave and dry alcohol. 'Don't worry about it. Just don't tell my manager, yeah?' He winks at me, then knocks back his shot before putting the other one in my hand. His fingers stay on mine for too long. I drink it quickly and launch myself into the crowd, leaving all my stuff at the bar with Nance.

I manage to get some words out on the way. 'I'm just going toilet quick.' I've never moved so fast in my life. I push through loads of people, not even looking. My eyes are scanning over everyone's heads for the toilets. I'm looking over a sea of bad hair extensions and Christmas hats.

I fight through a last little crowd outside the toilets, barge through the door, find the nearest cubicle, and lock myself in.

I just need a minute.
One minute. On my own.

No James.
No Nancy.
No mum.
No one.

Why do I feel bad for what just happened?
The guy just gave me a free drink.
And I took it.
Should I tell James?

It's not like I did anything, though. I didn't flirt to get it. I didn't lead him on. Or bat my eyelashes. Or push my boobs up under my chin, like Nancy. So, why do I feel guilty?
I shouldn't have taken it. I should've left the money on the bar and walked off.
I didn't do anything wrong.
I'm sure I didn't.
Then, why do I know I'm not going to tell James about this? If you hide something, you obviously know you've done something wrong – something that's worth hiding.
For fuck's sake. I only took a free drink.
But it's what it implies.
This night has been so shit. I just want to go home.
My phone has been vibrating in my hand since I got into the cubicle.
An incoming call from Nancy and a text from James.
I reject her call. I'd better reply to him.

Nance rings me again, straight after I reply to him. There's no point in answering. I won't be able to hear her over the music in the background. I'd better go back out and find her.
I walk straight out – not looking in the bathroom mirror because I know I look a mess and it'll put me in an even worse mood.
Nance is talking to the barman in the distance.
He's got his arms folded.
Looks bored.
He's walked away before I get back.
'Fucking hell, took your time. You got the shits or something?'
She's perked up. 'Oh shit, babes. What's wrong? You been

crying?' She wraps her arms around me and pulls me into her exposed, fleshy chest. I feel myself rubbing snot and my slight mascara on her warm skin.

She walks me away. Can't see where we're going, but we quickly end up outside in the smoking area.

I smell it before I see it.

I'm so embarrassed. Everyone's looking at me. I must look a mess. What must everyone think? I've turned into one of the girls that I'd see and think – *'look at the state of her'*; sat down in the smoking area, hugging my knees, eyes watering.

Classy.

I'm just missing a broken heel and an ASBO.

Nance has sat next to me and pulled me into her chest again, rubbing my head.

That's my hair ruined.

I can't hear what she's saying over the traffic of Piccadilly, but her voice sounds calm. It eases through the roar of bus engines going past. She's giving me goosebumps from speaking into my neck. I think she feels bad for having a go at me about the queue.

I haven't said anything since I got back from the toilet. If I start, I'll just go on a long rant about everything in my life. Plus, I don't want the whole world knowing my business. This isn't the time or the place. James is funny about me telling people if we've had an argument. He wants everyone to think that we've got this perfect relationship and never argue. Anytime we have an argument, he always asks if I've told anyone – or asks who was there with me if we were arguing on the phone. I get it… If we had an argument and his mum overheard – or he went away to confide in some other girl – I wouldn't be happy. I try not to tell anyone about arguments. Nancy will usually know, but that's only because she can tell. I don't like to tell her. There's no point in running to her every time we have a row. I think she gets annoyed that I'll complain about him one minute and be all loved-up again the next. Plus, because she doesn't like him, she'll just tell me to leave him and won't be much help.

My phone has started vibrating in my hand, again.
I lift my head up to Nancy, holding me.
    'Can we just go home, Nance? Please?'

17. RANDOM CLUB cont.

So, we didn't go home in the end. She talked me into staying.
'We've come all the way down here. No point going home now.
It'll make you feel worse. Just try enjoy yourself. You know I'm
here if you wanna talk.'
She's talking bollocks. She doesn't give a shit about how I'm
feeling. She blatantly just doesn't want to go home early and kill
her night.

We were outside for about twenty minutes until I psyched
myself up to go back in. I'm sure everyone was looking. The
whole club must've seen me run into the toilets and come back out
– crying. The tiny bit of mascara I was wearing has all gone now,
running down my cheek and staining Nancy's top.
That should make us even.
I went straight back into the toilets with her and sorted my face
out, while she pouted in the mirror over my shoulder – plumping
up her hair and straightening her bra from under her armpits.
'Come, let's just forget all this and have a laugh. No point us
moping about in here. People might think we're a couple lesbians,
keep running in and out the toilets together. Come – let's go
dance.' She's talking at her own reflection, barely noticing me
with my head in the sink, dabbing at the clumps of make-up
clinging to my eyes.
She takes my hand and leads me to the toilet door, muffling the
music outside.
I'm not in the mood for this.

On the way out, I read the text I got earlier from James. He would've seen from the read receipts that I haven't opened it. The message stops me in my tracks. I pause in the middle of the crowd as Nance tries to drag my arm to the dance floor.
My stomach has gone over.
The deafening music fades.

I see the words *'snake'* and *'liar'* before I read it fully.

It was sent about twenty minutes ago. I haven't done myself any favours by not replying straight away. I text back as soon as I read it – as soon as he gets notified that it's been seen. I don't want to make him any angrier. I just want to go home. Nancy's walked off without me and gone back to the bar. She's probably waiting for that same barman. I see where her priorities are.
I keep my phone in my hand, so I can feel if it vibrates.
There's an open pathway of people leading up to Nancy – tilting forward and balancing on the two front legs of a stool. She's on her toes, leaning right over so she can be seen by the barman; boobs spread out over the bar, fiddling with a straw in her teeth. She's going to go mad if I tell her that I want to go home because of James.
I'll have to make up something else.
I come to her from behind – crinkling my forehead and squinting my eyes. My words spill out as I slump on the bar next to her. 'Nance, d'you mind if we go? I'm getting a banging headache and I feel proper rough.' My arms are stretched across to the other side of the bar and my fingers are clenching my phone. I'm facing away from the bar staff. I don't want that guy to come back over and speak to me, again.
My phone has vibrated with a text. I read it straight away. It's a long one. That's never a good sign.

My eyes are drawn to certain sentences between name-calling.
'I proper hate you when you're with her.'

'I hope she dies.'
'Don't even bother replying to this.'
'I'm done with you.'

Nancy shouts over the music. 'Since when? You was fine a minute ago, I swear?' She's got a bit of a tone, now.
I don't need this.

I answer her a few seconds late, preoccupied with reading the text. 'Erm… I think it's from that little thing earlier.' Still scanning the text. '…Where I was crying.' Lock phone and look at her. 'It gave me a bit of a headache.' My eyes wander to my phone. It's started flashing with an incoming call.

'Got nothing to do with him then, no?' Her eyes beat over to James' name, pounding through my phone.

I hold it face down, pinning it to the bar. I *need* to answer this. It seems to ring out for ages under my hand, rattling the whole club. 'Nah, it's not. Can we please just go, Nance?' I grasp my phone tighter, hoping I don't miss the call.
She pulls the straw out of her mouth and flings it across the bar. She mumbles something to herself as she walks towards the exit. Usually, I'd care… But I really don't give a shit at the moment. I need to sort this out with James. I don't know where this even came from.
I don't need all this tonight.

Another text comes through as I trail behind her.
I stop dead over my feet and my entire body falls in line.
Certain words pop to the surface.
'Ignore me still?'
'Watch when I send that video all round the area and to your alcoholic mum.'

My body gets heavy over my legs.
He's never said anything like that before. And never mentioned mum like that. I try to ring him back, but he locks it off. After two

or three rings, it goes straight to voicemail. I feel my eyes welling up.
Nance is already outside, past the bouncers.

I need to get out of here.

18. WOOLWICH ARSENAL STATION

It wasn't a good journey home. The two of us hardly said a word to each other. I tried to at first – asking what she thought of the barman, how stupid we must've looked running around all night, me crying… She wasn't having it, so I just stopped bothering. The only time she spoke to me properly was to ask for the ID that she'd leant me.

We've cut through Woolwich Market, avoiding the river at the top end. It's too risky to go there at this time of night. I just want to get home, now. The sooner this night ends – the better.

The market is deserted. During the day, there's usually loads of people cutting through and loud music playing.

Now, there's no one around. It's scary. Too quiet.

I've taken my heels off and I'm walking to Nancy's in pumps, heading towards Woolwich Church Street. The balls of my feet have grown fresh blisters from sprinting hysterically around the bar all night. The colour from my flats has run onto my toes and my feet are stained with black dye. Cheap rubbish.

Nancy is a few paces in front of me and walking with a strop. She's got a swing of attitude in her step, strutting down her own cement catwalk. She's too good to be walking in Woolwich.

Those moves are wasted around here.

She belongs in Paris or Milan.

Flaunt those streaks of blotchy fake tan.

Flick them cheap, clip-on hair extensions.
Flutter those fake eyelashes.
Freeze.
And pose.
She's walking barefoot, occasionally stumbling off her path and
steadying herself from falling – not a good look with what she's
wearing. It looks cheap walking around barefoot after a night out
at the best of times. She must be freezing. I'm a lot more covered
up than her and I'm still cold. If she wants to dress like a slut, then
she has to deal with that. Her studded heels are clicking together
in her hand. The metal echo chases itself to the bottom of the
market and bounces back to us.
This is all a stage to her. She wants attention. She doesn't care
who it's from or what it's for, as long as she gets it.

I tried to check the time on the clock at the Royal Arsenal
Gatehouse. It was hard to see through the last clumps of mascara,
still resting on my eyelids. I don't want to get to James' too late,
that'll make things even worse.
She's really pissed me off tonight. I won't forget this. I was
looking after her when she was a mess before we went in.
Anything could've happened to her if I wasn't there. And when I
needed her? Nothing.
She saw what I was like earlier and now she's got the cheek to
blank me…
Sorry for cutting your night short and preventing you getting off
with some random guy, then going on about it for the next two
weeks – telling me how he's *'proper on you'* and boring me with
all that bollocks.
Let her get on with it. I'm not going to pander to the girl.
    We get to her front door and she turns to me. 'You coming in?'

Ha! Are you serious? You haven't said two words to me since
Piccadilly Circus and now you want me to stay over like nothing's
happened? No, thanks.

'Nah, I've gotta go James' now. I told him I'd stay over.' I can see her mum has put some Christmas decorations up around the windows and door. I wonder if mum's done the same… Stupid question.

'Cool. Bye.' She walks right in and shuts the door in my face. Stupid bitch. I know she'll tell her mum all about tonight… Make up some bullshit story that I made her go home because I wanted to leave to see James – when she knows that wasn't the case – then the next time I'm at hers, I'll feel like an idiot knowing that her mum knows all about tonight's drama.

We were due to fall out, really. And it's always because she's obsessed with James and makes out that he's a big influence on me and how I act. The last time we fell out like this was when she was trying to organise a girls' holiday to Malia. It would've been us two and two of the girls.

Nance was arranging this holiday and I said I *might* be able to go. *Might*.

It was just after the exams in the summer. Firstly, I didn't have the money to be going on holiday. It would've cost about five hundred pounds for the flight; then transfers; then travel insurance; then spending money… It would've been at least a grand – all in. That's too expensive for a week away. You could probably go travelling for that amount of money in hostels.

I thought it was all just talk. I didn't think it was an actual thing that she had her heart set on. I'd been with James for a little while. I knew he was funny about me talking to boys, and I'd already lost a lot of my guy mates from college over him by this point. A few weeks into the relationship, he made me go through my phone and delete most of my contacts on there who were boys. I didn't really want to because there were some people that I used to be quite close with – only as friends. He said, if I hadn't spoken to them for the last few months, they obviously weren't proper friends… So, there was no point in having them on my phone. He asked what I valued more – a few mates that I never talk to or him?

So, I deleted them.

I thought he *must've* trusted me after that.

I mentioned, in passing, that Nancy wanted us all to go on holiday. I thought, because there were no boys going, it wouldn't have been a problem. The way he put it made it sound a lot worse than it was.

'Four girls – three who are single – going on holiday to Malia.'

I know where he was coming from. Fair enough, the majority of people who go over to those places only go there for one reason. He was telling me about people he knew who had gone on these holidays. Apparently, the drinking games in those types of places are really sexual – like girls having to strip off or get with random guys. He said there was one game where girls had to race to give a boy a boner the fastest. Then, the winner would get free drinks all night.

One girl actually gave a guy head.

In front of everyone.

The whole club saw her sucking him off.

Obviously, I'm not like that at all. People say it's the drink that makes you do stuff like that, but I don't think so. I reckon you're either *that* type of person or you're not. No amount of alcohol could make me do something like that because that's not me.

I wouldn't have gone over there with any intentions of cheating or doing anything with a guy. If I'm not going to talk to boys on my own doorstep, why would I spend over a grand to ruin my relationship over there? No matter how much I explained to him that I just wanted a holiday because I'd never been abroad, he wasn't happy about me going.

So, I told Nance that I wouldn't be able to go.

No one ended up going – which made me feel really bad about the whole thing.

This was around the time that she'd broken up with her ex, who was James' friend. So, she didn't like him – even back then. She

started going on about how I'm letting him control what I do, how her ex was exactly the same; and since I'd started seeing James, I'd been acting different and hadn't seen her as much.
Which wasn't true.

All of a sudden – because I don't have the money to go on holiday – it means I'm being different with her and James is being possessive of me.
We've got a normal relationship. He's not dictating to me.
It was my choice not to go on holiday. He wasn't happy about it. Fair enough. But it was for a good reason.
Either way, it was my choice not to go. She's obviously not going to see it that way because she doesn't like him. She needs to accept that she can't be putting me in the middle of their rows. I'm with him. I don't want to lose her friendship. That's all there is to it.
She acts like she's looking out for me, but she's not. She blatantly just doesn't like him, and she lets it warp everything about our friendship. That's her issue. Not mine. It's not fair for her to put that on me, especially when James hasn't done anything wrong to me or her.
We didn't talk for a few days around that time. I hope we don't have a repeat of that. I don't like falling out with her. It always has to be me who makes the first move and apologise because she's so stubborn.
I always have to explain myself or justify what I do to someone, and it's really getting to me. I seem to spend my whole life apologising to someone.

I've walked through the estate on my own and just got to the park across from James'. It's really scary this way. It's deserted – only the orange streetlights making shadows climb up the concrete blocks of flats around me. Other than that, it's completely dark outside. He could've met me somewhere, so I wouldn't have to walk alone.

There's a pinch beneath my skin with every step I take closer to James'. My body is clamping a sharp blister between my pumps and my foot, warning me not to walk to his too fast.

I can make out some figures moving under the orange glow in the park. They disappear into shadows and come back into the dim light. They all have their hoods up, with the peaks of their hats poking out under them.

One of them has a dog and they're tormenting it. I hate seeing that. I don't know why someone would be horrible to an animal. They can't respond or tell anyone how much pain they're in. So, why wouldn't you do all that you can to make sure they're comfortable and happy? They're so defenceless and rely on people to be nice to them. I don't like seeing people abuse that trust.

These guys shouldn't be allowed dogs. They should need a license for a dog to make sure they aren't just given to any neglectful scum to look after. You wouldn't treat a kid like that, so animals shouldn't be any different.

No such thing as a bad dog – just a bad owner.

A few others on bikes join the group from around the corner. They appear all at once from behind the bins. They're pedalling slowly, their faces concealed under hoods. One figure on a stolen Boris Bike attempts a wheelie over the concrete slabs. The tyre slaps into a puddle, patting the sound all around me. The faint, tinny sound of music comes from a phone and bounces around the estate, chasing the agitated barks of the dog – trapping me under it all.

They all seem to stop moving and look over as I get closer. I know most of the people around here, so I shouldn't have any trouble. It's still intimidating to have to walk across here, especially all dressed up like this.

I don't look at any of them as I get closer. My eyes are fixed on James' blue front door. All the neighbours' doors are exactly the same. It's hard to tell which one is his. Luckily, I don't have to go into the main block. He's on the ground floor, so I avoid the piss-smelling staircases and broken lifts.

There are infinite rows of blue doors looking over the balconies, disappearing upwards – higher than I can see. They're all linked with clotheslines; hanging grey tracksuits and hoodies, flowing on to the next door along.

I keep walking, not taking my eyes off the frosted glass window of the front door.

I hear a couple of the boys talking, but still don't see their faces in the dark.

'Oi, where you from?'
'Bruv, she's blatantly sexy.'
'Look at her arse.'
'Allow it – I swear that's James' girl?'

I get to his front door and text him.

19. JAMES'

He kept me waiting outside for a while, blatantly pretending he didn't see my text. Eventually, he came down and let me in, but didn't say a word to me until we got into his room. I prefer that, really. The last thing I want is to be having a full-blown argument in his living room, where everyone can hear.

When we came into his room, he didn't say anything – almost like he was waiting for me to start talking, then he could react to it and say I started the argument. It's never a good sign when he doesn't say anything because I know he's just sitting there, waiting to kick off. He's never hit me or anything. He'd never do anything like that.

It turned into quite a big argument when he found out Nancy was in a state. I had to tell him why I wasn't texting him back straight away, and that just came out of my mouth.

It made him really suspicious of me, asking *'how much I'd had to drink?'*, *'did anyone get me one?'*, *'where exactly did I go?'*, and questions like that. I didn't mention the guy behind the bar because there was no point. It would've made things a million times worse. Plus, technically, he didn't buy me a drink. He just gave me *and* Nance one for free because he didn't charge either of us. Not just me.

I know he wouldn't see it like that, though. He'd want to take me out to the same place next week to suss the guy out and watch how I act around him and everything.

It'd be too much drama for something that's not an issue.

He lost his temper at one point. He sort of held me against the mirror – kind of by the throat – but more on the shoulders. It wasn't hard or anything. He didn't grab my throat to choke me. He just held me against the mirror as he was talking. He was getting angry because he was getting upset and he doesn't know how to deal with that – he would've been able to see himself in the reflection behind me.

It's still a bit sore, but I think that's more from where I was shouting in the club because it was so loud.

We're fine now, though. I said sorry for ignoring him, even though I didn't mean to. He said we should just forget about it.

I know why he gets like this… I do think he genuinely cares, and his ex totally messed him up with trust. It is difficult that he makes me pay for her mistakes, but he'll never point the blame there. It's like he doesn't want to admit that she had an impact on him.

He doesn't seem to think it's me or his ex that are the cause of it. Nancy is the cause of the problems because of how she is. He always says things like – *'if I didn't care about you, I wouldn't get so wound up, would I?'* and *'it's her I don't trust, not you'.*

It's about three in the morning and we're both in bed. It's been such a long day. He's already asleep, facing the wall. I'm on my back; staring at a tiny bit of light on the ceiling that's sneaking in through the window.

He made a good point earlier. For someone who is supposed to be my best friend, she let me walk all the way through the park on my own.

What if I got raped or something? That would've been her fault for letting me go to his place on my own. He's right.

There's no point in making an effort with the girl anymore. James was saying the same thing. She obviously doesn't value me as a friend that much; not if she's willing to let me walk through the estate on my own, while she's at hers – texting some guy, probably.

She can make the first move from here.
She's just too selfish.
I don't need her.
I'm done with the girl.

I've got James and he's never going to leave me.

20. AT MINE

'Hello, love. You want a bit of breakfast?' Mum shouts to me from the kitchen. Smells lovely in here – nice, greasy fry-up in the air.

'Hiya. Yeah, go on then, thanks. You're up early.' I drop my stuff by the front door and follow the carpet into the living room. It's so bright. The curtains are open and the white glow from outside is taking over the whole room.

She's put the tree up in the far corner, opposite the telly. It's scattered with blue and purple decorations and multi-coloured lights. Can't wait until Christmas – seeing the tree has got me feeling really festive.

At least I can scratch Nancy's name off the list of people I need to buy presents for.

Just James and mum to get this year.

In the middle of the room, there's an empty, faded cardboard box – wrapped in layers of brown tape, supporting bulging rips and tears. It's on its side, spilling out the same decorations we've had for as long as I can remember.

Tinsel.

Baubles.

Fake snow.

And on the coffee table, a little angel that I made when I was in primary school. I remember that day well. I was only about eight. We all had to flatten clay with a rolling pin, cut out a pair of wings, roll a little ball for a head, mould a cone-shaped body,

101

attach little worms for arms, then put it all together. They all went into an oven to harden, then we got to paint them how we wanted. Mine was the best. I remember wanting to make her look like mum. She's in a plain, white dress; with shiny, gold wings; and long, dark hair. She's got a bit faded and scuffed over the years, but she's still beautiful. She goes on the tree last – every year. When I was little, mum would pick me up and let me put her on top. She always said it was my special job because I was her little angel. She'd have to tie it with string after, so it didn't fall off and smash. It's nice that she's saved it for me to do.

'Awww, mum! You should've waited for me! I would've helped you put the tree up.' I shout into her from the living room and follow my voice into the kitchen. It looks clean. She must've been up for a while. Looks like she's given the place a good scrub. She's got her back to me as she shifts bacon around the spit of the frying pan.

'Ah that's okay; it didn't take me too long. I left you the angel to put on – I know that's your favourite bit.' Her voice speaks through a smile. I can't see it, but I know it's there.

It's our little tradition.

I go to her side and turn her towards me. She looks like she's losing a lot of weight. Her face is gaunt and her white pyjama top is just hanging off her. I put my hands under her open dressing gown and cuddle into her, pressing my head against her shoulders. We stand for a few seconds without saying anything; just rock with each other the tiniest bit. I can feel her bones through her loose top. I want to say something to her – tell her she should go to the doctors or something.
But I don't want to worry her.
She seems like she's in a good way.
And at least she's eating.

She pats my back and turns to the pan. 'What d'you want for breakfast? I'm doing myself a bacon sandwich with beans. That alright?' Her voice wobbles as she shields her face away from me, towards the mad popping of grease and fat.

'Yeah, go on then. Sounds nice.' My voice is soft as I stroke the bumps of her spine. I feel so much better in myself when I know mum is alright. I can finally relax.

Typical. Things go well with mum and now I've got dramas with Nance.

Fuck her.

Not even going to give her a second thought.

'Go on. Take your stuff upstairs and I'll give you a shout when it's ready, love.' She looks over her shoulder and angles a wet cheek towards me, with a wrinkled smile.

I give her a smile and go back to the hallway, grabbing my bag on the way upstairs. I can smell that she's sprayed air freshener on the landing. Usually, I'd be suspicious and think she's trying to hide the smell of drink. Not now.

Smell is one of the only things that can take you back to another time. It's the only sense that can give you déjà vu and instantly take you to an exact point in your life, making you remember everything so vividly.

That same vanilla air freshener hangs over all my memories of her slurring words and stumbling through the hallway. It drapes over all those times we both saw the problem hidden in plain sight and never spoke about it. When I'd come home and smell that, I'd suspect the worse – and I'd usually be right to.

Not today, though.

I'm still a bit on edge this morning. I woke up in a sweat earlier – maybe from all the drama last night; falling out with Nancy and the stuff with James. I don't remember dreaming about anything particular, but I jolted in my sleep and woke myself up; as if I was running and tripped over in a dream. That seems to happen a lot. I need a decent sleep.

I get into my room and drop my stuff on the floor. My bed has been made. That would've been mum. I usually just pull the duvet over and leave it like that.

I throw myself onto the immaculate bedding and pull my phone out of my pocket.

No texts.

I'm not expecting anything from Nance. We'll probably be like this until after Christmas; until she's at a loose end and has no one to go out with, then she'll act like nothing has happened and text me something stupid to break the ice – expecting me to just forget what a bitch she was.

She can go fuck herself. I bet she would… Loves herself that much. Then again, she'd probably get some random guy to do that for her. She was meant to check James' Facebook for me and see if he was talking to anyone. I doubt he was.

I go onto my Facebook and check his profile.

Nothing new.

I'll log in to his account and check his messages.

Email address.

Password.

Incorrect.

Strange.

No – his email is *'.com'* I think?

Email address.

Password.

Incorrect? Still?

What the fuck.

Has he changed it? Why's he done that? Did I definitely put in the right one?

I try it, again.

Incorrect.

Shit. He has. He's actually changed his password.

I load my Instagram app.
Log out.
Sign in.
James' email.
James' password.
Incorrect.

My stomach knots.
What's going on here?
Why's he done that?
I can't exactly ask him, can I?
I shouldn't have even looked… But he's obviously changed it for a reason.
What's he hiding?
I'll have to try his phone when I see him. If I can get hold of his phone, I can get a proper look. Am I actually going to do this?
I'm going to his tomorrow, so I've got time to think of what to do.
I'll drop some hints and try to find out what's happening… Before I go completely psycho.
I can't believe this. I've turned into *that* girlfriend.
Try not to think about it until I see him tomorrow.
But that's easier said than done.

I'm going to stay in tonight, anyway.
Want to have a bit of time with mum.

21. JAMES'

Apparently, I couldn't wait until tomorrow to see him. I texted him a few hours later and asked if I could come over; threw on a pair of leggings, a blue hoodie, UGGs, and made my way to his. I felt bad on mum for leaving – but she was going to bed, anyway. I'll give her a text later.

I was sitting on the sofa at mine and the password stuff was just ticking over in my head. I was probably letting my imagination run away a bit. I'm sane enough to know that much – that must be a good sign.
I was imagining him and his ex messaging each other. I don't know who else it could be because he doesn't speak to any girls. I know they had a bad breakup because she cheated on him, but she's still on my mind.
He *says* he doesn't talk to her anymore, but I'm not sure.
I was imagining them being friendly while we were first getting together. Then, after a while, they started meeting up more; just as we were getting serious. Then, probably around the time of my birthday, they started seeing each other regularly and probably having sex. Then, he'd ask me to come over and he'd fuck me in the same bed as that slag. They'd both be sneaking around and she'd come to his straight after I would leave, and they'd both just be laughing at me behind my back.
God knows what STIs she's left on these sheets – feel like I could catch something just lying here.
My body begins to wriggle on the bed.

I've always noticed his phone is face down – but now that I'm actually watching it, he's always got it in his hand. And he's always checking it. Or fiddling with it. Or walking away with it. We both know each other's passwords, but he never just leaves it on the side.

It's always with him.

If his lock screen password has been changed, then I'll know that something is going on.

All this over a changed Facebook password.

Really?

I need to get a life.

I'm probably just being paranoid.

I hope so.

We're both lying on the bed. He's asked me what's wrong a couple of times. He can tell there's something on my mind, but what can I say?

'Well, I was stalking your Facebook earlier to see if you were talking to other girls and I couldn't log in. Why'd you change your password? Oh… And can I have a look through your messages while we're at it? Sorry to ask you – Nancy was meant to look for me.'

Don't think that'd go down too well.

He's twirling his phone in his hand. I have to find out. 'What you got as your wallpaper now? Let's have a look…' He'll put his code in and I'll see if it's been changed.

It was 4753.

'Same one I've always had.' He presses the middle button for the lock screen to light up. 'Just my West Ham background.'

Bollocks. Plan B.

'Have you deleted that video from the other day, by the way?'

'What video?' He's still twirling his phone.

'You know what one…'

'Oh.' He laughs to himself. '*That* one? Yeah, I deleted it straight after you left.' He's smirking. I know he hasn't deleted it, but there are more important things to find out at the moment.

'Liar. Show me, then.' I say it in a jokey way, making it clear that I'm being playful and not trying to start an argument.

'Nah, you should trust me.' He tries to shut down the conversation.

'I do trust you, obviously. But I wanna see that you definitely have.'

...And see if you've changed your lock screen code.

'You obviously don't trust me if you need me to show you...' He's got an answer for everything.

I need to be careful what I say because I don't want to start him off. I really need to keep him happy to find out if his password has been changed. 'Well, the fact I even did the video in the first place should show I trust you.'

'Eurgh!' His face twists and he sniggers at that. 'Don't act like you was doing me a favour. It was a little thirty-second video. Nothing special.'

I don't even answer.

Feel like shit, now.

Thanks for that.

He climbs over me to get out of bed... Makes sure he takes his phone with him – obviously. He fiddles about with it while he's standing over me, then shows me his camera roll. 'See. Look. Gone.'

Why did he have to get out of bed, just to do that?

This can't be a coincidence.

He stood up for no reason.

Why not get his photos up when he was lying here next to me?

Is there another photo he doesn't want me to see on there?

He's blatantly hiding something. But how will I know for definite?

Fucking hell. I shouldn't have got myself into this.

He puts his phone on his chest of drawers by the side of the bed – face down, as usual. 'You gonna stop being miserable now, yeah?' He climbs on top of me and rests on his elbows, pinning my shoulders to the bed.

'I'm not being miserable. I told you, I'm fine.' I look up at him over me.

'Good. Well… Since you made me delete that video, you might as well…' He starts rubbing my head, just above my ears.

'Stop. That tickles.' I jerk my head away, maybe a bit too quickly.

'What the fuck's wrong with you?' He lifts the top half of his body and digs his hands into the mattress on both sides of my head, caging me in under him. His arms are tensed and I can see his veins under his loose vest.

'Nothing, you was just tickling my ear. Sorry, I didn't mean to snap.' My head retracts into my shoulders as I go into myself.

'Nah, don't try it. You've been weird since you got here. Don't ask to come round, then bring your shitty, little moods here. Otherwise – you can just go home now.' He's still on top of me, looking down his nose at me in my shell.

I don't know what I can say to him…

I'm upset about falling out with my best friend?
I think my boyfriend's cheating on me?
I did a pregnancy test and threw it away before I looked at it?

22. JAMES' cont.

I'm not stupid. To anyone else, I know it would seem like he was out of order earlier – but he knows me really well. If there's something on my mind, he picks up on it really easily. And if I don't tell him what it is, he gets really wound up; only because he wants to know what's on my mind because it makes me act differently towards him. And no matter what the reason is, that's not fair on him. Obviously, I can't open up to him about everything this time – just because it's about him.

I reckon it's me being stupid, now. It has to all be in my head. I shouldn't be acting weird with him because of something in my head – that's out of order. Despite what I think, he hasn't actually done anything wrong.

I gave him some story about mum in the end… Told him I was worried about her weight and said I was stressing about Nance a little bit; with what she might say to all our friends about me.

He tried to make me feel better about mum and told me that I can stay at his whenever I want to get away from things – that was nice to hear.

He didn't mention anything about Nancy, which I wasn't surprised about.

'So, you outta this little mood now, then?'

'Yeah, yeah – I do feel better now. Just gonna try not to think about stuff. Plus, I got my teaching placement next year to look forward to. I reckon, when I start that, that'll keep me busy and I won't have much time to think about anything else. Except you, obviously.' I give him a little smile.

I have noticed that… When we've got nothing to do, we seem to be at each other's throats a lot more. It almost feels like we've got nothing better to do than argue. That's why I tried to tell him about apprenticeships the other day. I reckon, if he actually did something, he'd be happier. He'd have something to look forward to and focus on, even if it was something little. And it would be an extra bit of money in his pocket. Then, we can actually go out to nice places rather than staying in all day and watching the walls. Now, he just sits indoors. One of his mates might come here to buy some weed from him, but that's about it. We need to get out a bit more.

When I start this school placement, things will get better with us – not that they're bad at the moment, but things will just be better.

We're sitting up on the bed. I've still got my eye on his phone. I shouldn't, but I'm going to have to go through it tonight – just to put my own mind at rest. Otherwise, I'll just be obsessing over it as soon as I leave. I know I will.

After that little talk, I genuinely don't think he'd cheat on me. I can tell he cares about me. But knowing me, as soon as I leave here, I'll start imagining all sorts again.

He angles his head towards me. 'Yeah, just don't think about all that. As long as things are alright with me and you, nothing else really matters, does it?' He puts his arm around me and brings me into his chest.

I love it when he's like this. He puts on a front of being the hard man who doesn't care about anything, but when I need him, I know he's there for me. He's got a really nice side to him that he doesn't show that much. He shows it at the right time and that's all that matters.

This side of him usually gets me a bit… On it.

I think he thinks talking about fighting and selling weed impresses me, but I prefer him like this. The whole *'bad boy'* image doesn't do anything for me. For me, bad boys are just that… Boys. This nice side *really* does it for me.
The affectionate, caring side that only I know.

Where I've cuddled into him more, I've basically ended up on top of him. He's shifted me up by my bum, so I'm lying completely on him. I start tickling his arms, from his wrists to the top of his black vest. His skin is lovely and soft.
So jealous.
I stroke the muscles on his arms under my nails. He's quite thin, but he's got nice arms. The hairs on his forearms stand up under my fingertips as my hands flow back down. I feel him digging into me. He's got dark grey tracksuit bottoms on and they're loose enough for me to feel him getting hard against my leg. I stop tickling him and grip onto his wrists, pulling them up over his head and pinning him down. He lifts his head up to me and kisses me hard. I push my lips against his and force his head back onto the pillow. I lock both his hands together above his head, using just my weaker left hand to keep him restrained. I drag my right hand down his chest, past the drawstring on his bottoms, and onto his left thigh; then slowly ease my hand in between his legs and rub back up to his chest. I can feel him – warm and hard through his bottoms – giving him a teasing rub up and down, then bring my hands back up to his. His body wriggles about under me.

I go in to kiss him again, but just lick from his chin and over his lips. 'Getting too much for you, is it?' My voice falls down onto him and spreads out over the bed. He doesn't say anything, just lets out a deep breath through his nose and smiles. He gets these little dimples when he smiles. So fit. He pushes through my hands and grabs my hips, squeezing them tightly. I raise my arms to put my hair up, and he pulls my hoodie over my head before I can resist. I look down at him, biting my bottom lip and smiling through it. 'Cheeky.'

I bring my arms down straight away to cover my belly and lean over him – before he sees any of my rolls; this isn't the most flattering position in the world. I've got my arms on both sides of his head, caging him in under me. He starts rubbing my bum and squeezes it. He slaps through my leggings, before pulling them down a tiny bit to look at my knickers. 'Not matching for me, no?' An eyebrow raises through half a grin.

It takes me a second to get what he means. I'm wearing black knickers and a cheap, grey bra. It's not a nice one at all. I should throw it away, really. 'Well, I didn't know I'd be coming over. Just make sure it doesn't stay on for long.' I give him a teasing smile. I try to take his vest off, but he doesn't lift his body to help me. I make sure I'm leaning forward the whole time I'm on top of him; hopefully, my boobs will cover my belly.

He grabs my back and pulls my right boob towards him.

I'm sure that one's bigger. That's probably why he always goes for that one. It must be at least a cup-size bigger than my left one. Easily.

What's that about? They're the same age. They were put in a bra at the same time. They've had the same support their whole life.

One decides to be awkward.

One decides to just do its own thing.

Typical.

I get lost for a minute, until he slips my boob out of the bra and dips it into his mouth. I can feel his tongue moving around the nipple between his teeth. This gets me really on it. I could have him do this for ages. He starts squeezing the other one through my bra, pinching my nipple through the material. He tucks his hand down inside my bra and does it again, rolling my nipple between his thumb and finger. He starts to get a bit harder with his fingers and I feel myself starting to make noise. It hurts a bit at first, but it's a nice pain. When he starts using his teeth a bit too much, I pull myself away and pin him to the bed again, dangling my boobs in his face.

He loves that.

I can see him wriggling around and getting frustrated when he's restrained. He overpowers my right hand and starts picking at his mouth. 'Eurgh, man. What the hell?' He casually scrapes his tongue, wipes his fingers on the bed sheet, then puts his hand back under mine again.

No way.

Don't.

He didn't just get a hair in his mouth.

From my boob.

Fuck. Off.

He's started kissing me again, but my eyes are wide open. Are we just going to pretend that didn't happen? Are we just going to pretend that I'm not some big, hairy yeti? Do not tell me I'm getting hair on my boobs. I know my arms have fair hair on them, but never my chest. I've officially got a hairy chest. Brilliant. What am I? Some fifty-year-old man in a seventies night club? Maybe I should get myself a medallion and a white suit for Christmas. Really commit to the role.

Does every girl get this? Not the kind of thing I can ask mum, is it?

I'm really self-conscious now and I can feel myself pulling away when he's trying to bring me closer to him.

Fucking moulting... Unbelievable.

I've realised he's been fiddling with my bra, trying to get it off. Maybe the bra got caught with my lead, since I'm clearly a big rottweiler. He sits up quickly and throws me onto my back. My body follows where he wants it to go. I love it when he takes control like this. I don't put up a fight, just flop onto my back and do whatever he wants me to do. I love the feeling that my body is his. He can do whatever he wants to me. He's started kissing my neck and squeezing my boobs really hard, pulling at my bra. 'Take this off.' He kisses around my belly as I quickly fiddle under my back. I pull it off my arms and throw it on the floor.

What is it with him and bras? It's two little hooks, and he always has trouble. I've got to being able to take it off with one hand. He gets so flustered trying to get it off.

That's education for you.

They taught us the science of what's inside a boob – but not how to unhook a bra.

They taught us the breakdown of the uterus for periods – but not the breakdown of a relationship.

Pass exams. Fail life.

He starts pulling on my leggings, so I have to lift my bum up to help him get them off. He rolls my knickers off with them. They're tangled in each other as he tosses them over his shoulder. No idea how this is fair… I'm totally naked and he's still fully dressed.

He starts kissing my hip and licks the inside of my thigh, then stops just before he gets between my legs – gives me goosebumps when he does that. I love it.

I look horrible from this angle. I can barely see him over my belly. My body has spread over the bed like a doughy pizza base. Got big love handles going on at the moment, too.

Stuffed-crust.

I pull the top of his vest over his head while he's down there. Let's try to even things out a bit. It comes over his head with one pull and he doesn't try to resist, just carries on teasing around my hips and thighs.

A massive chill goes through my body. His house is usually really warm, but when you're naked on top of the covers, it's a different story. I start pulling at the corners of the duvet to cover us, trying to keep my legs as still as I can.

Don't want to interrupt his… Flow.

Not sure how I'm going to get it from under me. I can feel myself wriggling about more and more. Feel like a fat, naked fish – flapping all over the bed.
Bet I look like a lava lamp.

He stops. 'What you doing?'
'Huh?'
'Can you keep still?' His little eyes are looking up at me from between my legs. Looks quite funny from up here. Can't laugh, though. That'd be a real mood killer.
'Sorry, I'm just cold.' I use my arms to hug myself warm and cover my rolls as he looks up. This can't be a flattering angle. 'Can we snuggle under the duvet?'
'What? You not on it now, no?' He's rolled on his side, still between my legs.
'Nah, course I still wanna. I just wanna be all cosy under the duvet because I'm freezing.' My teeth click together as I talk.
'For fuck's sake.' He slides off the bed, just in his tracksuit bottoms. They're loose and riding his boxers up. He pulls the bottom corners of the duvet and whips it from under me. I wobble on the bed, like a big table of unsteady cutlery and plates. He drapes his duvet cape over his shoulders and flops on top of me, sliding back between my legs. I feel his tongue push through me straight away. He's not hanging about.
Luckily, I shaved the other day.
My hands follow down there after him and I feel him breathing through his nose on my fingers. If there's no lead up to it, it can get too much – so I put my hand there to try to control it.
I pull myself up to his tongue to help him into place. I wouldn't move his head. I'd rather fit myself around him.

Both of my arms flop to my side and grip the bed sheet. My whole body tenses. My back arches itself upwards and my head tilts back – rolling a faint groan up through my throat. My body falls back onto the bed and my hips start lifting up, pushing myself into his face. As I push my hips up from the bed, I feel him grab my bum and squeeze it between his fingers. He breathes heavier into me and moans.

Just as I start to relax and let go of myself, he crawls up the bed – kissing and licking my body as he comes up to my face. He emerges from under the duvet and pushes through me. I feel every bit of him as he gets deeper. My hands grab his bum, feeling where his boxers are slightly pulled down. He's got his elbows on each side of my face, caging me in under him. His hips push hard and fast for a few seconds. My boobs bounce up and down with his body. I'm really aware of it as it happens, so cover them with my hands. He brings his body down to rest on top of mine, then nuzzles his head in my neck and starts kissing my right shoulder. He starts slowing down, going in and out smoothly, but still just as hard.

I feel like he wants to say something. He keeps looking back at me from my neck, never making eye contact.

He grabs my hair with his right hand and pulls it. With his left hand, he pins my arm to the bed, then starts going harder. Something's got him more in the mood.

Our hands link into each other – as his body tenses on mine, we both squeeze together. He stops again after a couple of seconds and lifts the top half of his body off me. He looks me straight in the eyes – serious. 'Let me anal you.'

I stop. 'Huh?'

'Let me put it in your arse.' He looks over my body.

I did hear it right – explains why he's been squeezing my bum so much. I work my body up under him and rest on my elbows to sit up. '…What's brought this on?'

'Just try something new. It's meant to feel better because it's tighter.'

Tighter? Like I've got a bucket…?

'Erm, I dunno. Won't it hurt?' My voice softens. I *really* don't want to do this. Surely, it's going to hurt… But if I don't do it, he'll think I'm frigid.

Did his ex do that sort of thing?

'Nah, it's meant to feel nice.' His eyes don't leave me. His hands start tickling my stomach, rubbing across my hips and bum. They're guiding me to lie on my front. He kisses me on the lips, and his voice gets sensitive and reassuring. 'If it starts hurting, just tell me and I swear I'll stop. You know I'm not gonna hurt you.' My eyes glance over at his phone – face down on the side. My whole body follows as he starts rolling me over to my left side. He starts kissing my ribs, licks down to my hips, and onto my bum. He pushes my body onto its front and squeezes me, harder than last time. He starts kissing the left side and works towards the middle.

I'm nervous, now.

I'm lying on my front, resting on my elbows with my head down. My fingers start knotting up my hair. My arms are tight against my head.

He's still kissing over the bottom of my back and bum, like that's going to get me in the mood for it. It's just drawing out this horrible feeling I have in my stomach.

I feel like such a slut.

Barely seventeen – and I'm doing anal.

I really don't want to do this. But I can't exactly stop him now, can I? God knows how he'd react.

The bed starts rocking from where he's sat up on his knees, looking down on me. He brings my hips up towards him, putting me on all fours. He's started rubbing himself between my legs and I can feel where he's bringing it up to my bum.

He's really hard.

This is going to hurt.

Just hurry up and get it over with.

I haven't even showered properly.

118

He brings it up and pushes himself between my cheeks. I can
actually feel where it's rough and dry, so he tries to wriggle from
side to side to get it anywhere close. My body pulls away as he
tries to force it in, arching my back up. He presses his hands into
my hips and drags me back onto him. It's starting to hurt where
he's forcing it through.
This isn't going to happen, I can tell.
He breathes heavier into a frustrated grunt behind me. My hair
falls to the side as I look up at him from over my shoulder. He
sticks his fingers in my mouth and makes me suck on them, then
puts them between my cheeks. I clench up straight away, but his
hands overpower me and rub my spit in as far as he can reach –
then he pushes inside more.
This is really hurting.

'I just got the tip in. Does that feel alright?' His voice bounds
down my back.

I bring my head down. My chin is on my chest and I bite both
of my lips together. My face clenches up and my hands are
gripping the sheet. 'M-hmmm.' I can't manage any actual words,
just trying my hardest not to pull away from him.

He's started moving in and out harder.
I can feel everything.
The strain in my back.
My knees digging into the metal springs of the bed.
His fingers clenching my hips.
The rough, dry feeling when he's inside.

I try to ignore it, burying my head in his pillow and groaning
into it. That makes him go harder – probably thinking I'm
enjoying it.
This is the worst feeling.
He spits on his hand and wipes it on me, then gets harder and
faster. Through the pain, his body tenses suddenly. His fingers dig

into my hips and he finishes. I feel him pull out and my stomach cramps. There's a warm drip down my bum and leg.
I feel so disgusting.

He tosses me to the side and my body collapses on the bed. His body drops – face down next to me. He's on his front, with his head facing the wall. 'Fucking hell, that was nice.' His voice is low and bounces off the wall back at me. I start to lie on my side and feel it dripping more. He lifts his body off the bed quickly and looks down at me. His face is twisted up in disgust. 'Oi! What the fuck, man? Don't get any of that on my sheets!' He pushes my body away from the bed, and I have to use my leg to steady myself from falling off.

'What do you want me to do?' I'm standing up beside the bed, using the edge of the duvet to shield my bare skin. I have to curl my body over slightly to cover myself and stop the rest of it dripping onto the floor.

He's already pulled his boxers back up and he's reaching for his phone. 'I dunno. Go get a flannel from the bathroom or something.' His face is lit up by his phone and he doesn't even look at me.

I want to cry.
I'm so embarrassed.
I pick up my clothes and hold them against my skin, trying to protect as much of my body as I can.
I don't stay in his room to get changed – just go straight to the door, biting my lips together and clenching my eyes, trying so hard not to cry.

23. BED

I couldn't even look at myself in the mirror. I feel so disgusting. And on top of that, I'm in a lot of pain. I had to wipe myself down with a freezing-cold flannel and I can still feel where my leg is sticky. I got dressed in the bathroom and had to be really quiet in case his mum heard. It would be the worst if she heard me and came out.
What would she see? Me – scrambling naked to the bathroom, hugging my clothes.
God knows what she heard. Her room is only next door and the whole flat is silent.
I bet she thinks I'm a proper slag. She'd be right.
I feel like one.

When I came back into his room, he was already asleep. The light was still on, his laptop was open and locked, and his phone was back on the side.
I had to ease myself into bed because it hurt to sit down. When I got back in bed with him, he turned away and faced the wall. I heard him mumble for me to turn the light off before he fell back to sleep. I'm lying in a tiny space now, just staring at the ceiling.
God knows what Nance would have to say about all this. I forgot that I'm not speaking to her. She's probably told her mum a fake version of what happened, then she'll tell the girls the same thing and they'll all think I was out of order. They'll all start hanging out together and talking online without me, and I'll start missing out on stuff that gets planned and get left out of everything.

Then, that'd be it. I would've lost everyone.
I feel my eyes getting watery. The little piece of light I usually
look at on the ceiling has gone. I'm focusing on a tiny chip in the
paint and it blurs as I start welling up. I try to control my
breathing and close my eyes. I take a deep breath, open my eyes,
and look over to the right. He looks like he's in a deep sleep; his
shoulders rise and fall with his breath.
I turn to the left and stare at his phone on the side.
4753.

My stomach knots.
I look back over at him and lift my body to sit up, trying to move
the bed as little as I can.
The pain comes back as I get up above him, but I try to fight
through it.
My eyes are on him the whole time.
I take his phone off the side as slowly as I can, then twist my body
to cover it – just in case he turns over.
I hug it towards my head on the pillow.
4753.

I look over my shoulder at him.
Still asleep.

Everything I do is making so much noise.
I hear my heartbeat inside my head.
My breathing gets louder and heavier, so I make each breath
shallower and weaker than the last.
I can hear the bed creaking every time I move – or even breathe.
I look over my shoulder at him again and bring his phone into my
chest, then try his password.
It lights the entire room, more than it should.
4753.
Incorrect.
What?

Lipgloss

I don't hesitate.
4753.
Unlocked.
Must've hit the wrong button.
I guess it's a good sign that he hasn't changed his password.
My hands are sweating and my legs are wanting to fidget.

I look over my shoulder.
Still asleep.

I turn my body more – as if I'm sleeping on my left side – and
bring the phone as close to me as I can.
The light squints my eyes and bounces up to the chip in the
ceiling. Hopefully, it doesn't wake him up.
I'm not sure what to check first – Facebook or WhatsApp?
I'll try normal texts first.
He's only got a few conversations open – all the rest have been
deleted.
I go through them one by one.
They're harmless.
Maybe, I was wrong.
What's the point in even doing this?
If I can't trust him, I shouldn't be with him.
I want to be with him, so I need to trust him.

I look over my shoulder.
Still asleep.

I'll quickly check WhatsApp and Facebook. After that, I'll forget
about all this. It's ridiculous. Look at what I'm doing; sitting up at
one o'clock in the morning, scrolling through conversations
between him and his mum.

Open WhatsApp.
The most recent conversation is with me.

Next one down is his mum.

Next one down is one of his mates – nothing in there to worry about. I actually looked through it and enlarged the profile picture; checking to see if it was a girl and he just changed the name of the contact... There's something wrong with me.

Next one down is a group chat.

Another one of his mates.

Group chat.

Charlotte.

Who the fuck is Charlotte?

That's not his ex.

Still... Who the fuck is Charlotte?

I look over my shoulder.

Charlotte?

I'm going to have to read this.

24. NANCY'S

'Come on, babes. Try and get some sleep, yeah? You'll feel better in the morning, I promise.' She rolls over to face me, taking up less than half of the single bed. Her head rests right beside mine and she drapes an arm and a leg over my body, shielding me under the duvet. 'We'll go out and get some breakfast, do some shopping – whatever you want. We can talk about it more tomorrow.' Her voice gets softer and quieter with every word. 'Everything will be better in the morning.' She kisses my left cheek and gives me a tight, warm cuddle. 'I promise.'

I'm lying on my back with my eyes fixed on the ceiling light. I haven't moved or blinked since she turned it off about an hour ago. She went to sleep about half-an-hour after; she must've just woken up and sensed that I was still awake.
I tilt my head to her alarm clock.
The red digits are piercing through the dark – there's no light coming in the room at all.

05:14

I got here at about two o'clock. I left his and went straight home. Don't remember much of the journey. One minute; I was in bed with him – the next; I was on my door step, fumbling in my bag for my keys.
Mum wasn't in. I went straight to her room, trying to find my footing in the dark. Anything I could make out was misshapen

125

and twisted from the tears clumped at the bottom of my eyes. I was falling over clothes and loose pairs of shoes on the stairs and the landing.

No lights were on upstairs.

Her door was open.

Her telly was on, but there was no sound.

Her sheets were hanging off the bed.

There was no sign of her.

I went straight to my room, grabbed whatever I could carry, and went to Nancy's. I really didn't want to – not after how she'd treated me yesterday.

I just couldn't be on my own.

I had to see someone.

I rang her when I was on her doorstep, but I was worried she wouldn't pick up. It seemed to ring out for ages. She must've been asleep because there were no lights on and all of her Christmas decorations had been turned off. When she did finally answer, I could barely get any words out. I was still crying and sniffing, and my teeth were clicking together with cold that I couldn't even feel. She came to the door straight away; hair down, tying up her pink dressing gown. I didn't have to say what it was about. As soon as she opened the door, she knew it was him. We looked at each other, she took a deep breath in and out, and her eyes closed. She hugged me as close as our bodies could get, then took me straight up to her room, leading me by the hand through the dark. I followed her footsteps, my UGGs soaking the carpet on the way up. She sat me on her bed and closed the door behind her.

I broke down as soon as I got in there.

She just sat beside me and cuddled me, rocking me gently until I stopped.

She didn't probe.

Didn't ask questions.

Didn't go on a rant about him.

She just sat and rocked with me – holding me into her, occasionally kissing my hair.

When I'd finally calmed down, I managed to tell her about the texts. I thought she would've given me a lecture – used it as an opportunity to slag him off, recycled the empty words of how I'm better off without him... None of that would've helped at all.
She didn't do any of it. She just sat and listened to everything that poured out of me.
She asked me if I was sure I wasn't reading them out of context.
There's no other context to *come round and suck my dick*.
There's no other context to the photos in their shared media.

I feel so embarrassed. So ashamed.
This girl had probably seen me walking to his at some point – and had just...
She obviously knows about me. She must do.
When could they have met? How long has this been going on?
What did I do wrong? I've always tried to put him first, no matter what. Even if it's meant losing friends, I've done it. I really thought things were going well. Things had been looking up for us and I was so excited about the future.
I feel like such a fool. All the plans we'd made; me sitting there and imagining our kids, thinking of baby names.
I feel so humiliated. Why did she have to ruin it? Things can never go back to normal.
All the things we'd done together – he was doing with someone else.
Her.
The little things I knew he liked – she was doing for him.
Is that who he had been texting the whole time? Would he text her when I was with him?
Charlotte.
I'll never forget that name.
Charlotte.

I don't know any *Charlottes*.

But now, I hate everyone with that name.

What did she do different to me?
Was I too ugly? Too much of a child? I didn't wear make-up around him that much and never really dressed up for him. But that's only because we never went out and he wouldn't like me wearing it.
Was I too boring? Too depressed? Sometimes I'd be in a mood, just because of things with mum and it'd stress me out. I always said I didn't want to burden him with my problems, so I'd try not to talk about it around him. It was him that would be asking me what was wrong and he'd get annoyed when I wouldn't tell him, so he'd make me say. I never wanted to. No one else knows about mum's problem. Just him and Nancy.
I thought I could tell him everything. I thought I could trust him.
I loved him.
I love him.
I know I sound pathetic. But even after all this, I can't just switch off my feelings.

I can't be with him. Not after this. Things will never be the same.
But I need him.
I can't not be with him.
I can't picture a life without him.
I don't want to.
A life without him wouldn't be a life. All the things we'd planned. All the private jokes we'd have that no one else would find funny except us. I can't have that with anyone else. I don't want to. It makes me feel sick to think of him like that with someone else.
I can't be without him. I can't ever end things.

I want him to feel this. I want him to feel exactly what I feel now; to be in this much pain and to know that he caused it.
I tried to make him happy. I did everything he wanted me to do and didn't do anything he wouldn't let me do.

And it wasn't enough.

I feel so stupid. I'm up at half past five in the morning, still crying over him; while he's sleeping – not giving this a second thought.

I knew I shouldn't have looked through his phone. I didn't want to. But by the time I'd read one text, it was too late. My eyes saw the texts before I'd even read them, and I was getting hotter and panicking more with each one that I read.

And he's going to wake up tomorrow and be angry because I'm not there.

I didn't exit the conversation. He's going to know.

What's he going to say?

What's he going to do to me?

I wish I could just go back to earlier on. I would have never gone through his phone. It's my fault for looking. I would rather live in that moment, not knowing any of this. At least then, I was happy. I could've avoided all this pain if I'd just gone to sleep.

This doesn't feel real. I wish I could wake up tomorrow and it would be this morning. I would do everything differently.

I should have just stayed at home with mum.

I just want to lose this hurt.

But I can't.

This feeling is never going to go away.

Everything's ruined.

25. NANCY'S cont.

'Morning.' She speaks in the softest voice. 'I brought you up some breakfast – the classic *'Nancy speciality'*.' My eyes ease open to Nancy tickling my ear and pushing the hair off my forehead, stuck there with cold sweat. I open my eyes fully, without moving any other part of my body. Nancy's sat on the bed next to me. She smooths her hand over my clammy cheek. My phone is on the side. There's a bacon sandwich and an emptied packet of crisps on a plate. 'Cheese and onion. I made them myself – opened the bag and everything. Who needs one of them poncey chefs when you got Nancy, eh?' She smiles down at me and kneels beside the bed to my level. 'How you feeling?' She pushes my hair back behind my ears. 'Silly question, probably. Sorry. You let me know what you wanna do today and we'll do it, yeah?' Pause. 'Or let me know if you wanna talk about… Things.' Pause, again. 'Or if you just want me to shut up talking for five minutes. I've never done it, but I can give it a try.' She smiles gently at me. I can't say anything to her. I wouldn't know where to begin. 'Sorry about the other night, as well. I was a proper little bitch… As usual.' She rests her head on the edge of the mattress. Still, I can't think of anything to fill the silence. 'Anyway… You eat up and come down when you're ready, yeah? Use my toothbrush if you wanna brush your teeth. The pink, electric one is mine. Mum's out – so it's just you, me, and some shitty daytime-telly all morning.'

Morning. I thought this would never come.

130

A new day. The day after last night
My eyes roll over to her alarm clock. The numbers are dimmed in
the sunlight coming through the window. The room is completely
whitened – unbearably fresh.

11:44

Nancy gets up and tightens her dressing gown. The light takes
over her whole body, blinding me. I can barely see her outline,
just strands of hair catching the sun and reflecting it all over the
room. I see her clearer as she gets further away from me, leaving
the blanket of sunlight covering the room.
She follows the carpet to the door – turns back to me and smiles.
She pulls the door closed, leaving it slightly ajar. Her muffled
footsteps grow fainter as she goes downstairs. She dragged the
smell of oily bacon around the room as she left. It usually smells
nice, but not today. It's a sickly smell, hanging stale over the
room.
I ease an arm from under the duvet and the sun catches it,
instantly warming my skin. I reach it past the sandwich to my
phone.
Three missed calls. Unknown number.
One new message.
Loading.

Swears.
'Go through my phone.'
Names.
'Too stupid to exit the convo.'
Words.
'Watch when I see you and that whore.'

My stomach cramps.
My hands shake.
I feel my body get hotter.

My forehead get sweatier.
My breathing get heavier.

The smell of the bacon traps itself at the back of my throat. My stomach knots, harder than before – unbearably. I push past the heavy duvet and run through the light to the bathroom.
My legs collapse under the weight of my body and drop at the toilet, resting in cold puddles outside the bath. The water seeps through my pyjama bottoms and soaks my knees. I drop my head into the toilet and my body strains behind me, forcing up sick through my nose and mouth at the same time. The splash of sick hitting the water echoes around the bowl around my head.
Quicker than they left, Nancy's feet chase up the stairs and arrive at the bathroom door behind me.
I rest my head in my hands and spit loose parts of food into the dark mess of the toilet. The smell hits me in the face and tenses my nose and throat for more. From my feet to my head, my whole body strains behind me again, driving lumps of food and hot mush through my mouth and nostrils. My throat burns with the force and my insides ache from the stress.
The smell floats around the rim.
Right on time, Nancy flushes the toilet. The new, fresh water cools my face as it clears away the brown chunks.
She snatches off piece after piece of toilet roll, then wipes my nose and mouth from behind me.

'It's alright, come on.' She rubs my back with one hand, while the other pinches at my nose to clean it. 'You finished? Is that all of it? Wait here, I'll get you some water.'
I think it's finished, but keep my head on the cold, white rim. My teeth grind together in my mouth. They're rough and dry against each other, as if they haven't been cleaned for years. The acid from my stomach has eroded my mouth.

Nancy returns, almost instantly. 'What brought that on? It weren't my bacon sandwich, was it? It was cooked, I swear!' She giggles nervously to herself and rubs a cold flannel to my forehead. 'Here – have a sip of this.' She brings a cold glass of water to my lips. I take a little sip, swish it around my mouth, and spit more loose pieces into the toilet. She sits on the edge of the bath and stretches down to put the glass next to me, but quickly stops when she sees my hand; red and damp with sweat, still clenching my phone.

She kneels down beside me and reads the text.

26. CAFE

Nance suggested we get out of the house, just in case James did turn up at the door.

I don't know what would've brought that on earlier; I didn't eat anything, so I wouldn't have had anything to bring up. I think it was the smell of the sandwich, combined with the nerves of getting that text. I don't usually get sick like that, especially not first thing in the morning.

This cafe isn't really helping things either. That same thick, oily smell hit me as soon as we walked in. Nance brought us in here because it's the last place James would think to look for us.

He wouldn't do anything, but it's best to just stay out of his way when he's like this. He's never hit me, but when he gets really angry, he'll start punching walls or throwing things around.

That's why he's got the Scarface poster on his bedroom door – we had an argument a few weeks ago because I was texting in bed and he thought I was trying to hide my phone from him. I wasn't shielding it. It was just angled towards me because of how I was lying. My head was resting on his chest – so the phone was facing towards me – and he thought I was hiding the screen from him. When I showed him my phone, he accused me of deleting my texts in the split-second before I showed him. He sat there for ages, looking through my messages and the times they were sent. When that proved I hadn't deleted anything and I didn't have anything to hide, he ended up punching his bedroom door and putting a hole in it because he was so wound up.

He had to put the poster up to hide it from his mum when she cleans. He said it was my fault and I was lucky he did it – and that if he didn't hit the door, he would've hit me.
And the whole time… He was texting behind my back.

'Are you sure you don't want anything? Just a cold drink or something?' She empties out the coins from her purse. They scatter across the table, running away in different directions. A couple have rolled onto the floor, so I reach down through a cramped stomach to pick them up. The brown tiles of the floor are sticky to the touch. 'Cheers, babes. Milkshake?'
I shake my head.
My throat is burning and it would be an effort to talk. It was still hurting from where he grabbed it the other night – and being sick just made it worse.
I pinch my sticky fingers and thumb together. When I prise them apart, the skin strains; pulling pale and bouncing back under the stretch. I look up from my seat and Nance is ordering at the counter. I can't hear her words because there's a telly on, playing the news at full volume.

'Cost of Olympics sores to nine billion pounds.'
'Tax payer foots the bill.'
'Speculation over whether the Olympic Village will be ready on time.'
'Part of an investment programme for East London.'
'The sporting legacy of the Games will continue for years to come.'
'MPs say it will bring thousands of jobs to the area and improve the lives of the local people.'

I don't care about all that.
It won't change my life. Nothing will.

Nance throws herself back onto her seat opposite me, blocking the telly and sliding a cold bottle of water over the table. 'There you are – have a drop of water. Go easy on that, it's hard stuff.' I giggle a little at that. She's such a fool. Her face lights up at my slight smile. 'Oi! Oi! Look who's smiling!' She stretches over the table, pinches both of my cheeks and pulls them up to make my smile bigger. 'It's nice in here, don't you think? I've never been in here before.' She keeps my cheeks held up in a smile as she talks to me.

As we came in here, I found myself walking in with James when we first met. We came here when we first started seeing each other. He took me one day after college; met me at the gate and we walked down the riverside together. I think that's why I like walking that way – it reminds me of better times.

We took a slow walk along the Thames to this cafe. He got a Full-English and I got a fried-egg sandwich. He made fun of me because the guy asked me if I wanted my egg *'sunny-side-up'* and I'd never heard of that.

I thought an egg was an egg.

He thought it was well funny and teased me about it for the whole day.

We sat in there for ages, just talking. We knew each other from school, but we'd never really spoken. We'd see each other around, between periods and in the canteen, but we didn't have any mutual friends – so he never had a reason to talk to me. I didn't know that Nancy's boyfriend was his friend back then because she didn't mix him with our friendship group. Besides seeing him every so often between lessons, I'd never actually spoken to him. Then, one day, we ended up on the same bus going home and we just got talking. Nance was off that day. She bunked off to meet her boyfriend, so I went home on my own. Me and James were at the same bus stop together. I had my headphones in to stop people talking to me. Sometimes, I would just put headphones in and not have any music playing. It was just my way of leaving my surroundings, so

I could sit back and observe while everyone thinks I'm in my own world. A peeping-tom of conversations to go with my people-watching addiction.

The bus pulled up, going towards Woolwich Road. I let all the younger kids fight their way on the bus first, then got on after them. The poor bus driver looked tired and didn't even check to see if they had Oyster Cards.

James was just behind me as I got on. I was really aware that he was looking at me – even from behind. It made me uncomfortable at first, but I kept my eyes on the floor the whole time and just tried to ignore it. I swiped on and he swiped straight after. Our hands almost touched on the way.

All the younger kids fought their way upstairs, but I usually stay on the lower deck if I'm on my own. I sat a few seats from the back – by the window – and he stood a couple of feet away from me. There was a spare seat beside me, but he didn't take it. I had my head aimed down at my phone and could still feel him coming through the top of my head.

I stared out the window for the first couple of stops, really aware that he was still there. I didn't know when he'd be getting off because I'd never seen him on my bus before. I was always too busy talking to Nancy to notice, I guess.

Hard footsteps and bulky school shoes would run along the aisle of the top deck, making the ceiling shake. When that stopped, the bell would ring a load of times, then the next herd of school kids would come pushing down the stairs and pile out of the doors like ants. They always look so small and their bags would be huge. You could literally push one of them over and they'd be there for hours trying to roll over, with their little arms and legs clawing at the sky.

While I was watching the next stampede of rucksacks bundling through the back doors, I accidentally caught James' eye. I felt myself go red straight away and my eyes dropped to the floor. I saw the beginnings of a smile come on his face before my eyes fell off him.

I felt bad at first – as if I'd left him hanging.

As we approached my stop, I saw him edge towards the doors… Before I'd even got up myself. I was nervous the whole time. I didn't know if he knew it was my stop or if it was just a coincidence. I stood behind him and followed his footsteps off the bus. It drove off – carrying dozens of screaming kids, bouncing off the steamed windows of the top deck.

I was still a few paces behind him as he walked down the street. He started to slow down, so I was forced to come alongside him. I tried to overtake him quickly, so we wouldn't have to do that awkward side-by-side walk. As soon as I came next to him, I heard his voice over my shoulder – *'You following me?'*

I can't remember exactly what I said back; something jokey and playful – *'Don't flatter yourself.'*

Later on in the relationship, he said he liked the way I seemed feisty when we first met. It's because I wasn't falling for any of his lines and I was quite dismissive at first – not in a rude way, but I wasn't really entertaining a conversation. He was really nice, and I felt bad for giving him a hard time at the beginning. He seemed quite shy, but I could tell he was trying to mask it with the *'hard man'* image. As we walked home, it seemed like he was trying to rush through as many topics as possible because he didn't know when we'd go our separate ways. He was expecting me to turn onto a side road at any point, so wanted to make a good impression as quickly as he could. That self-doubting and anxious part of him was really endearing, and I loved the way he was trying and failing to cover it up.

It was so obvious. It was cute.

I missed my turning to talk to him more. I obviously didn't tell him that – couldn't be giving him a big head so early on.

We got to his turning on Woolwich Road and he started slowing down. He was fumbling his words and tripping over himself long before, but he managed to ask if I was free after school the next day to go out.

He suggested the cafe before I even said I was free.

It's like he had this plan before he even suggested it… He'd already arranged where we'd meet, where we'd go, what he'd get, what we'd talk about…

He seemed so unsure of himself when he asked. It took him ages to say nothing. He was like a little boy.

I loved it. He was adorable.

I had to say yes.

And that's how we met.

I was waiting for him at the gate the next day and we came to this cafe. The wait at the gate seemed to last ages, and I had butterflies the whole time.

I knew after that day – as he teased me about eggs across the table – I knew that we would have a future together.

I never thought that future would lead me back here.

Back in this very same place; feeling very different about the future, but exactly the same about him.

Despite myself. Despite him. Despite everything.

I'm still at the gate.

I'm still waiting for him.

27. WOOLWICH MARKET

Charlotte.

She could have been in that cafe.
She could have been the girl who came in to get a drink and then left.
Maybe that was her and she recognised me, so she left.
She could have been one of those girls on the table behind us.
Maybe that's why they were laughing.
Me.
The idiot.
James' girlfriend.
The girl who got cheated on.
Sitting there, still having not said a word since I woke up.
I could have walked past her on this street a thousand times.
She could be this girl walking towards us. Behind us is the way to James'. Maybe she's going there.
In a way, it's worse that I don't know who she is. If I knew her – or even knew of her – I could tell everyone what she'd done.
I could tell everyone that she'd…

I shouldn't jump to conclusions. I don't know what's happened with them. I'll never know, not for definite. He's not going to tell me the truth. And it will somehow be my fault that all this has happened. He'll probably say one of his friends had his phone and was texting her for a joke.

Maybe, that is what happened? – That's why he got so annoyed and sent that text this morning; because I just assumed the worst of him and left without saying anything or even giving him a chance to explain it.

That would annoy me – if he assumed that I'd done something and I knew I didn't.

Why am I still giving him the benefit of the doubt?

He wouldn't have any reason to do stuff with another girl. The reason Nancy's boyfriend cheated on her was because they weren't sleeping together as much as they were when they first started seeing each other – that's what James told me; he seemed to think that was a good enough excuse. I don't think we would have that problem. I'm at his every other night, more than I am at my own house. I'm always really conscious of knocking him back if he wants to do stuff. The only time we wouldn't have been able to do anything would be when I'm on my period. And even then, he would tell me we could do *'other stuff'*. And we would still end up doing something, even if it was just for him.

I need to know for definite what's happened. And if anything has happened, I need to know why.

Why did he do it?

What did I do wrong?

Who is she?

How long has it been going on?

But I won't find out anything by running away and hiding in cafes.

A final question floats at the back of my mind.

Is it just her? Are there others?

I push the thought down to the pit of my stomach.

Don't think about it, and don't make it real by talking about it.

We're walking away from the direction of James'.

No matter how far away I get, I can still feel that he's watching me.

I begin to notice the cracks in the pavement and my feet are drawn to step evenly on each one. When I try to ignore the urge to step on them evenly, I feel my body pull me back. My body is trying to balance itself out and I'm not even in it.
I'm a passenger in my own head.

I pat myself down in a panic, frisking myself for my phone. Did I leave it at the cafe? My whole body heats with nerves and my stomach cramps, threatening the same sickness as this morning. I calm down when I remember Nance made me leave my phone at hers. She did the same; saying that nothing good would come from bringing our phones out with us. She's got a point, I guess. He's got Nancy's number, too. He made me give it to him a while back – in case my phone ever dies and he needs to get in touch with me through her. She must've known that he'd be ringing and texting us the whole day… I can imagine him doing that. I didn't want to, but I left it indoors. I turned it off and put it on charge before we left. That way, I could say the battery went. If he rings – it will go straight to voicemail.
If I left it on – it would ring out and he'd think I was just not answering.
I don't think Nance would've done the same. I'd be surprised if he tried to get in contact with her. I would've preferred it if she brought her phone out with her. We could have gone through Facebook to try to find out who this girl is.

I feel myself scowling at every girl around our age.
Every girl walking in the opposite direction and towards James'.
Any of them could be her.
I hate every face that walks past and I compare each one to mine.
Hating their badly drawn, permanently-surprised, caterpillar eyebrows.
Hating their mismatched, uneven contour.
Hating their pouting, dewy, filler lips.

Nancy is linking my arm and she tightens as a cold wind hits us. Neither of us have said anything since we left the cafe. I still haven't said anything all day. Nance was trying to talk to me in there, but I couldn't think of anything to say.

I feel so drained – so exhausted; mentally and physically.

Time seems to be dragging today. I got a look at the clock in the cafe before we left and it wasn't even half past one.

Will the rest of my life go this slowly and I never lose this feeling?

I feel so naked without my phone – frantically patting myself down every so often, forgetting I haven't got it with me; feeling for phantom vibrations in my back pocket from texts I'm not getting.

I keep imagining text after text coming through – while my phone is on the floor on charge at Nancy's.

Missed call after missed call.

Voicemail after voicemail.

Post after post being uploaded about me, slagging me off to everyone I know.

My body pulls faster towards the cracks in the pavement, while trying to stay calm and not veer too far off my path.

I manage to squeeze some words out through the acidity of my throat. 'Can we go back to yours?' My breath escapes in a white cloud of cold and chases itself behind me, disappearing towards James'. I know it's not a good idea. I know I'll be sitting there, going through messages, stressing myself out, getting upset… But I have to talk to him.

'If you wanna… But I'm not sure it's wise, to be honest. I don't wanna tell you what to do, but you'll feel better if you're out and keeping yourself busy. Y'know what I mean? We can go back if you want, but I wouldn't advise it.' Her footsteps slow against the wind.

It is a bad idea. I know it is.

'Yeah, I just feel like a tramp.' My throat burns with each word, begging me not to speak. I've still got the coarse taste of sick in my mouth that floats to the surface with every word I force up.

I'm in the same leggings and blue hoodie that I wore to James' last night. Can't stay in these any longer – I feel contaminated with bad energy and the germs of memories.

Her footsteps finally slow to a stop and she turns me towards her, lifting my head to meet her eyes. 'I tell you what… Why don't we pop back to yours, grab a change of clothes, and have a shower? Then, we'll go Westfields for a bit, come back to mine, and have a girls' night in. We can put a box set on and order in a pizza. Sound good?'

28. WOOLWICH CHURCH STREET

Everything seems harder, now. A simple thing – like going home – meant we had to decide the best way to get there. We could have gone the long way, down by the Thames. That's the way we originally planned to avoid going through the estate. The memories I have of that walk are good, and I don't want to taint them by creating new memories today. In my head, I'm still walking along there with James in the summer. I'm still there with him; full of hope, nerves, and anticipation of the future.
I don't want to think of the river and remember how I'm feeling now. I don't want to mix those two memories in my head and corrupt the good times with badness.
Nance pointed out that, if we did go that way, it's secluded. If we did bump into him, there wouldn't be many people around. She's talking about him like he's a violent criminal, and I genuinely don't think he'd actually do anything horrible to us if we saw him.

We decided to go along John Wilson Street to get onto Woolwich Church Street. Again, that has its downsides. It's a main road. If James is going anywhere, he'll take this road to get there. Walking down here, we'll be totally exposed from all angles. Because it can get quite busy with cars and people, it'll be hard for us to be aware of everyone on the road.
Nance was saying he'd be able to see us from a distance. There are so many little side roads he could be on and we wouldn't even know it.
It's the most direct route to mine, so I suggested going this way.

I genuinely think she's overreacting about what he's capable of and what he would do if he did see us. I know him better than anyone – he wouldn't do anything. I doubt he's even left the house.
But right now, I don't want to see him.
I can't.
I feel like I want to accidentally bump into him, but my head is all over the place and I don't know what thoughts to listen to for the best.

I'm making an effort to walk at a quicker pace, keeping my eyes fixed straight ahead. They're daring me to wander off my path, but I can't.
I won't.

It's only a short walk down Woolwich Church Street until we get to mine. I don't live that far from James, and Nancy lives a few doors down from me. He wouldn't have any reason to come down this way – unless he was meeting me. He rarely comes over, anyway. It's always me going to his. I don't like to bring him to mine… Just because I'm never sure what state mum will be in.

I wonder what estate Charlotte lives on…
She could live right near me.
I don't want to think about this.

This is the longest time before anything can get better.
I haven't even lasted twenty-four hours and I already want to die.
This is just the beginning.

29. WOOLWICH CHURCH STREET cont.

The houses on our way are concrete clones of each other.
Identical cages; made to keep people like us in one place – and out of sight.
Council flats.
Two floors.
Neglected paved garden at the back.
Brick wall separating the house from the street.
Wooden gate leading to a concrete front garden.
White-bordered windows that only open from the top, like the ones you'd see in a school. They're on most of the buildings around here; probably to stop people from jumping out of them. Living this life will have that effect on someone.

Even though they all look the same, I'm instinctively drawn to my own place. Without having to consciously think of where it is, I know exactly where to go. It's almost like a sixth sense to be guided to where you know you belong. Although, I rarely feel like I belong here. I don't have many good memories of living around here. I'd love to escape and start somewhere new.
I could leave London if I got into university. But I don't know if I'd have the guts to leave. It takes a certain kind of person to get up and leave everything they know behind. As much as I'd like to be, I'm not that person.

I'm addicted to all the bad stuff that keeps me where I shouldn't be. Instead of moving away and starting fresh, I stay with the familiar things that wear me down – because at least I know them. I was born here.
I live here.
I'll die here.

I can't think of anywhere else I could go. My family have lived here for generations. Nan used to live here, only a few doors down from us. Mum would take me and Nance over for Sunday dinner when we were younger, and she'd give the two of us pocket money every week. Nan didn't know anything different to Woolwich. She lived here for nearly eighty years and died in the same house she was born in. Mum took it really badly – she was the last thing mum had. Nan belonged to a generation that actually cared about the area and took pride in their environment. Her house was her home, and everyone was made to feel comfortable. She'd always look her best, even if it was just to go to the Post Office to pay the rent and buy us some penny-sweets. She knew everyone and everyone knew her. Any time I would go anywhere with her, it would take us ages because everyone would stop her for a chat.
London doesn't want that, now. There's no money in those kinds of people. It doesn't matter that they built the areas up into what they are today… Just price them out and get them out of the way, as quickly and as quietly as possible.
I think that's partly why I'm not connected to this place – how can I care about a place that doesn't care about me?

I would like to see the world. I'm jealous of those people who can just get up and go. The ones who are always on holiday and *'living their best lives'*.
If I could, I'd go off to Australia for a few months – maybe waitress or be a beach lifeguard. I always enjoyed swimming when I was younger. We would go on a Tuesday morning in

primary school and I looked forward to it every week. I'd wear my little, pink swimming costume underneath my uniform, so I could get changed quicker and be the first one out of the changing rooms. I'd be waiting at the poolside, shivering and dancing from foot to foot to keep myself warm. I was in the top group, so we got to go in the deep end and practice diving – while the other kids kicked around the shallow end, balancing on chewed-up floats and clinging to the filthy edge of the pool.
I think I'd be a good lifeguard.

Then, after a few months, I'd go to Thailand and do some travelling out there. There are supposed to be lovely beaches out there. I follow a couple of travel pages online and I've fallen in love with it from the pictures. They have a Full Moon Party where everyone goes onto the beach and spends the whole night there. I'd love that. It's so far from what I'm used to.
I've never felt hot sand between my toes.
I've never felt my foot sink into a wave and leave an imprint.
I went to Southend a couple of times when I was younger with Nancy's mum, but I can't count that.
They seem to get a lot of tsunamis out in Thailand, so I wouldn't stay for too long. And I've got bad luck as it is. Lifeguard or not, you're not swimming away from a tsunami.
I'd start there and travel across South-East Asia. I'd have to be back before Christmas, though. It'd feel too weird to be away for that period. Plus, Christmas has to be cold. I couldn't be abroad for it.
Stay in London for a few days over the holidays, then get out to New York for New Year's Eve.

After that, I'd do most of Europe. Only the main countries, though. I'd go to some little villages in Italy, then get off to Rome. I'd spend a lot of time in Italy. It's got a lot of culture, and I'd actually take the time to look around and enjoy it. I'd prefer that to the usual holidays in Magaluf, Malia, Kavos… How many times

149

can you go out, get drunk, and not remember it the next morning? It must get boring after a while. And you can do all that in London.

Same thing – just a bit hotter.

I don't even do that here, so maybe I'm just boring because I don't drink that much. We'll go in a big group and drink in the park – if the weather's nice and we can actually get alcohol – but I never get crazy drunk.

I'd go to Spain. Barcelona, maybe. I wouldn't want to see any of the bullfighting. It's barbaric. I'm amazed it's still allowed to happen. I wouldn't want to be part of that... Seeing a poor bull get tortured and killed in front of hundreds of people. Why would you pay to see that happen? – And clap for it? I'd be the only person hoping to see the bull win... That'd get my applause for definite. I imagine a lot of places in Spain are full of English tourists, but I'd want to experience a different culture. I wouldn't want to go somewhere I could find *beans on toast* on the menu.

I want to not be able to understand the menu.

Order the wrong thing.

Think it looks horrible.

Eat it.

Be surprised at how nice it is.

Want to order it again, but not know what it's called.

That's what I want from travelling.

That's why I couldn't go travelling with Nancy. She'd hate that.

It would be fun to go on a girls' holiday, but nothing longer than a week or I'd die.

I'd like to think that, if I was confident enough, I could go to these places on my own. Maybe not now, but in a few years. Saying that, as much as I'd love to do Italy, there's no way I'd go to Venice on my own. Loads of loved-up couples, holding hands, gazing into each other's eyes, and slurping spaghetti to a kiss –

while I'm sitting there, just about ready to throw myself overboard
of a gondola.
No, thanks.

On my big world tour – that I have no idea how I'd even pay
for – I'd have to stop in New Zealand at some point. I looked it up
online during a Geography lesson, and that's almost the exact
other side of the world. It's the furthest away I could possibly go –
without drowning – before I have to start coming back.
There would be an entire planet between me and my old life. I'd
just lie there and enjoy it; look at an entirely different sky – a sky
I would never see.
My old life would be at my feet. I might even stamp on the
ground… Just because I could.

Those are just dreams, anyway.
What I'd like to do – and what I will do – are two very different
things. I doubt I'll ever leave the Borough of Greenwich, let alone
leave the country.
I'll have to find happiness here; try to find some light in the grey.

Back in reality, we cross the road to get to mine. Nancy takes
my hand and leads me halfway across the road. The crying of
seagulls, flying overhead towards the Thames, bring me as close
to a beach as I can be. A few insignificant cars speed in front of
us, followed by some white vans. A bus growls past, forcing wind
and thick, black smoke into our faces. Nancy squeezes my hand
and guides me through the darkness across the road. My eyes
follow a plane above us. It's taking a new load of people to go and
live my dreams for me. It crosses the road with us, disappearing
into the blinding white of the clouds.
We follow the grey conveyor-belt of concrete to the entrance of
my front garden. Nance slows her stride and takes a step behind
me, allowing me to go in first. The gate swings open with the

gentlest push. Usually, I have to lift the rusted, brown bolt and give it a hard nudge with my body.
Not this time.

I don't look for my keys.
I don't need to.

My eyes follow the crooked slabs of paving stones up the front garden.
A plastic plant pot has been knocked over and is lying on its side.
Soil is scattered across the concrete.
The doormat is kicked at an angle.

The front door is open.

30. AT MINE

Nancy is to my side, standing slightly behind me. I feel her clinging to the side of my hoodie, stretching the fabric across my stomach and pulling it taut. My hand trails up the side of my body and covers hers, feeling the fabric crease and bunch in her fist. She's cold to the touch, as her stiff knuckles pierce through my palm. The blood has drained to her legs, ready to carry us both away to safety.
I won't let her.

My eyes haven't left the strip of darkness between the door and the frame. I strain my eyes, searching for anything familiar inside. Nothing.
The wind shouts from the street behind me, taunting us and daring me to go inside. My feet are firmly cemented into the ground. My body leans forward and my neck is outstretched, peering as far as I can without moving forward.
Still, nothing.
Nancy's grip loosens and the material relaxes over my body. She gives me a reassuring squeeze and her thumb strokes the back of my hand. My head turns slowly towards her – my eyes following cautiously behind it. She looks blankly at me; eyes wide, sucking her lips into her mouth and biting them together. She gives me a slow nod. I feel comforted. Enough – at least – to shuffle forward with her. We take our first steps towards the white door frame. The world has gone quiet.

153

My eyes are back on the deep strip of blackness. I don't dare to blink and miss anything inside. My left hand guides me forward, and I use it to press against the frosted glass window of the front door. The cold, rough surface eases away from my pale fingertips, swinging open to expose the hallway.

The traffic on Woolwich Church Street has stopped, and the world is watching over my shoulder in anticipation of what is inside.

James?

I step inside, with Nancy trailing behind me.
The world is gone.

The hallway looks normal.
In front of us – loose pairs of shoes scattered up the side of the staircase.
To our right – coats and jackets hanging from dull, brass pegs.
Upstairs – just darkness.
Ahead, past the staircase – the tiling of kitchen floor covered with shards of something; maybe plates or mugs.
Something has been smashed.
My footing gets more urgent, but is still controlled under my body.

Burglar?

More shards appear as we go further into the hallway. My body creeps along the wall to the right, peering around the door frame to the living room. There's enough light coming through the veil of net curtains to see the whole room.
Photographs of unknown relatives – knocked off the shelves.
Old ornaments – broken and tossed from their usual places.
The Christmas tree – lying on its side and resting precariously on the coffee table, decorations desperately clinging onto it.

The angel – my angel – on the floor next to it, only one wing still attached. I go straight over to it with a few unthinking steps. I pick up both pieces and try to lock them together. It's a clean break, but I can see where the other wing is cracked. Parts of the body shatter in my hand as I hold it, and flakes of paint crumble between my fingers.

I look over to Nancy, standing in the doorway. She's not coming in after me and she looks on edge. Her legs are ready to carry her away any minute. Her hands are gripping the door frame, keeping her from running away. The whites of her fingers, pressed against the frame, are merging with the cream paint.

She's not going to leave.

I know it.

As I place the shattered clay on the coffee table, glass photo frames crack under my feet.

I suddenly become very aware of how much noise we've made since coming in.

Is there still someone else here?

The two of us are frozen in position.

A silence takes the whole flat.

I make the first move towards Nancy, treading carefully over diamonds of glass, glistening from the light outside. I reach her and we look blankly at each other. My eyes are drawn through the banister and up the stairs, into a dark hole of nothing. We both know we will have to go up there together.

This doesn't feel like my house. I feel like a stranger, realising it all for the first time.

Nancy's eyes shake under a glaze of water.

A loud, damp thud shakes the ceiling.

The whole flat rattles around us.

Nancy grips my hand tight and backs off from the staircase.

'Mum!' I shout through the shadows and follow my feet towards the bottom of the stairs. My arm swings my body around the banister and it drags behind my feet, jumping two steps at a time. I couldn't hear Nancy over my feet slamming through the carpet.

I get sucked into the darkness.

I've lost her.
I'm alone.

I feel my way across the landing. My pace slows, trying to find familiar surroundings to guide me through the darkness of the hallway. My breathing gets deeper, and I let out small amounts of air to make no noise. I need to hear everything. 'Mum?' Softer and quieter than last time. I tap the edges of the walls. There's a light switch here somewhere, but I can't feel it. All the doors up here are closed, so there's no sunlight coming in from outside. Something is wrong.
The bathroom door is always open if there's no one in there. I cling to the wall and scale it to the entrance of the bathroom, then fiddle with the handle to open the door. Some dim light makes its way in through the frosted glass. I pull the light, getting as much visibility as I can. The fan roars across the bath and chases the fading light down the hallway.

I follow the carpet to the next door – my door. I ease it open, twisting the handle as gently as I can. I don't know what to expect. Nancy hasn't followed or called up to me.
I'm on my own.
My head peers around the door.
Nothing.
It's lighter – everything is as I left it.

Downstairs was completely smashed, but upstairs looks untouched.
I kick my rubber doorstop under the door to allow more light in the hallway.

Mum's door is at the end of the carpet.
I follow the shadows into darkness.
My feet are making no noise under my body.
I seem to float all the way to the wooden door.

I pause.

Do I knock?

I tap the door – twisting the cold, brass handle at the same time. I whisper into the painted wood. 'Mum?' I can barely hear my own voice over the deafening silence.

The door swings open with the whistle of the hinges.
Her room is dark.
The curtains are drawn.
As I open the door, light from the hallway floods inside; while a stale, sickly smell escapes.
It looks the same as downstairs.

Nothing is where it should be.
Her drawers are pulled open – clothes are hanging out and have been thrown across the room. One drawer is pulled out entirely and the front panel is broken off.
Her wardrobe has been emptied – it's exploded with clothes and shoe boxes. The doors are open, with coat hangers coughed out onto the floor.
Her mirror is cracked – it's fallen away from the wall, hanging on by one corner. Something has been thrown at it.

The lamp shade above the bed is clinging to the light bulb – it's swinging slightly, looking down and dangling over the room. It could drop onto the bed at any moment.

And on the bed… Mum.

She's lying in sick. Her pillow is browned and her mouth is crusted over with it. She's on top of the duvet, lying on her side and still wearing her dressing gown. It's undone and she's got nothing on underneath it. One slipper is flopping from her toes. I go over to her, kicking pairs of jeans and anonymous tops out of my way. I pull her dressing gown over her, trying to cover her up as much as possible. I keep my eyes focused on her face, as my hands fondle with the fabric to cover her naked body.
I'm embarrassed for her.
Her hair is stiff and matted with grease, snaking away from her head in all directions. Her eyes look baggy and exhausted, even in her sleep.

Nancy arrives at the door behind me. She doesn't say anything, but I feel that she's here with me. I'd almost forgotten she was in the flat. She comes to my side and picks up a heavy, dark coat from the floor. She sees me frantically struggling to pull mum's dressing gown from under her body, so she takes me by the shoulders and guides me away, then drapes the coat over mum.

I turn away from them.
I can't look anymore.
My eyes fall to the mess at my feet. As I look closer, I notice trails of sick on the floor, making a pathway to the bed.
My eyes gather with tears.
Nancy staggers back quickly and knocks me from behind.
I don't want it to, but my body turns to see what she has stepped back from.

Mum has started waking up. She's got an arm outstretched, reaching out from under the thick coat. Her fist is clenched and it begins to loosen.
A photograph relaxes and unfolds in her hand.
I take it from her quickly and smooth it out under my fingers.
My dad.
…What I know him to look like.

Mum fidgets under the coat. Her eyes open slightly and her words slur out, spilling carelessly off her tongue. 'You look just like that cunt with your hair that colour.' She turns onto her other side and faces away from me. 'You're just like him. I never liked either of you… Pair of…' Her voice trails off, back into her sleep.

My feet carry me out of her room and down the stairs.
Nancy's footsteps echo behind me.

31. AT MINE cont.

No matter how many times I see her like that, I never get used to it. After all these years, I would've thought I'd be desensitised to seeing her in that state.
Today was different.

I can't really call the guy in the photo *'my dad'*. I don't know him. He's only my dad genetically – that's the only input he's had in my life. I could walk past him in the street and not recognise him; he hasn't done anything for me and he's never been there for me. He's a stranger.
I have a vague memory of a man on a Christmas morning. It's the last time I remember being really happy. I had no worries – everything was easier. I can only assume that it's him – my dad – that I'm remembering. He's the only man I can remember growing up. He's the only man I've ever seen mum with.
One moment, he was there; the next, he was gone.
And I never understood why.

When I think back to when I was younger, it seemed a lot brighter. Every memory I have from around that time is in a white haze. I don't remember any specific days, just snippets of memories under a blanket of white. There are no seasons, no hot or rainy days – just a single memory, untouched by weather or anything outside of that one moment.
I couldn't have been much older than five. We were living here, as we've always done. I remember sitting on the floor, surrounded by

presents, the small ones were at the front and they led up a shiny mountain of reds and greens, all the way up to the biggest ones at the back. There were thousands.

Mum and the man were sitting together. He was on the armchair and mum was on his lap – his arms were wrapped around her while they both watched me open my presents. I turned around after each one that I opened and waddled over to bring it to them; thinking they had no idea what Father Christmas had brought me. Mum had a smile on her face all morning. I haven't seen her smile like that since. She'll be happy at times, but it's not the same. She used to paint a smile on her face some days, wanting to keep up appearances that everything was alright.

Now, she doesn't bother.

Her eyes always give her away… I always felt she had a sadness in them that wanted to tell me something desperately horrible that had happened – but she couldn't bring herself to say it and inflict it on me; almost like the thoughts and the words were contagious, and she was shielding me from them.

I've watched her face slowly melt downwards over the years, weighed down under the strain of the words she couldn't bring herself to say. The bouncy smile in her cheeks has deflated. Now, she has no expression. Her emotions hang off her face. Her fresh, rouged skin from back then dangles off her gaunt, yellowed cheek bones.

The glowing mum in the memory was so bright and enthusiastic with every toy I brought over to her. She'd sit with me on the floor when the man disappeared into the smell of turkey to the kitchen. She'd help me pull off the toughest corners of Sellotape, so I could rip them open easily. I remember how the two of them would look at each other after looking at me. I've never seen that look anywhere else.

Films.

TV.

Even with James.

I've never seen that deep, intense love since then.

I can't remember eating Christmas dinner that day. My memory fades after I'd opened my presents.
I don't remember him after that moment.
He could have disappeared that day.
I don't know.
I'll never ask.

I don't hate this man. I don't know him enough to hate him – I never loved him enough to hate him. The way I see it, he left for a reason. If I wasn't enough to make him stay, I'll never be enough to make him come back. I haven't gone anywhere; he'd know where to find me if he really wanted to.
I made peace with my situation a long time ago. I've grown up fine without him, so I don't need him now. He left for a reason, and I'd rather not know what that reason was. I don't want to delve into the past. If I find out something I don't like, I'd have to live with that knowledge for the rest of my life.

It would've been nice to grow up in a *proper* family – but I didn't. I'd love for things to have been different growing up. Things wouldn't have been so hard with some more money in the house and an extra pair of hands, but there's no point in wishing away the future by chasing the past.
I think the past determines a lot of your future.
The way you grow up shapes your character. I wouldn't be the same person if I grew up in a different place or with a different family. There are times when I'd rather be someone else – when I look at my own life compared to other people. But there are a lot of people in a worse position than me.
Why should I complain?

I wouldn't dare ask mum about him.
Those are the topics we never talk about.
Her drinking. My dad.

It's an unspoken understanding. We know they're there – or not there – but we both just get on with it.
No point in talking about things that can't change.

I don't know if he left because of her drinking or if she started drinking because he left.
I'm always giving people the benefit of the doubt, even when they don't deserve it.
Fact is – if her drinking made him leave, he would've taken me away with him. I'm glad he didn't. I don't know where mum would be otherwise.
I don't know if she would even still be… Here.
Despite how she may be, she's still here with me – she has been from the beginning. There may be times when I will have to check on her, put her to bed, even make sure she's eaten…

Maybe not always as a mother, but she's still here.

32. NANCY'S

Since we got to Nancy's, neither of us have mentioned what happened at mine. She met me at my front door after I ran downstairs. The light of outside was blinding after being in mum's cave. Nance followed behind me and cradled me on the doormat when she caught up. She disappeared back inside after a few minutes.

I was sat on the doorstep with the front door open behind me, facing away from the house. I could hear the shards of plates being scraped across tiled floor. When I did finally bring myself to turn around, I saw Nance clanking big pieces of crockery and sweeping smaller pieces into the corner. She said, if mum was to come down, she probably wouldn't notice the mess and slice her foot open.
I felt bad for not helping clean up, but my legs wouldn't let me go back inside.
She took a bucket from a sticky corner of the kitchen next to the fridge, rinsed it through in the sink, and took it up to mum's room. She came back down for a glass of water, then vanished back upstairs. When she came back down, she told me that she'd left two paracetamol tablets by a glass of water and turned mum on her side to face the bucket. If she was lying on her back and got sick, she could end up choking on it.
She'd cleaned up the sick around the bed and left a fiver by her bedside lamp. She said mum would probably be hungry when she woke up, so she could use it to get food.

I'll make sure I pay it back.
I hope she uses it for food.
I don't want to think about mum waking up.
The mess she'll be in.
How disorientated she'll be.
She won't even know what day it is. There's no clock in her room.
With the curtains drawn, there's no way of telling when one day ends and another begins.

It's starting to get dark out. We're in Nancy's living room. She draws the curtains and sits back down next to me on the sofa. The orange streetlights were shining in through the window, but it was getting too dark to see each other. We turned the lights on – which meant people would be able to see in through the window.
It's best to close them completely.
She put a DVD on a little while ago. I've got no idea what it is or what's going on. It keeps jumping from modern times to the war. The only part that took my attention was a sex scene. That's only because of the awkwardness of watching it with someone else. I never know where to look – or where not to look. We sat in an uncomfortable silence during that. Even Nancy wouldn't think it was appropriate to make a joke. Not today, anyway.
Other than that, my eyes have been looking straight through the telly. The sound has been coming from miles away.
Weirdly, I haven't been thinking about anything in particular.
There's too much to think about at the moment.
Mum.
James.
What the test would have said if I'd have looked.
There's only so much that one mind can think about, before everything starts overlapping and getting confused.
All the problems merge together; merge together as one life.

My phone is still charging upstairs. I haven't looked at it yet. I should go and get it soon. I don't want it to overheat or have the battery melt. It could start a fire.

I'll have to check it in a minute.

Before we left, Nancy brought some clean clothes down from my room. I haven't got changed into them yet. I'll save them for tomorrow. I'm wearing her clothes for the night; a pink vest top and a purple pair of pyjama bottoms.

She's cuddled up to me on the sofa, leaning on me. I'm slouched over onto the arm, supporting my head on my palm. It's all I can do to keep my body still. My exhaustion is battling with an overwhelming urge to fidget. I'm just a passenger in my body, trapped up here inside my own head.

Nancy's mum is upstairs with her boyfriend. We haven't seen them since we got here. It's good, really. I wouldn't want her to see me looking like this, and I'd rather not have to tell her about what happened earlier on. I wouldn't want her to think mum is rough – I'd rather she didn't know about mum's problem. I doubt Nancy has ever mentioned it.

The less the world knows about my life, the better.

'Are you hungry yet? You've barely eaten all day…' She talks over the dialogue of a man and woman on the screen. They look like they're a couple who got separated at some point. Now, they're coming back together after years of being apart.

I force some words up through my throat. 'I am a bit hungry. I think.' My stomach and head are taking turns to give me sharp, stabbing pains. If I eat something, maybe at least one of them will go away for a while.

'Alright, one minute. I'll order us in some pizza. You wanna share one or have one for yourself?' She stands up and walks in front of the telly, interrupting the two on-screen lovers before they kiss by a lake.

'I won't eat a whole one.' The thought of food is getting me unnecessarily hopeful. This must be how comfort eating starts.

'Ah, let's just get one each. Then – that'll be breakfast sorted, as well. I'm so fat… Look how many menus we got here!' She sifts through dozens of menus and minicab leaflets in a bowl by the telly. She throws herself onto the sofa beside me. As she walks in front of the telly, the two lovers have had their moment and the camera leaves them, holding each other and drenched in the rain. Real life isn't that easy.

She throws down a pile of leaflets on the coffee table and spreads them out like a deck of cards. The food is plastic and undercooked. She picks one from the middle. 'This one's lovely. Remember we had it before, when mum went out and we had the girls over? It was proper cheap, as well. I think it's free delivery… Or you have to spend over a tenner.' She gets lost in the menu. I remember the night – Nancy's mum was going out with her new boyfriend for the first time. They'd only just met and it was the first time they were going out – just the two of them. She asked me to come over and help her get ready. I'm really good at doing eyeliner flicks, so I was on make-up duty. After a while, Nancy asked the girls to come over and give us a second opinion on her mum's look.
We helped her choose an outfit that suited the night out.
We wanted her to look sexy, but not easy… Make people look twice, but not like she'd made a proper effort.
She looked lovely.
She had this gorgeous dress which really suited her. It was a dark, midnight blue and made her eyes pop. It hugged her body and fitted her like a mannequin. Her hair was done beautifully and her skin was so fresh. She's really glamorous for her age. I hope I look that good when I get older.
I remember being really surprised at her hair. It had such a nice curl to it and it was even all the way around the back.

I know she's a hairdresser, but I assumed that meant she's really good at styling and cutting other people's hair. I didn't understand how she'd be able to make her own hair look so good.

While I was doing her contour, I told her I'd always wondered who cut the hair of a hairdresser. Whoever cut a hairdresser's hair – they must be the best person to go to; even other hairdressers think they are good enough. No hairdresser wants to be walking around with hair like a stack of hay… It's a bad advert for them, so they're going to go to the best person for the job.

That seemed like a normal thing to wonder.

She thought it was hilarious I'd think something like that. She told me I'd always been curious and questioned everything for as long as she could remember. She said I saw the world in an innocent, child-like way, and I should never lose that.

I always thought it was just me being stupid.

'You alright with this one then, yeah? Let me guess… Margherita, no toppings?' She pats down the side of the sofa, forcing her hands between the worn leather of the arm.

'Yeah, that's fine. Thanks.' I'll probably only manage to eat half.

She carries on searching under the cushions for something, then drops to her knees and looks under the sofa. 'Margherita… You boring bitch.' She shakes her head in joking disapproval and giggles at me. Her head pops back up from under the sofa – flustered, with wild hair. 'Babes… Have you seen my pho – ' She slams the words back inside her mouth. 'It's okay. I'll use the house phone.' She makes an awkward, little smile at me.

'I think it's upstairs, ain't it? You want me to get it for you?' I start pushing the sofa away from under my body, ready to stand up.

'No, no, it's fine. Honestly. I'll use the house phone. It's no worries.' She's covering a panic in her voice. 'I couldn't wait that long, anyway. I gotta order this bad boy now!' She grabs the house phone from the side of the telly and starts dialling.

Again, she's standing between the two lovers.

She turns to look at me while she waits to place the order, giving me a little smile. 'Hiya, are you still open for delivery, yeah?' She swings her body back around towards the menu, flattened out next to the phone dock.

She turns the volume down on the side of the telly, leaving it resting ominously on *thirteen*. Her voice trails off on the phone and I get fixated on the numbers.
Thirteen.
One. Three.
My body is restless under me, fingers running across the leather stitching of the sofa. I start to feel the volume bar, etched on the telly, coming to life in front of me. The numbers engrained on the screen are growing and I feel them invisibly arching over the room, corrupting everything with bad energy. The unbalance of the numbers pushes down on me, deep into the pit of my stomach – and it bubbles with fear of the bad luck that has been and is still to come. I'm caught inside an airtight pocket of unease and dread which blocks out the rest of the world. Something bad is going to happen. But I don't know what. I need to do something about it. But I don't know what. The fear builds and unbearably heats my entire body. Against me, my mind focuses on my breathing to try to cool me down. I take deep breaths in, but can't manage the air that I'd usually take. No matter how hard I breathe, the air won't fill my body. I fight through a tightening chest to stop from suffocating under an invisible weight. The short breaths out get rid of more air than I can take in. I only inhale more anxiousness and nerves that clog up my throat and lungs.
Nancy speaks in silence – a million miles from me, getting further away.
I fondle frantically for the remote control, forcing my clammy hands down the creaking side of the sofa until I feel it. Finally, I

tear it out and adjust the volume down to ten – bringing the room back to life as quickly as it faded.

'Okay, cool. Thanks. Bye.' She slides the phone back into the dock and looks at me with a laugh. 'That is shameful. Y'know they had my address saved on their system? I dunno if they recognised my voice or if it comes up automatically when I dial from the same number. That's bad though, ain't it? They probably recognised me and thought *'oh that fat bitch again'*, don't you think?' She throws herself next to me.

I force out a laugh, being as genuine as possible and bringing myself back into the room. I fan myself down, pulling at my top to cleanse my body with new air. 'How long did they say it would be?' I'm concentrating more on the telly now, trying to stay in the moment and not get lost inside my own head.

'They said about half hour. I didn't order any drink because we got mixer and some proper drink in the fridge.' She leans her body back onto mine.

I'm searching for any excuse to go upstairs and check my phone. She knew I only offered to get her phone so I could check mine. I don't know why she's stopping me.

What if it does overheat and cause a fire? Her mum is up there with her boyfriend. They'll be trapped if a fire starts in Nancy's room. Then, they'll only wake up when it's too late. By the time the smoke wakes them up, the fire would have taken over the entire hallway.

And it will be my fault.

Why else would I need to go upstairs? What can I say? I can't go upstairs to the toilet when there's one down here. I can't go upstairs to her room for no reason.

I'll have to wait until we go to bed. Again, she's standing between the two lovers.

33. NANCY'S cont.

We slept on the sofa.
Annoying.

I'm not annoyed at her. She's been really nice about this whole
situation over the last couple of days. I'm just annoyed that I
haven't got the confidence to tell her I need to check my phone.
She's my best friend – she'd understand. But I know she'd think
less of me if I caved in, and she'd be right to.
I'm just really anxious when I don't have my phone with me.
I enjoyed those first few moments of waking up. The few seconds
when I forget why I am where I am. There's a small window of
not remembering anything about life.
That's the moment I sleep for.

Our pizza came at about half past ten. I only ate half of it, with
a couple of chicken strips. Then, I kept yawning and hinting to go
to bed. When one film would finish, she'd insist on putting
another one on. I woke up to the menu screen of some random
film. I have no idea what it was; I don't even remember watching
it. I do remember that the main menu theme song has been
playing for about eight hours straight and it's doing my head in.
Nancy is still asleep. We've slept in the same position that we sat
in all night. We only got up to get our food and pour our drinks.
My legs are aching from not using them for so long. On top of
that, I've got pins and needles in my right arm from Nancy
sleeping on my side. She's cutting off the circulation to my hand.

If I lift my arm, I think my hand might stay behind. I'll see it resting in the same position and I'll have a little stump at the end of my wrist.

My arms are poking out of the vest top and sticking to the leather sofa with my own sweat. As I peel them off, my skin stretches pale and bounces back to my body.
My face is stiff with dry skin and grease. The grease from the pizza is oozing out of my pores and has congealed on my nose, forehead, and cheeks. It pulls and stretches when I open my mouth to yawn, burning deep to the bone.
I need to moisturise.
I need to shower.
I need to go upstairs.
I ease my arm from under Nancy's head, trying not to wake her. My bare skin sticks to the side of her head, so I use my left arm to support her while my right arm makes the escape. I have to twist my shoulder and contort to get out from under her. My fingers are hanging limp at the bottom of my sausage arm.
I finally free it – still, in complete silence.
The looping theme song of the film has started to play louder, emphasising certain instruments and clips of the loudest scenes, trying to wake Nancy.
The remote is out of reach.
The clock starts drumming each second, louder than the one before. It was hard enough to sleep through that ticking and now it's started again, just as I need the silence.
I use the side of the sofa to pull myself up, preparing one of the cushions to support Nancy's head to feel like I'm still there. The dry leather creaks and scrapes against itself as I slowly stand up.

'This fucking song is doing my head in.' Her eyelids flutter and crinkle. Awake. Brilliant. I collapse back down onto the sofa. She looks up at me. 'I never wanna watch that film ever again. That fucking song! Did it keep you awake, as well? I swear it actually made me dream differently.' She sits up and stretches towards the ceiling.

I stretch after her, as if I've just woken up with her. 'Yeah, it was really annoying. I kept waking up with it. I would've turned it off, but you was pinning me down all night.' I laugh to myself. 'By the way, d'you mind if I have a shower quick? I can literally feel the grease dripping off me.'

She laughs and reaches for one of the leftover pieces of cold pizza, stuck in damp grease and cardboard. 'Oh shit, I must've been crushing you all night!' She gnaws through the tough, red rubber of pizza base, speaking through it. 'Yeah that's fine, babes. Make sure you use my shampoo and conditioner up there. Mum's one is the bottle for *old people* hair. Don't use that – it might make you go grey or something.' She throws the chewed crust back into the open box.

What a waste – crusts are the best part.

I make my way to the bottom of the stairs, before she calls back to me. 'Actually, lemme get you a clean towel. You don't wanna use my fishy, old one, do you?' She launches herself off the sofa and scrambles over to me.

Again, I know what she's thinking.

Her footsteps echo behind mine as we go upstairs.

On the landing, she pulls a towel from a pile in a cupboard and hands it to me. It's warm from being next to the water heater and the new softness strokes against my hands.

We stand awkwardly for a moment that seems to drag. She cuts the silence. 'Listen… I know you're gonna think I'm getting involved. And feel free to tell me to *mind my own business* or whatever. But please – don't check your phone just yet. I've been where you are right now. I know, the only thing you wanna do right now is text him and see what he's said. Trust me… From someone who's been in this position. The worst thing you can do right now is speak to him. You'll get pulled into an argument and nothing will ever get resolved over text. You need to wait until *you* know what *you* want to do. The way you handle this at the beginning will judge how this turns out. You're seventeen. You do what you want. You don't have to listen to me. Or him. Or anyone else. All I can do is advise you. You know what I mean? You're my best friend and I love you more than anyone. I only wanna see you happy, which is why I'm telling you what I wish someone told me. Think about what you're gonna do and don't get pulled into his games over text. The minute you play his games – you lose.'

She's right.

I launch myself into her and she holds me, tighter than I've ever been held. I whisper into her neck. 'Thanks, Nance. I love you.' She squeezes me into the warmth of the towel between us. The world stops for us. We stand alone in the hallway, rocking softly together. My sniffing breaks the moment and I have to let her go to wipe my nose.

Her eyes shimmer under a coat of water. 'Go on. Get yourself in there, you smelly bitch. Before you get me going, as well.' She wipes her eyes and opens the bathroom door for me.

34. SHOWER

This is what I need.
A hot shower.

I never know when I'll have hot water at mine, and there's nothing worse than having to wash your hair in freezing water. It's not just the water that's cold. It makes the white surface of the bath even colder, too. As soon as it starts, you know you've got ten minutes of hell waiting.
Well, not hell – hell would be a bit warmer.
Then, I'll get out and have to dry myself with a damp towel, which will make me even colder as soon as it hits the goosebumps on my skin. Finally, I'll have to find a way of getting back to the temperature I was at before; all in an absolute igloo of a flat.
It's enough to make someone not wash.

It would be nice to not have to worry about whether the meter has been topped up. I could put the heating on when it gets cold and not have to worry if me having a shower means mum won't have any hot water.
No one in London in 2011 should have to choose between being warm and washing.
I'll be able to help out a bit more with bills when I get on my placement. Hopefully, that'll make things easier. The last time I had a proper wash was before West End the other night – and that was only because I was at James'.

I have no idea why people would prefer to have a bath instead of a shower. Lying in your own filth. You'd be dirtier after a bath than you would be before it; floating in murky, cloudy swamp water. Then, when you get out, there's a layer of grime from where the water has settled on the edge of the bath. Showers are so much more hygienic. You can actually get clean.

I need to enjoy this for as long as I can. I don't want to take advantage and use all their hot water, but it's such a relief to be able to control my own temperature.

I turn the hot tap up to the maximum and control the heat by putting the cold tap on slightly. Teasing my hand under the shower, my skin tightens and recoils under the blast of new water. When I get the temperature right, I follow my body into the bath. My head scales the shower hose up and down, letting the fresh heat drip down my back. The shower curtain is cold from the air in the bathroom, so I do my best to avoid touching it as I turn around. The hot water smooths my hair down my back. I feel all my problems flow from my shoulders, trickle down my legs, and disappear into the plug hole. I tilt one shoulder under the hot spray, while the other shivers in the cold air. I alternate each one, so they both get the precious heat. I use her two-in-one shampoo and conditioner, working it through my roots and scalp. It burns from where I must have been scratching my head without knowing. I pull the soapy lather down my hair and it flicks off the ends. The white foam clumps on my fingers and splats into the puddle at my feet.

I love the feeling of having just washed my hair. It's nice to have disgusting hair that's thick with grease and oil one minute – then to wash it and have a nice softness and bounce to it.

I take her shower gel from the side and work a lather into my skin, making sure it won't be too harsh on me. I've got sensitive skin and want to avoid breaking out. Stepping away from under the pouring of water, I ease the soap all over my body before it washes off. I appreciate the warmth more when I step back under it. It soothes my body and washes the white droplets off my fresh skin. My eyes follow the trail of white down my legs as it disappears into the enamel of the bath. As I turn, I try to keep my whole body under the shower.

I'm inside a white shell. Pure light is flooding in through the frosted glass, catching every corner of the room. Tiny drops of water bounce off my shoulders and vanish into the steam around me. I hold my arms out as the soap washes away, and my skin glows with the room. The white around me gels with my fingertips, and the bridge between me and my shell disappears. I lose myself in the steam. I look up to the shower head and let the fresh water hit me in the face.
For a brief, necessary moment, I forget the world outside of my shell.
As I wipe my eyes, I see my fingertips wrinkle in front of me. I've got the hands of an eighty-year-old. I must have been in here a while. I shut off the taps and the noise that has kept me company ends abruptly. The shower head burps out its last drops of water through thick, chalky limescale. The plug hole calls me back with a gurgle as I step out of the bath.
I feel reborn… Like a new person.
My body is sticky with heat. I can't tell sweat from the clean water. Every part of my body melts in steam. I take the clean towel to my face, then use it to wipe down the body-length mirror opposite the bath.
It's not surprising that Nancy is so confident. You need to have some confidence to be able to look at yourself naked as soon as you get out of the shower – without being sick everywhere.
I try not to look at each fleshy part of my body.

My eyes take themselves down to my stomach. There's a faint line of fair hair below my belly button, disappearing downwards – my snail trail. I haven't seen this on anyone else. And there's no way I'm shaving it, just for it to come back thicker and coarser.

My eyes are drawn back up to a love bite on my neck. It's quite fresh. It was done when James was on top of me and had his head there.

He's left his mark on me.
I hope it fades.

I turn and look at my naked body from the side.
My hands take themselves to my ribcage and smooth my skin down.
They rest on my belly and stroke.
I pause.

He's left his mark on me.

35. WOOLWICH ADVENTURE PLAYGROUND

I wish I'd put a new bra on when we were last at mine. I've been wearing this one for a few days, so it's starting to smell of sweat. No matter how much deodorant I use, it gets that musty smell after a while and begs to be put in the wash.

That's not even the worst part.

When it gets really annoyed about not being washed for a million years, it decides to release the underwire and the sharpest part sticks out from under the cup. A metal prod under my right boob has managed to rip a hole through my bra and continually poke my chest. I don't know how it happens, but most of my bras come to the end of their lifecycle by doing that. It'll leave a red sore on the inside of my chest and a gaping hole in my top if I try to protect my skin with it. The metal tears through any top, no matter how thick it is. A little hole doesn't look that bad; it looks trampy, but not too noticeable. It's just a warning that I need to throw it out – a *warning hole*. And it's always the right side – the slightly bigger boob that's just playing by its own rules and makes me look all deformed and horrible. I need to be careful how I hold my arms. If it continues for too long, it will look awful. I'll have a chest like a fat block of Swiss Cheese; a big, pasty slab, with dozens of holes poked into it.

I'd like to get measured and fitted properly. I've never had it done before. I shop blindly for underwear. I'll get things that look nice, but I never pay much attention to the size or how comfortable they are until they start hurting. I think I've intentionally avoided getting measured properly. I know that, if I get measured somewhere – and the double-D cup, supermodel sales assistant tells me that I'm actually a B cup and not a C – I'll die.

Me and Nancy took a walk down to Woolwich Adventure after my shower – a wooden playground on Woolwich Road. It's been raining today, so there's no one here. A lot of the playgrounds around here are usually empty, although you might get a few from the estate when it starts getting dark. There will be a cloud of choking smoke over the woodwork and the burning smell of weed. At this time of the afternoon, they're still in bed – stoned from the night before.

The wood that I'm sitting on is damp under my body, slowly easing its way through my jeans. Nancy is sitting on a bench, easily visible from the main road. I'm under one of the wooden obstacles, out of sight. My eyes are following each individual plank of wood, connecting it to the next. I'm drawn to each of the knots in the wood, looking for any weak points in the structure. She's mouthing something to me, but it's difficult to hear over the traffic that's shouting to us from the main road. She signals to me to come closer to her. I stand up, with caution. My eyes are scanning everyone in sight. I don't think James would come here. I don't come here that often, so he wouldn't think to look for us here. He would always tell me that he has no reason to come this far down Woolwich Road. He always moans about some other football team down this way. I don't know if they're rivals with West Ham, but he would always complain when I would suggest going somewhere that involved coming this far down the main road.

It's not an option for him.

Nowhere outside of this area is an option for him.

As I make my way towards Nancy's wooden island, my eyes dart across Woolwich Church Street.

Lipgloss

I see James.

    He's walking from the roundabout that connects us to Woolwich Road. He's walking differently, but I can see that it's him – even from a distance. The sky is a deep grey behind him, swallowing the background and leaving nothing but him. My stomach knots and Nancy's voice fades into the murmur of traffic. He's wearing jeans and a smart coat; different clothes to what he usually wears. He's talking into headphones, but his expression stays. The flashing of cars disrupts my view of him, but I make sure to keep my eyes on him the whole time.
I won't let him disappear.
My eyes shake inside my skull as I try not to blink.
I won't let him disappear.
They begin to water and my eyelids beg to close.
I don't allow it.
I won't let him disappear.
He waits for the flow of traffic to ease, then commits to a slow jog; coming to our side of the road and heading straight for us. His head swings from left to right, avoiding the metal shells of oncoming cars. He charges heroically through every obstacle to get to me. His pace slows as he steps onto the pavement.

My body has frozen with the rest of the world.
Everything but James has stopped.
His eyes glide across the park.
Through the woodwork.
Through Nancy.
Through me.

In one tragic moment, he's looked through my entire life. He's seen all of me – and all that I have to offer – and maintained a stride away from me.
He continues in the other direction.

His face morphs through my tearful eyes as he wades through my watery vision.

His face continues to manipulate itself.

The face of James has disappeared.

The face of a man – an unrecognisable, unfamiliar man – walks away.

That's not *my* James.

As he walks out of my life, Nancy runs towards me. She interrupts my view with a confused, bewildered expression. I urge myself to tell her, forcing up my words. 'That's James.' My voice shakes in a cold breath.

Her body follows behind her head, already examining the road in front of us. There's no one else in sight, so she can't help but notice him. 'Where? I can't see him.' She scans the road and the streets around us.

One lonely figure is in our sights. He's still visible, but getting less recognisable with each step he takes away from me. I don't even recognise him, now. His face is different to the one that I first saw crossing the road.

I point to him, directing her vision to the only other person around us. I cough up my breath, telling her that it's James – over and over again.

She looks straight at the man in sight.

She doesn't see James.

36. WOOLWICH ADVENTURE PLAYGROUND cont.

Nancy spent a long, frustrating time looking for him. She was convinced that he wasn't there. She looked right at him and said it wasn't James. She didn't see him anywhere.

I know what I saw – and I know that was him.

Not having my phone won't make any difference. I can keep running from my own life forever, but it will always catch up with me. I might not be with him, but he's with me.

I don't know if I can outrun that.

As tempting as it was to leave, we decided to stay here. There's nowhere else to go. We will be chasing a continuous loop from my house to Nancy's, until circumstances force me to confront James. I need to face up to my own issues. I can't keep relying on someone else to protect me and bail me out.

This is the longest period of time that we haven't spoken for. Even if it was speaking through text, we've talked to each other every day since we first met at the bus stop.

It might've turned into a bit of a habit. I wouldn't want any particular day to be the first day we hadn't spoken to each other. I would try not to text him, just to get over the idea and not be needy, but he would text me to ask what I was doing. It turned into a routine of speaking to each other, just for the sake of talking. It would sometimes feel like we would run out of things to talk about, so we'd just recycle the same stories that we'd told before.

Other than checking up on me, it would always be me making the effort to speak to him. He wouldn't phone me to see how I am or ask me how an exam went. We got into a routine where I would text him in the morning and a conversation would start, then continue until we met later that day. And if I didn't text in the morning, he would wonder why I hadn't texted him.

Not talking could just as easily cause an argument.

Even if we were in an argument, we'd still be speaking to each other. I hate the idea of not being in contact with him, even if it's just to argue. I'd rather talk and argue than not talk at all. In an argument over text, if one of us was to stop texting, that person would be the one ignoring the other; it would be down to them to break the silence and get back in contact.

I would always make sure I didn't ignore a text or be the person not to reply. If we completely stopped talking, I was worried that would give him time to move on and adjust to not speaking to me. Then, I know I would see photos of him on Facebook with another girl and it would break my heart. I think he felt the same way because he would always ask me what I was doing or who I was with – even if he hadn't replied to my text from the night before.

I feel like, without my phone, I've fallen off the radar. I'm dead to the world if I'm not online in some way. And it makes me uneasy to think what I might be missing out on. In a way, I hate having my phone with me. It's like an anchor. Everyone's life is lived online, now. If you're not there, you don't exist. And it will just get worse with time.

I've seen it. A group of my mates from college will sit together, and all of them will be on their phones – probably posting about what a great time they're having.

Heads down – in another world.

I don't like to be part of that. But I need to, just to keep up.
Everyone's sitting there, hoping that people will want to take an
interest in the most boring parts of their life that they put up. Or if
that doesn't work, they'll make up an entirely different life
altogether that isn't even theirs, just to make everyone else
jealous.

Constantly on holiday? Sure.

Filming yourself with a drink in your hand while twirling around
a really busy club? Can't be having that much fun if the only thing
you're looking at is the front-facing camera.

I'm really starting to see through this. It doesn't make me happy
anymore, and I'm not sure if it ever really did. It's more important
to look like you're having a good time than to actually have a
good time. Everyone is *'living their best life'*. But rather than
living, they talk about living. Take a photo of your food, shove a
filter on it, upload it. Don't forget to tell everyone where you are.
Can't possibly forget the tag. Otherwise, were you even there?
Eating the food comes second. And now, you're eating a great
looking, freezing-cold dinner.

Everything is public.

If I was to advertise all my problems on Facebook, I would be in a
very different position. I would have loads of *'friends'* offering me
a cyber-shoulder to cry on.

'Hope you're ok.'

'PM me!'

If you were my friend, you'd know about my life – not my latest
status. You wouldn't have to wait for me to post one of those
annoying quote pictures on Instagram that's meant to look all
ambiguous and subtle, but is blatantly just attention seeking. And
if you don't market your life like that, you get overlooked. If you
don't tell the world your problems, people assume that you don't
have any. Attention is for the people who crave it. And there's so
many people who crave it, there's no room for the people who
need it. It's only ever the loudest voices that get heard, not the

ones making the most sense – and online, everyone's got a microphone… Plugged into a megaphone.
If that's the alternative, I'd rather no one know my business.
I'm tired of seeing my own friends scrolling through Instagram, stalking everyone just to criticise how they look – then liking the picture to get a like back. I hate seeing my friends like that. It brings out a really bitchy side to them that isn't even there in real life. I'm struggling through my issues, trying to keep some self-respect… And I have nothing better to show for it. There's no privacy or dignity in going through hard times.
Maybe I've just been born at the wrong time.

Without my phone, I can't see what James has told everyone. I can't see if he's shared that video of me online. I don't know if he's telling everyone about us. He doesn't like people to know if we've had an argument because he likes people to think that everything is fine. To him, a crack in our relationship would be an invitation for another boy to step in and fill it. Best to make everything look fine for everyone else. Doesn't matter what is going on beneath the surface.
He doesn't like me telling my friends, but I don't know what he'll tell his.
Everything I do is to benefit him.
Everything he does is to benefit him more.
I'm so sick of it.

It's not just him. Everyone is like that. Completely self-obsessed. Everyone's a celebrity… Taking pictures of their own baby photos and uploading them. Throwback? That just means you've got nothing new going on in your life. No one cares what you looked like when you were five. It was only ten years ago. And you basically look the same as everyone else now, anyway… I guess that's what happens when you're watching the same make-up tutorials as everyone else and modelling yourself on the exact same people.

I think even that will change. Baby photos won't be dusted out of an old biscuit tin at the back of a cupboard like mine are. If someone wants to see photos of their first Christmas, they can scroll a bit further down their Timeline and find everything. It's all changing – and not for the better. *Baby's first portrait photo* is turning into *baby's first profile picture*. Parents won't keep a photo of their kids in their purse like mine and Nancy's mum do; they will just send them a Friend Request instead.
Everyone is in on it.

Life is lived online.
Without my phone, I don't exist.
And the more time that goes on, I don't know if that's such a bad thing anymore.

37. WOOLWICH CHURCH STREET

Today has lasted for days. I've got no way of telling what time it is, but it hasn't started to get dark yet. We woke up quite early, which means I have to be awake for longer and face a longer day. I'll try to have a lie-in tomorrow.

We are walking further down Woolwich Church Street, on our way back to Nancy's. We stopped off at a shop to get some food.

A few bars of chocolate.

Milkshakes.

A bag of cheese balls.

Not proper food.

I try not to look at the people passing us on the street. I feel like they know all about me; that my face tells them all the details of my life. Luckily, it's a miserable day, so the streets are quite empty. Just the occasional car slipping across wet road and gliding away from us into the grey.

I keep my head down, following the cracks in the pavement and making sure I step evenly on each one – never letting my feet unevenly touch the pure paving stones. My eyes are scanning all the lumps of trodden chewing gum that pepper the pavement in front of us, ruining the purity of the clear path ahead.

As well as the sword sticking out of my bra and nudging me for attention, my jeans haven't been washed for a while. I wore these jeans to Westfield the other day. They were skinny jeans that day. Denim is weird and annoying like that. When I wear a pair of jeans for a few days without washing them, the material gets really loose and baggy. A pair of skinny jeans on Monday turn into a pair of flares by Thursday. I keep having to pull them up from the waist and they bunch around the knees as I walk. These are a size ten – after a few days, they're a size fourteen. They'll probably fit me after I get through that big bag of cheese balls.

Nancy seems to be wearing new stuff all the time. She always looks nice, even when we are going to the shops in our pyjamas. I need to get her something nice for Christmas. When I come out of this phase that I'm in, I'll get her something.
I know this will be a phase. I won't let it be anything more than that. She's been so good through all this. I know I can't be much company at the moment, so she's done well to put up with me. I owe it to her to get out of this.
I know she wants a onesie. I'll get her a llama one. I think she'd prefer an animal one. She wants to be a vet when she gets older and she's obsessed with llamas, so that will be right up her street. Without any hint from her, I know exactly what she would like. That's how I know she's my best friend.
I don't want to keep bothering her with my problems, and I know she's probably got her own issues going on. I'm more of a listener than a talker, so this is all new to me. All my talking is done to myself, inside my own head. Things always sound stupid when I'm saying them out loud. They make perfect sense in my head, but – out loud – they sound childish or just stupid. I don't want to keep boring her about myself. My life really isn't that interesting. I'm no different to any other girl.

There is something that has been bothering me, but I wouldn't like to say it to Nance. I feel that, if I say it out loud, it could be true. If it's just a thought in my head, then that's where it will stay.

Seeing mum in that state got me wondering about my own future. What's the difference between me and mum? She's on medication for depression. When she doesn't take her medication, she'll have a funny turn and start drinking. Recently, I'm looking at her and seeing myself. What if I end up... Like her?

I'm not a happy person.

Not at the moment.

I haven't been happy for a long time.

Is this how depression starts?

Do people with depression know they are depressed? At the start, they must just feel down. That's how I feel now. So, what's the difference between being depressed and being unhappy? How would I know if I had depression? I'd need someone to tell me. But no one would ever do that. James has mentioned, especially recently, that I'm always in a mood.

But is it more than that?

Am I causing all this?

Is there something wrong with me?

How long will it be until I am *mum*?

38. NANCY'S

I tried to push all the stuff about mum to the back of my mind. I noticed that I was staring out and daydreaming for a long time. When I'd think about it, my mind would leave my body – unresponsive and empty. That could be how those conditions start. Need to keep my feet grounded. When we got to Nancy's, her voice got further and further away as I drifted into my thoughts. In the end, I had to shake off and bring myself back. No one is going to get me out of this rut except me. It's been really tempting to leave myself and get lost in my own head.
I'm scared of where that might take me, so I'm forcing myself to be occupied – don't think about it, and don't make it real by talking about it.

We got to Nancy's and watched some rubbish telly for a while, feasting on the stuff we bought from the shop. I was making myself pay attention to what was on. We were channel hopping through all those shows where they try to find out who the father is. I was making the sound of laughter at some of the stories and Nancy was loving them. I don't know why people would drag themselves on telly to settle stuff. People don't watch it to see conflicts getting resolved – they watch it to laugh at the people on there and compare them to their own lives.
The stupid, poor people – one of the last groups of people it's still alright to make fun of.
How else are you going to feel better about yourself?

I think that's why people are obsessed with sad songs and films. They want to know someone else is worse off. Either that – or they want to know other people have been through the same thing they're going through and voice it in a way they can't. People want to know they're not on their own in love, fear, heartbreak… All those things. They want something to relate to – and hear someone say what they feel in a proper way.

There were a few stories involving pregnancy, so I had to really concentrate on making a convincing laughing sound. I had to get the timing right; not go too over-the-top, but be loud enough to look like it wasn't something that would affect me.
I was almost robotic.

I think it's too early to do another test just yet – don't think about it, and don't make it real by talking about it.

We've had a bit of a scare before. The first time we had sex properly. The first time I'd done anything.
He knew I was a virgin. When I asked him if he was, he would always give a different answer. It would never be a straight *yes* or *no*. He'd give an answer like *'I've done stuff before, but not fully'*. I still don't know what that means. Whether he was too embarrassed to say anything different or he genuinely had done things with loads of girls – I'm not sure.
I had no idea what I was doing the first time, but I made sure I shaved when I knew I was staying the night. I was lying there most of the time, letting him do everything. He was making a lot of groaning noises, and I didn't know if I should do the same. I would've been too embarrassed to make any noises, so I just didn't. I remember staring at his ceiling light most of the time, feeling really conscious that his mum might hear the metal twang of the springs in the bed. She knew we were upstairs on our own, and she wouldn't have heard any talking. I kept wanting to talk or put a film on.

Anything.

Anything to make her think that we weren't doing what we were doing. A film would make background noise and explain why we weren't talking – we'd be too busy watching a film to be talking. She must've known what we were doing and that made me feel like a slut. I was only sixteen at this point, so I thought she'd think that was too young to be doing anything; and she'd think less of me for it.

I really didn't want to see her the next morning, so I waited until she left for work before I went downstairs and went home. I still do that now. It would be an awkward little conversation at the bottom of the stairs. We both know what's gone on up there. What else is there to say?

'You sleep well?'
'Yeah, thanks.'
'You have a good night?'
'Could say that.'
'What did you do?'
'Your son.'

He wanted me to go on top after a few seconds of trying to squeeze it in.

I didn't want to. It was the first time I'd been naked in front of someone else since I was about two – in the bath with mum. It took me long enough to take my bra off in front of him, let alone get on top of him naked. I made sure my body was under the duvet the whole time. I wanted to keep my top on, but he convinced me to take it off. I had to beg him to do it with the lights off because I was so conscious of my body. He did – in the end. He likes to keep the light on now, though. I'd like it off, just to feel more comfortable. But he says there's no point in doing anything if you can't see it, and I should be flattered that it feels better for him to see me.

He seemed to expect a lot from me, considering that it was my first time. It made me wonder if he had done stuff with other girls

before or if he'd just had a warped idea from watching too much porn.
He was only sixteen himself, so he couldn't have done that much...

I felt like he expected me to know exactly what to do for him to make it feel good. I've never watched porn, but I would imagine the girls know what they're doing. I'm not some crazy feminist, but guys watching porn at a young age can't be good. It obviously gives them unrealistic ideas of what girls – *real girls* – are like. They expect all girls to be sluts as soon as the lights go off... The *'good'* kind of slut that they want to sleep with, not the *'bad'* kind of slut that they don't want to go out with.
Plus, the girls in porn are actresses. They get paid to *act* like they enjoy it, and they must pick up a rough idea of what feels good for a guy along the way.

I had no idea what felt good for him. He would squeeze my hips and grab a handful of my hair really tightly in his fist. I remember it being quite aggressive for something that's meant to be nice. He'd started pushing against me quite hard as soon as he'd started. There wasn't much of a soft lead up. He'd pushed through and started from there, going at the same quick and eager pace the whole time. I was in a bit of pain, so I just bit my lips together and tried to bear it, wondering if there was something wrong with me. If it was meant to feel so nice, why was it hurting?
He kept his head buried into my neck and chest, so I didn't see his face the whole time. I did see that he had socks on at one point, which freaked me out. I still don't know why. It's just weird to think he'd be naked except for a pair of socks.
After a few times of pushing against me under the duvet, I heard him call my name.
Then, I really didn't know what to do.
Do I call him back?
Do I answer him?

I just stayed silent; still staring at his – by that time, fascinating – ceiling light.

As quickly as he'd started moving, his body stopped. His head was still hidden in my neck and shoulder as he was on top of me, and I felt him kissing at it between deep, heavy breaths.

I got a sharp, stinging sensation as he pulled out. My legs tensed under the pain. I felt they were a bit wet and they'd hit a cold patch as soon as I'd moved them. I didn't know exactly what it was at first. When he rolled off me, I put my fingers down there and dragged them back up. I tried to do it as subtly as possible because I didn't want to look weird.

It was faint, light blood – almost pink. My first thought was – *'I've just come on my period at the worst possible time in the history of Earth.'* I realised, quite quickly, it couldn't have been that because I'd only recently finished. I got really scared at first and didn't know if it was normal to bleed after sex – no one had ever told me what was normal and what wasn't. I'd started panicking inside myself, but I didn't want to say anything to James. He was busy covering his face with his forearm and panting away next to me.

If there was a mood, I didn't want to ruin it with this.

I was using my knickers to pat myself down and pressed them between my legs to make sure no blood was coming out. I thought I'd look down and see a crime scene.

My legs.

The sheets.

The duvet.

All splattered with blood.

So, I just didn't look. Not until my body forced me to and James wasn't looking.

Eventually, he stopped hiding his face from me. He kept asking me if it was okay. I didn't know what was okay and what wasn't, so I just told him that it felt nice.

He seemed quite smug and proud when I told him it felt sore.
When he took the condom off and eased it from under the duvet,
there wasn't much inside.
It had split.

As if bleeding and being in pain wasn't bad enough – the condom
had split.
I always thought the first time I'd had sex should make me feel
special and more loved.
I'd spent it awkward, bleeding, and probably pregnant.

39. NANCY'S cont.

After hours of watching box sets and all the soaps on telly – trying to catch up with the plot lines – we were spread on the sofa like two sloths.

We'd eaten our weight in rubbish.

I felt a lot better that my mind was occupied. I focused on the problems of EastEnders characters and was able to escape my own for a little while.

Between episodes, Nancy decided to paint my nails with one of her bright, girly colours.

Neon pink. It was a lovely shade.

She could do it professionally. She did such a good job on mine. I was sat on the armchair and she kneeled on the floor beside me, hardly looking up. She was so engrossed in doing it.

She put a clear base coat on first and added the pink when it dried. After that, she put a special coating on which stops them from chipping. She's got a proper kit with loads of different colours. I really liked the glitter one she had, but it's a bit too flashy for me. It was nice to have them done properly. I don't usually do them myself. If I do, I just splat on the colour closest to my hand while I'm getting ready. Then, I'll pick at it throughout the day and wonder why I bothered putting it on in the first place.

Because she took such care in doing them, I want to be just as careful with them. I've had to make a conscious effort not to pick at them or bite my nails.

I've made it a challenge for myself to see how long I can keep them looking nice. If I start picking, I'll be annoyed at myself. This is the nicest they've ever looked and I'm determined to keep them this way.

Before she'd added the last coat, I'd forgotten my nails were wet. I went to scratch my cheek and push my hair back – and ended up smearing the paint across half my face. I realised straight after and Nancy started laughing. She took a picture of me on her phone and showed me. I looked like an ultraviolet soldier. I had neon pink war paint and was ready for battle. She saved the picture and set it as the wallpaper on her phone. I thought she'd be annoyed because it took her ages to do and I'd messed it up in five seconds. She just thought it was funny.
I haven't seen her get stressed about anything in a long time.
She used spit on her thumb to wipe my face, like a mum would do. After she'd touched-up the smears, she gave my hand a playful slap and told me to be more careful.
I sometimes think I'm just not cut out to be a girl. I don't have the patience to be primping and pruning constantly. It's nice every once in a while, but it's a lot of maintenance to be a full-time girl.

After a while of keeping my hands flat on both arms of the armchair to dry, I decided I should probably go to bed.
I felt exhausted.
As I stood at the bottom of the stairs, Nance gave me a look from the sofa in the living room. She didn't say anything. She just smiled slightly, as if to say – *'do what you have to do.'*
She knew I'd go up to check my phone.

I've been lying in her bed for a while, now.
Small light is coming in through the blinds. Enough to look by, but not enough to see.

Lipgloss

I'm on top of the duvet, staring at my phone on the floor by the door. I switched it off as soon as I came up. I know it couldn't overheat and cause a fire, but it'll save on their electricity bill.
It was tempting to pick it up there and then – just through habit. I unplugged it from the wall altogether a few minutes after – disconnecting it from the power – but left it where it was on the floor.
That phone is going to drag me back into a world that I don't want to go to.
That phone is going to force me back into a life that I don't want to be part of.
That phone holds the future of my relationship.
But, so do I.
I need to start taking some responsibility and sort out my own life.
I can't keep running to someone else when things get tough.

I sit up on the bed and edge back towards the pillow, hugging my knees. My eyes are fixed on the phone as I shield myself. The headlights from a car outside force the shadows across the room, then they settle as they were as it drives past.
I swing my feet to the floor and sit on the side of the bed. I feel my body pulling towards the phone. Another car drives past the window. The room lights up and darkens just as quickly.
I stand up, walk to the corner of the room, and stare down at my future.
Stare down at the arguments – waiting for me as soon as I switch on the phone.
Stare down at everyone online – asking me what's happened.
Stare down at my past – disconnected from the power socket.
And stare down at James – hugging his knees in the corner of the room, tightly clenching his phone.
Shadows swing across the room with another car driving past, falling back down as fast as they grew.

Darkness takes over again – but I see clearer.

I turn away.

I pull the duvet from the sheets and climb into bed. I squeeze up against the wall, so Nance will have enough room to get in later. My body rolls onto its side and I turn my back on my first relationship, still on the floor in the corner.

I'm lying in darkness, waiting to fall asleep with my eyes open. Another set of headlights pour into the room. Shadows snake up the walls, and James is lying behind me on the bed; lost and looking to me – hoping that I'll turn around.

Then, darkness.

The beams of another car straight after. This time, only creased, empty bed sheets in the light behind me.

Shadows take over.

Darkness, again.

40. AT MINE

I'm not stopping. I came back to pick up a few things that I couldn't get before, then I'm going straight back out. I had my keys in my hand from the moment I'd left Nancy's. I don't want to waste any time – either indoors or out here.

I went to bed yesterday feeling stronger than I'd felt for a long time. I was able to overcome myself and take charge of my own life for once. I had the opportunity to cave, but I didn't. I'm not sure how long it'll last... Maybe I'm fooling myself, but I don't want to live upset and feel down anymore. It could just be a case of *out of sight, out of mind.* But I'll take that for now.
I want to keep that feeling with me.
Nothing scares me anymore.
I can't keep being a passenger in my own life.

This morning, I woke up to Nancy spooning me. She had her arm around me and I was holding it into my chest. Our fingers were locked into each other. I can't remember the last time I woke up to James cuddling me – or even touching me. We don't even hold hands when we walk down the street. He'll have me under his arm and hidden beside him, but we wouldn't ever hold hands. Nance woke up at the same time as me, and I told her all about my epic triumph over not texting James or even switching my phone on to check it. She seemed really surprised and said she was proud of me. I was waiting to tell her from the moment I'd done it, so it's the first thing I said to her in the morning.

We've arranged to go into the West End today, just to get away from the area. I can't go dressed like this, so I needed to get a change of clothes. I need to get toiletries, too. I can't keep using Nancy's toothbrush. I brush a lot harder than her and my toothbrush ends up getting frayed into a toilet brush.

When I told Nance about not texting James, the two of us kept flinching over each other's morning-breath. Hers was worse than mine. It was like talking into a sewer. Unless that was my breath bouncing off her.

We kept making fun of each other.

She started it…

'Did you comfort eat a lump of shit during the night?'

My comeback was better…

'It's probably you! You're the one who's always talking shit. Now, it's on your breath.'

She's such a fool. I'm so lucky to have her.

I get to my front door and have the key ready to put in the lock. The brass scratches together as the key goes in and turns. I slam the door behind me, wanting mum to hear that I'm home and not happy with her. I don't know if she'll remember what she said to me – or even if she'll remember speaking to me at all. I won't make any excuses for her. As far as I'm concerned, if she knew she'd started drinking, she knew she'd behave like that. She's responsible for whatever she said, whether she remembers it or not.

I storm up the stairs, pounding the carpet. I don't care if she's asleep. She can wake up. I take a look in the living room through the banister and can see it's been tidied since I was last here. I get to the top of the stairs and the hallway is bright with sunlight. Not sure if she's in.

I go into the bathroom and grab my toothbrush. There are only two of us that live here, but there are about five toothbrushes for some unknown reason. I try to hit a few of the old ones out of the holder as I grab my own. I want to cause maximum chaos while I'm here. As I walk past it, I make sure I knock the damp towel off the towel rail. It's a petty thing to do, but makes me feel better.

I go straight into my room and grab some clothes. I'll get dressed at Nancy's – don't want to stay here any longer than I have to. On my way over, I made a mental list of things that I need. As I grab them, I tick them off.
Toothbrush.
Face wash.
Moisturiser.
Few pairs of clean underwear.
Bra.
Change of clothes.
Make-up bag.
Some hair clips and hair bands; they always go missing, so I take a handful from my drawer.
I pile everything into the biggest tote bag I have. I manage to squeeze a smaller handbag inside, so I can transfer my essentials before we go shopping. I leave my packed bag on the bed, bursting at the seams and overflowing with clothes.

I go to the mirror, straighten up my body, and stand proud.
Chin up. Shoulders back.
My head angles to look at the love bite on my neck.
It's fading – only visible when I stand strong and don't hunch over. The taller I stand, the deeper the scars.
I can feel his grip on me loosening as it heals. His hold is getting weaker by the day. I'm worried that he might have had a bigger impact on my body than just a love bite. The real effect he's had on me goes deeper than the skin.

I shake myself out of any looming daydream and make my way to the stairs. I drop my full bodyweight on each stair, shaking the whole flat under me. I see mum through the banisters, standing in the living room. Her dressing gown is slumped down one shoulder, falling off her pyjama top. She looks like a zombie, just been dug up. 'Hello, love.' I don't answer. 'Where you off to?'

I don't look at her. Just continue to thump down each stair as I leave. 'Nancy's.' I talk to the front door ahead of me.

I don't stick around for any more questions. Just walk straight out.

I do feel bad. It's not in my nature to be rude or ignore people. But she needs to know that she did something wrong and I'm not happy with her. Otherwise, she'll do it again.

She will, anyway.

But this way, she'll know it affected me.

41. OXFORD CIRCUS STATION

The traffic of Oxford Street growls past the two of us as we hold hands at the crossing. Nancy stands to my left and we wait for the green man; our hands squeezing with every taxi honk and cyclist's shout over the bustle of shoppers. Shopping bags graze us and shoulders pound us from all angles. Arms that aren't attached to a body weave through crowds and disappear into the grey backdrop of shops. A sharp wind laces through the traffic, dragging a dull smog over a thousand shouting voices to the end of Oxford Street.

Madness down here.

Standing at the traffic lights, two prams arrive. One stops beside me and the other stops next to Nancy.

I look at the one on my right side.

Through closed eyelids, a sleeping baby looks up at me.

A beautiful little girl. I only know she's a girl from her gorgeous, pink blanket – thick and comforting, protecting her from the world.

She's a perfect canvas.

Strawberry-blonde tufts of hair under her knitted hat.

Fresh, new skin.

Rosy cheeks.

A sleeping porcelain doll.

She looks less than a year old. Brand new, full of hope and promise. Her face scrunches up for a moment and her tiny hands clench in a pair of mittens. She relaxes after a few seconds and her soft, silky skin smooths itself back out. Her blankets are rising and falling slowly, with each innocent breath. Her eyelids ease open and she looks into me with delicate eyes that are impossibly blue. She blinks deeply and slowly. She's dropping back off to sleep in her soft cloud of blankets.

I look at the mother. She's not that old and looks middle-class. She's dressed smart and a lot taller than me. There are bags hanging from the side of the pram, stretched and taut from the amount of presents inside. She must have money to be shopping for toys down here. She's preoccupied with talking on her phone, not appreciating the bundle of perfection she's got in front of her.

The lights change and the traffic stops.
Green man.

Both prams on either side of us push forward at the same time. The pram on Nancy's side forces ahead, moving faster than mine.

'For fu – ' Nance hops up and down, steadying herself on me. 'Why would you bring a pram to West End? Look how packed it is down here – and they still bring them! Ran right over my toe, the bitch. Not even a *'sorry'*, y'know! What am I? Fucking invisible?' She gestures after the pram, flinging her arms up and down.

My eyes follow my pram across the road as it disappears into the anonymous crowd of shoppers.

We cross the road while the green man is still signalling for us to walk. We make our way towards the entrance of one of the department stores. People are pouring in and out of all available entrances. We have to ease past cliques of girls; they link arms as they walk and it's impossible to get between them.

Inside, it's even worse.

Swarms of posh girls float from stand to stand, fingering through hangers and trying to find the last size six.

Nance takes my hand and we walk to the escalator in front of us. 'Jesus Christ. Don't worry, babes. We won't be in here long; I just gotta look for one top downstairs quick.' We take our jackets off and Nance stuffs both of them into her bag. Nan got us into the habit of doing that when we were little.

'Take your jacket off indoors – otherwise, you won't feel the benefit.'

I try not to look in the mirrors on the way down the escalators. It's hard because there are mirrors to the left, the right, and straight ahead of us as the ceiling lowers. It's just in case the vain girls in here start panicking that they haven't seen themselves for five-whole-minutes.

A hair might've fallen out of place in that time and someone might see. That's their career as an *'influencer'* – over.

Nancy is in front of me on the escalator, pouting into the mirror on our right and flattening the back of her hair as we go down. 'This fucking crown! Can you see this kink at the back of my head?' She gently pats her hair down.

There's a serious chunk of hair sticking up on top of her head. I've only just noticed it myself, now that she's pointed it out. I try to push it down for her, but it bounces up under my fingers.

'Yeah, that ain't going down. It's been straightened like that.' I laugh to myself and point her to the mirror. 'Look how bouncy it is!' I press gently on it.

'Okay… So, it's literally your fault for straightening it like that – mugged me right off.' She scruffs her hair up and shakes her head like a dog. The chunk has disappeared in a mountain of dye and extensions. She turns around to face me on the escalator and raises her head slightly. Her hair is all over her face. She pulls a blank expression through the thin, brown strands. 'Does it look better now?'

I burst out laughing as we get closer to the lower-ground floor. She's such an idiot. Half of the shop is looking at her as we get off the escalator, but she doesn't care.

She pulls her hair out of her face and ties it back. 'Right – let me ask someone quick. One sec, babes. I won't be able to find it in here on my own. D'you wanna have a look around? I just need to get this one top and I'm done in here.' She edges towards the nearest sales assistant. She seemed to avoid asking the female ones for any help. I don't blame her. They're worlds away from us, so I can see why she would. They're the type of girls who would judge us straight away and think they're better than us.

'Nah, I don't have to get anything in here. I just need to go Primark and that's me.' We could've gone to Stratford to do this, but we both decided it would be nice to get out of the area for the day. Just have a girls' day out, without the threat of bumping into anyone we know.

We get pointed to the Information Desk by a guy who looks like a rocker. He's got his ear lobes stretched and a sleeve tattoo down to his knuckles. The tattoo will look ridiculous when he gets older, but it looks alright now – only because everyone else in the world has them. Sleeve tattoos aren't really for rockers and bikers anymore. They're for baristas and hairdressers, scaffolders and accountants, personal trainers and plumbers. Anyone with arms, skin, and no personality. I get why people have them... How else will I know how hard and cool and individual and alternative you are, unless you look like everyone else?
I hate everyone.

'He was quite fit, weren't he? I don't usually go for them types, but he was nice.' She speaks into me and keeps looking back at him as we walk towards the Information Desk. I turn around and see he's looking at her, smiling. He seems to love himself. He's holding his chin up in the air, expecting that every girl is looking at him. Nance turns around with me and brings me in closer to her. 'He's looking at you, y'know.'
He wasn't.

He wouldn't.

Even when her hair was all over her face, she still looked nicer than me. I'm wearing a red checked-shirt; open – with a white tank top underneath, a pair of skinny jeans; washed – so they're actually skinny for a change, and white Converse.

Nancy's wearing a denim shirt, thick pair of black leggings, and a white pair of Vans.

She fingers tops as we pass hangers of overpriced winter jumpers, with weird pictures and random writing on them. We follow the aisles until we get to the Information Desk. I hold back while Nancy speaks to the girl at the till. After the girl types into the computer, Nance comes back to me. 'Right – she said they've got one more in a size twelve and it should be on the wall over at the back. So, we gotta get there quick before some other fat bitch gets it first.'

Size twelve is *not* fat. And she's only that size because of her boobs. I'm a size ten because I haven't got any.

She walks ahead of me. I took her stuff off her, so she could get there quicker.

The tattooed sales assistant comes over to me and I feel my stomach knot. 'Did your friend find what she was looking for?' His voice travels over my shoulder.

I try not to look at him in the face. My eyes are darting around the whole shop. 'Oh, yeah. Thanks. She's just run off to get it. Thanks for your help.' I turn my body to the direction Nancy ran in, hoping she'll come back quickly and rescue me. I sense the guy is still standing near me, but I don't turn around to check.

'Wow, she's away. She must really want that top.' He comes to my side. 'You not getting anything in here?' We are standing next to each other, looking out for Nancy. He's obviously sticking around and waiting for her to get back.

'Nah, I've gotta save my money. I need to buy something for my boyfriend for Christmas.' I emphasise it… *Boyfriend.*

I see Nancy in the distance. She stops and hides behind a mannequin when she sees me and the guy talking.

'Ah, well. Make sure he gets you something special, won't you? Make sure he knows how lucky he is.' His voice fades.
I smile at him.
We stand in an awkward silence for, what seems like, ages. I'm still waiting for Nancy to come over.

'Got any big plans for New Year's Eve?' He fills the silence. Nancy makes her way back towards us. I feel more comfortable talking now because I know the conversation will have to end.

'I'm not too sure yet. Still gotta make it through Christmas dinner before I can make any sort of plans.' My eyes are on Nancy.
He laughs through his beard and whitened teeth. I didn't realise that came out as a joke. I was being serious.
I laugh with him.

Nancy comes over with a bag. She obviously bought the top in the time I'd been standing in silence with my new best friend. I bundle our things together, getting ready to go. She seems rushed as she approaches us. 'Alright, babes. I'm gonna go upstairs for a minute. But I'll come back down after and meet you here, yeah?' She smiles at me, then him.

As she gets ready to walk off, I take her hand. 'Oh, no. It's okay, I'll come with you. James is still upstairs, isn't he?' I give her a knowing look; my eyes tell her to take me away.

Her eyebrows get lower with confusion. 'Oh, *is he*? I didn't know. I'll tell him you're down here, then. Don't worry. You stay here, though.' She sucks a grin into her mouth, trying to hide it.

I turn to the sales assistant. 'Nice meeting you. Have a good Christmas.' I link onto Nancy, but she doesn't walk away. That's just made me look weird.

She points to a tattoo on his neck. 'What does that *'G'* stand for?'

He looks blankly at her and sighs, 'It's a *'C'*. It stands for *Chris*. My name.' His voice is dead and unimpressed.

She tries to hold in her laugh and I attempt to pull her away before she can explode in his face. 'Looks like a *'G'* to me. You sure your name isn't Gerald? Or Gornak? Or Guntherdink? You look like a *Guntherdink*.' She tries to get out some last words as I drag her away. 'Nice meeting you, Guntherdink. Her name is – '

'Come on, Nance.' I drag her to the escalator and we both laugh our way up. We probably knocked his ego a bit. He looked quite flash and Nance just brought him down to Earth.

'Someone's gonna be getting that tattoo lasered off tonight.' She laughs into me and pushes her forehead against my shoulder, collapsing her body onto me. *''James is upstairs'* y'know… What were you thinking?' She laughs more with that.

I grab her shoulders and hold her away from me. 'Yeah, thanks for sticking me in it!' I fight back a laugh and try to hold a serious face, but I don't manage it. 'And who the fuck is Guntherdink? Is that even a real name?' My head bulges with laughter as we go up to the ground floor.

'You looked like a right dick head! And you went all red, as well!' She laughs more, as the bright sky becomes visible over the top of the disappearing escalator. 'I told you he was looking at you, though. Didn't I? You sexy bitch. Come – let's go McDonald's and eat.'

42. McDONALD'S

'I asked him for three barbeque sauce, two sweet and sour, and a curry sauce. What d'you think he gives me? Fucking – two ketchups!' Nancy's head is buried inside her food as she peers up at me. She tears open the brown paper bag and an avalanche of chips tries to escape. The rest of the sauces are in my bag. But I'll tell her that when she finishes her rant because it's entertaining me at the moment.

She ordered large chips, six chicken nuggets, and a Coke.
I asked for a cheeseburger, medium chips, and a banana milkshake.
No banana.
Chocolate?
We're out of chocolate.
Nance laughed.
Strawberry?
Strawberry's fine.
Put your card in please.
There's me – raffling off all the different flavours like some fat milkshake fiend.

While we waited for our food, Nance took some coppers and change from her purse, dropping them into the donation box. Someone had dropped a fiver in. That must have been an accident. They were probably messing about and it slipped out of their hands – no one would put that amount in on purpose. There were some coins in there that weren't English. The writing looked like it was Chinese. It must be scary for someone to come to the West End if they're not from here. It's bad enough for us and we speak the language. It's worlds away from Woolwich and we're still in the same city. You have to be quite brave to come here and try to settle down. I don't think I'd be able to live in this part of London.

'Seriously, d'you think the sauce comes out of their pay? How am I gonna make this little bit last me the whole time? I'm sure they do it on purpose.' She studies her buffet of tiny sauces.
I laugh to myself as she goes on, looking at my cheeseburger and comparing my food to hers.
I've missed these days out. Even though we aren't really doing much, it's nice to have a proper day out with her and not have to worry about checking in with someone or keep an eye on the time. It's good to have my life as my own for a change.
It's still quite early in the afternoon and the day is ours to do what we want. We are sitting downstairs in a booth in the far corner. We were lucky to get a seat – there were no free chairs upstairs and the whole place is packed with shoppers, squeezed onto the smallest tables to be sat with each other.
I'm on the seat facing the wall. I don't like to face people when I eat; always feel really self-conscious as if people are looking at me with disgust. It's impossible to look good while you're eating. And I always manage to catch someone's eye, just as I've got food hanging out of my mouth.

We talk through mouthfuls of chips and burger, and she teases me about how red my face was earlier. Through her laughter and incoherent chomping of words, she spits a piece of chicken that bounces off my lip. She saw it happen and I react instantly. 'Oh my God – come on!' I wipe my mouth, scrambling through the rubbish and dirty serviettes to find a clean one. 'Seriously?'
She laughs more and buries her head into the table, vibrating with laughter. She's trying to control herself – and not choke on the chunk of food she's still chewing.

'Stop!' She shakes her red head. 'I'm dying!' Mashed food pushes through the gaps of her clean, white teeth.

I rinse the joke for as long as I can, trying to entertain her more. 'Unbelievable.' I wipe at my face, hands, and forearms; where my sleeves are rolled up. 'Spraying all your diseases on me.'

Her eyes are watering, her thick mask of foundation creasing around her eyes and mouth. 'Well, at least you know I spit and don't swallow.' She sticks her tongue out, peppered with mushy food.

I look away from her, shaking my head with embarrassment and hiding my face. 'You're so grim!' This is the reaction she wants from me. I talk to the whole room. 'I'm not actually with this girl, everyone.' I animate myself to be more disgusted, trying to make her laugh.

She only *acts* the part. She hasn't had sex since her ex. That's what makes her so funny.

I know it's a joke.

She knows it's a joke.

Guys are intimidated by her because of the way she acts. They all think they can have her. Everyone thinks she'd be easy, but they're all too scared to approach her because they know she'll knock them back.

Mentioning diseases out loud has planted a seed of thought in my head. I try not to water it by thinking about it more, but I can feel the roots burrowing deeper into me.

What if this *slut*, Charlotte, had… Something?

I try to let my mind wander onto another topic.

It doesn't.

Don't think about it, and don't make it real by talking about it.

The roots dig deeper into the pit of my stomach.

In the distance, Nancy laughs in silence.

James doesn't use protection.

If James didn't use anything with her, he could have something.

Lipgloss

If he's got something, I've got something.
My mind is stuck on that.
If he's got something, I've got something.
I try to maintain my smile, but it gets harder with each second.
I've got something.
I don't know what.
But I've got something.

If he's got something, I've got something.

The sentence plays on a loop in my head.

43. McDONALD'S cont.

'But I haven't had any… Symptoms or anything.' I talk slowly and quietly, as if not saying it loud will make the words less real. If I don't say it out loud, I'm still just thinking it. But Nance can hear my thoughts.

'I swear there's some things that don't have any symptoms, though?' She talks as quietly as me, leaning in over the torn McDonald's bag between us.

I had to tell her that it was on my mind. I could feel myself panicking over it and my legs started to shake under the table. That initial thought had just triggered something inside me. The thought that I could have something was enough to get me worried.

As soon as I acknowledged it, I felt an urge to do something. Anything.

The first thing I did was go to the toilet. I was able to go normally. I wasn't in pain and there wasn't anything unusual – not that I could see. That calmed me down a bit. I didn't consider that some things might not have any symptoms. That's brought back my anxiety. Now, I know that I could have something and not even know it.

I've completely lost my appetite. Half of my stale burger is lying on the paper it was wrapped in, and my chips are floppy and cold. 'What d'you think I should do?' I look desperately at her, hoping she will effortlessly make everything better.

'Wouldn't you get...' She leans in towards me. '...Checked?'
Her eyes are gazing over the grease-stained bag. I see worry in her
face as I occupy myself with tidying our space.
I wrap my burger in the paper and put it in the bag with the other
rubbish. I bundle all the dirty napkins, sticky with sauce and salt.
It's important to keep them all separate. There's nothing more
annoying than going to wipe your mouth and not being able to
find a clean one. I pile all the dirty ones and isolate the clean ones
to protect them. I place each clean one on top of the next, keeping
them uncontaminated, trying to recreate the symmetry of the
original stack we got. I click the lid off my drink, take all the
rubbish from the bag, and squeeze it into the plastic cup. I put the
cupful of rubbish into the bag. It's better to condense all the
rubbish in the cup, so it doesn't fall out of the rip in the bag when
we get up to put it in the bin.
I look up to Nancy. I still see the same worry painted on her face.
I can't find the other wrapper from my straw. We took two straws,
but I can only find one wrapper. I frantically look under the bag of
rubbish and all around me to find it. My eyes dart around the
table, across the chairs, and scan the sticky floor. The other one is
by my foot, so I bend down to get it – hiding behind the wall of
rubbish I've built between me and Nancy's fear. She's really
strong, so it's got me scared that she's worried for me. This must
be serious. I pop the lid off the cup again and tear it from the
straw hole in the middle. The plastic is sharp against my cold,
sweaty skin.

I can't find anything else to do.

I fondle with the clean serviettes, but Nancy stops me.
Her hands drop onto mine and relax them on the table. She
squeezes them under hers, and the frantic scramble to tidy our
area stops – suddenly, but gently.

'Listen. If there is anything… *If…* The sooner you get it looked at, the sooner it will go away. *If* there is anything at all. Anything it could possibly be, they'll have something to give you for it. But you'll only know if you get checked out.'

We use the word *'it'*. None of us want to admit what we're talking about. We are two seventeen-year-old girls. This shouldn't be a topic of conversation.

'What should I do?' I've got nothing left to distract me. All the cards are on the table and I'm waiting for her instructions. I need someone to tell me what to do. I've been made to have to rely on James or someone else for so long, I'm not cut out to make big decisions like this.

'I can't tell you what to do. But if I was you? Genuinely – I reckon you should get checked while we're down here. There must be a walk-in clinic or something about.' She leans in, flattening the bag and the wall between us. 'The thing is – literally, no one knows us down here. If we go back home, you won't wanna do it in case we bump into someone. I don't blame you; I'd be the same. We're far enough away from home to not be recognised if you do it down here.'

'I'm just really scared, Nance.' I feel my eyes start to water. So much for feeling strong this morning. Even when he's not with me, he's still got a hold on me.

'Hey… Come on.' She pulls me over to the seat next to her and I let my body follow. 'Tell you what – whatever test you get done – I'll have one done, as well. That way, we'll both go through whatever it's like… Together.' She takes me under her arm and presses me into her.

I feel bad for dragging her into this. I just had to mention it – or it would be playing on my mind. I wanted a second opinion to know if I was just being paranoid. I didn't think she'd be as worried as me.

I have to go and get checked.

44. WALK-IN MEDICAL CENTRE

I don't know where we are.

Nance looked up a load of different places on her phone. There were a few different ones that were near us, but I didn't care which one we went to. We got on a bus and she followed the map on her phone to this place. We travelled the whole way in silence. Nothing could be said. There was no point in talking.
We were both having conversations with ourselves, in our own heads – asking how we'd got here.
Her answer was a lot simpler than mine.
She's here out of friendship.
I'm here out of naivety and stupidity.

I have no idea where we are. I'm totally out of my comfort zone doing this. The entrance to the clinic is beside a hospital, next to a big train station. At the entrance, everyone on the street knew why we were there. We walked past a few times, asking each other if we were definitely comfortable going in. We were both hoping the other would pull out at the last minute.
In loyalty to each other, neither of us did. We had to stay strong for each other.
I didn't want to go in. I didn't want to be seen going into an STD clinic by anyone. It doesn't matter that I don't know them. If they live or work near here, they know who goes into this building. You're either a nurse or a patient. And we don't look like nurses.

We waited until the street was at its emptiest before we committed to going inside.

I don't know if this place just checks for STDs. There were signs for family planning, too. I'm going to decline if they suggest a pregnancy test. I'll make something up.
I can't.
Not yet.

It doesn't matter because everyone knows what I'm here for. It makes me feel dirty just walking in. Nancy does most of the talking to the old lady at the reception. They talk quietly before she pleasantly points us down a long corridor. She smiles to me as we walk away, and I'm torn reading her expression for reassurance or pity.

A short walk down a long, empty, wooden tube – and we stand under a sign… *Sexual Health and GUM Reception.*
No hiding.

The whole area is sterile. The walls are too white and the floor is immaculately clean. Yellow signs illuminating *wet floor* are dotted on either side, setting up a makeshift pathway and boxing us in, giving us no way out. The wood gleams and brightens our way forward, towards a small queue of people at the second reception desk. I study the back of each of their heads, wondering what their story is.
There's a middle-aged man in front of me.
A young woman in front of him.
Two boys at the front; maybe a couple of years older than us.
The queue moves forward – quicker than I'd thought, but slower than I'd hoped. We're made to stand a few feet away from the person at the front of the queue. I guess he's telling the lady at the glass window what's wrong with him.

We're next.

The guy walks away, and there's a hundred feet between us and the second receptionist.

She calls us forward.

Nance looks to me with a nervous smile.

She gets ready to step into the hole of space in front of us, but I step in before her – taking the first stride into making this situation better.

The old lady looks at me, then to her computer screen.

She speaks loudly, and the whole waiting area listens in judgment to the questions she asks and the answers I give.

Have you been here before?

No.

Name?

I answer, quietly.

Date of birth?

Again, quietly.

She picks up a clipboard, attaching a small card and a sheet of paper to it. She talks in silence through the glass, pointing towards the sections on the sheet.

There are check boxes on the paper.

I am under 20 years old.

I have symptoms.

I have no symptoms.

I've had unprotected sex with someone who has told me they have an STI.

I've paid for/been paid for sex.

I've had unprotected sex with someone who injects drugs.

I don't read the rest of the boxes. I know which ones apply to me.

I'm here for a routine check-up. That's all. I haven't got any *diseases*.

She slides the tattered clipboard through her isolated window hatch, then points to a pile of pens and tells me to take one.

Why doesn't she give me a pen?

Does she not want to touch me?
I'm not contagious. I probably don't even have anything.

I walk to the waiting area and sit in the furthest corner from the entrance. Nance speaks to the old lady and fills out the same form. She's asking Nancy the same questions, but a lot quieter than she was asking mine. She wasn't speaking to the receptionist for as long as I was, and sits next to me within a few seconds.
We don't talk while we read through our forms. I lean on the wall and tilt my clipboard away from her, making sure she doesn't see what boxes I tick. I don't think she'd tick the same boxes as me.
Certain words keep flashing up into my vision.
Symptoms.
Sex.
Positive.
Anal.
Unprotected.
HIV.
Drugs.
This can't apply to me.
Still… The words are scratched onto the inside of my eyelids and flash the reality back to me every time I blink.

Nance breaks my mind from wandering too far. 'Did they give you this little card?' She points to hers. I pull the page off the clipboard and the same small card is underneath – and a number, starting with *F*. Nancy's is similar. She turns her card over to examine it. 'That *F* must mean female. They probably have different waiting rooms for men and women.' She folds it in her hand.
I never thought of that… This is only the beginning. We still have to wait to be taken through and wait to be seen.

From the next window, my number is called. I get up straight away, so they don't repeat it. I've stared at it for so long, it feels

like my name. Everyone knows that this number is for me.
They're all anonymous numbers, except mine.
I twist the blue plastic of my clipboard down and bend it out of
shape. I carefully slide my card out and delicately place it at the
front of the clipboard, careful not to ruin it. When I get to the next
window, another woman is waiting for me. She is younger than
the other two receptionists, but judges me just the same.
She asks me to confirm my name and date of birth.
I rest my body on the desk and speak softly.
I hand her my clipboard and she asks me, again, if I'm here
because of any recent symptoms. I lean in to tell her that I haven't
had any.
I'm not like the other people here.
I was a bit sore after sex the last time, but that's only because of
the type of sex it was. I don't mention this to her. I ticked that box
already and made sure Nance didn't see it.
Her eyes scan my forms. She puts all my information into the
computer, then points me to the Female Waiting Room.

I look past the people we shared a queue with and look to
Nance. She gets called up straight after.
I walk alone – past sexual health leaflets, posters, and judging
eyes; all wondering what a seventeen-year-old is doing here.
She must be a slut.
I follow the sign for *Female Waiting Room*, forgetting where the
receptionist pointed me. My eyes are fixed on the floor and I
guess my way forward; only holding my pristine card – delicately
and carefully by its corner. I go deep inside to the chairs at the
back of the room, facing away from the entrance. I thought I'd see
someone I know as I walked in – or someone would recognise me
and call me back.

As I find my seat, Nancy comes from behind me and sits by my
side.
She takes my hand.

45. FEMALE WAITING ROOM

It's so quiet.

I get nervous whenever I hear the echoing footsteps of a nurse. She'll stop at the entrance and a number will be read out. We're sitting at the back, furthest away from the entrance to stay hidden. It means we hear the numbers the quietest, so have to concentrate on the silence.

Being furthest from the entrance also means being the closest to the toilets. We're the most seen. Everyone who gives a urine sample has to walk by us. Some put a small tube in a hatch and then walk past us, trying not to make eye contact.

I haven't been able to see how many people are in the waiting room. I was looking down as I came in and I haven't looked around since.

No one is talking. Everyone knows why everyone is here. There's no hiding. If you're in here, you're in here for one reason. At some point, you were stupid enough to have sex with someone you obviously can't trust. I knew I shouldn't have done anything without a condom. I didn't want to. I should've said no.

But I didn't.

And now, that could have given me anything. That stupid decision could ruin my life.

There are thousands of pamphlets with the names of different diseases on them. I won't read any. I'll read them and get the symptoms straight away. I know I will.

I could have any of these diseases.
My eyes scan the bold words on different coloured pamphlets.
Chlamydia.
Gonorrhoea.
Syphilis.
HIV.
Herpes.
I stop looking. It's not helping my anxiety.
When I look away, I catch someone's eye as they walk out of the toilets. I turn away quickly and she does the same.
To stop my eyes wandering, I fix them onto the wall in front of me.
It's beige. Chipped. Scuffed. Not as clean as the reception.
It makes me feel dirty, so my eyes start to drift and focus on each poster and notice on the wall. There are hundreds of signs saying the same thing.
Do not pass urine until you have been seen by the nurse.
I don't know if I need to go at the moment. How will I give a sample?
I might have to come back another day.

The next number is called.
It's not mine.

Now, I really need to go to the toilet.
I can't hold it. How long will it be until I'm called? I can't hold it in for that long.
Maybe I should go home – get checked another day.
My body wants me to leave and my mind isn't putting up a fight.
I force my body into the hard cushion of the chair.
No.
I'm here. Nancy was brave enough, so I owe it to her.

I study the purity of my card to take my mind off everything.
The running water.

The toilet flushing.
The gurgle of the water cooler.

The writing on my card is crisp – centred perfectly.
The edges are sharp – straight and flawlessly flat on my hand.

My head is aimed at the floor.

We aren't here.
Me and Nance are in a park at the back of Oxford Street, after a long day of shopping in the West End. We're huddled together on a bench, talking about old times when we were younger. We came straight here after McDonald's. I didn't go to Primark to get her onesie. I'd like it to be a surprise, so I'll get it from Westfield Stratford another time. I might go with James on the weekend. I'm glad I didn't look through his texts the other night. It would've been an abuse of trust. I wouldn't do that to him. He got cheated on by his ex. The last thing he needs is a girlfriend who doesn't trust him. A strong smell of pollen is sticking to my nose and pigeons are bopping around my feet. I don't think it's fair that people call them *'rats with wings'*. They're harmless. They just look for some food, then go on their way. They're not out to hurt anyone. If anything, they try to stay away from people. I should've brought a bigger jacket with me. I didn't think it would be this cold outside. The wind tunnels through the bushes and collides with us. It looked sunny when we left, but the sun only warms your skin when you're standing right in it. Out of the sun, we get the full force of the cold.

Nancy nudges my arm. 'Was that my number they just called? I thought you would've been before me.' She gets up and unlinks my hand at the last moment. I turn back to reality and see her disappear around the corner with a young nurse.
I bury my head straight away. In case I'm seen.

My eyes swing down to my card. It's creased and the edges are bent inwards. It's soaked with sweat. I focus all my effort and attention on straightening it, trying to recreate its purity from before. It's dirty, and it's making me dirty. It's contaminating my number and contaminating me in the process. It was so clean and smooth when I got it – now, it's ruined. It has rips around the edges, and the torn coloured pieces are scattered on my lap and dotted around my feet.

I don't want to pick them up.
I don't want to touch the floor.
I don't want to get a drink from the water cooler.
I don't want to use the toilet.
I don't want to sit on these chairs.
I don't want to catch anything.
I roll my sleeves down to cover my hands.
If someone has been here with a disease, what if I touch something they've touched? What if I get the same thing?

What if James' ex cheated on him – with a guy who had something?
He would've given it to her.
Then, she would've given it to him.
Then, he would've given it to me.
What if Charlotte had something?
She would've given it to him.
Then, he would've given it to me.
I've got double the chance of having something.

My number is called.

46. CONSULTATION ROOM

My brain switches off.

My eyes don't leave her pen, as she scratches my most intimate details onto the paper. As my answers leave my mouth, they disappear from my memory. I can only focus on the next question that might be coming.

'Okay… Before we begin – can you just confirm your name and your date of birth for me?'

'Right… Just to let you know – I will be asking you some questions about your sexual history. They may seem intrusive and you might not be comfortable with answering some of them. But it's really important that you answer them as accurately and as truthfully as you can. That way, we can give you the best help. Okay?'

'So, why don't you start by telling me what's brought you here today?'

'And is this a regular partner?'

'Okay. And it says here that you've had no symptoms. Is that right?'

'No itching? Discharge? Bleeding during or after sex? No pain during vaginal sex?'

'Good. And are you on any method of contraception at the moment?'

'And you use them all the time?'

'That's good. And when was the last time you had sex of any kind?'

'What type of sex was this?'

'And was this sex protected or unprotected?'

'Okay. And did you give or receive oral sex?'

'Right. Have you had any sexual contact with anyone else within the last three months?'

'Okay, good. And how long have you been sexually active for?'

'Roughly...'

'And your current partner, he's been your only sexual partner in this time?'

'Good. So, besides vaginal and oral sex, have you had any other sexual contact with this partner?'

'And was that unprotected, also?'

'Please don't be upset, these are just routine questions that we have to ask everyone. It's just so we can assess what tests you may need.'

'We're not here to judge you. Our job is to protect you. Anything that's said in here is kept in the strictest of confidence.'

'Are you here with anyone else? Would you like someone to sit in with you?'

'Don't worry; you take as long as you need.'

'Are you happy for me to continue with my questions?'

'Okay, you're doing really well. We've nearly finished.'

'Did this form of sex occur within the last two weeks?'

'Okay. We're almost done, I promise you.'

'Besides the penis, were any other instruments or toys inserted into either your vagina or back passage during sex?'

'Okay, good. You'll be happy to hear that my questions are finished now.'

'Right – because of the information you've given me, I'm going to suggest that we test for the infections written on this form. If you're happy to, we'll be doing a blood test to check for some of these. For the others, the tests will require me to examine you. And I'll need to take a swab from your vagina during the examination.'

'No, no. It shouldn't hurt at all. It may feel slightly uncomfortable at first, but the swab itself isn't known to be painful.'

'Now, some of the tests may not show definite results for at least two weeks from the point of sexual contact. It's because some viruses take about a fortnight to appear in the blood. I would advise that you come back and take a blood test again at the end of next week, as this will be two weeks from your last sexual contact. If you visit your GP, they can arrange this for you – if it's too far for you to travel back here. You're at a low risk, given that you've not had sexual contact with anyone who injects drugs or anyone that's known to have an STI. But given the type of sex you've told me about and the fact that it was unprotected, I would recommend doing another blood test just to definitely rule out any possible infection. Is that okay?'

'Trust me; you've done the right thing by coming in. It's best that we do these tests early. You've done very well so far, and the most important thing is that you came in to be tested. That's the hardest thing for a young person to do. If everyone had your mentality, our job would be a lot easier in the long run. I'm sure afterwards, you'll feel far better that you actually came in to see us – rather than not coming in and worrying yourself silly every day.'

'For future reference, it is worth noting that all forms of sex need to be protected – not just vaginal. Of course, continue using condoms for vaginal sex. But be aware that infections can be passed from person-to-person in multiple ways, so just remember to protect yourself during all forms of sexual contact. Before you go, I'll give you some condoms and a contraceptive advice pamphlet for you to have a look through.'

'Right… Are you happy for me to continue with the tests?'

'They shouldn't take longer than a few minutes. Then, the nurse will take a small amount of blood from your arm and you'll be free to go.'

'And you said you'd like to receive your results via text message. Is that right?'

'That's fine. Is it the contact number you've supplied here?'

'Not too long. You should receive them within one or two weeks. Obviously, if you haven't received them by then, give us a call on the number that's on your card.'

'Okay, I'm going to step outside for a moment. If you'd like to go behind that curtain and remove the bottom half of your clothing, I'll be back in a few minutes.'

47. NANCY'S

'Strawberry, banana, vanilla… They've thought of everything! I feel like a slut in a sweet shop! I actually wouldn't mind giving head if I was using one of these. But why would you use vanilla? The most boring taste in the world! I'd rather the taste of the di – '

Nance emptied out a little bag onto the bed. We were both given one after the tests.

Condoms.

Spermicidal lubricant.

A few pamphlets on sexual health.

Instructions on how to put a condom on.

The condoms came in different flavours. I didn't realise why they were flavoured until Nance mentioned it.

How naive am I?

I wouldn't have thought to use a condom for that. But apparently, you can get an STD from going down on someone. I didn't even know that was possible. After knowing what can happen and seeing the reality of the consequences up close, there's no way I'm doing anything without using protection. Ever.

I probably won't even have sex again.

Nancy takes her jacket off and throws it on the floor beside her. She's sitting at the head of the bed, under hundreds of photos of us and the girls. They're decorated around her head, framing her against the wall. The room is barely light enough to see in, but it's not dark enough to need the light on. There's a crisp, blue, summer's evening coming in through the open blinds. It feels unusual – so close to Christmas.

She picks up a condom and holds it up in front of her, studying it. 'Y'know what? Even though guys are *so* against wearing them – y'know, because they're always *so tight* around their *massive dicks* – all guys are walking about wearing big, human-sized condoms. They all put on this shield and try to hide what they're really like. They'll cover themselves up, but expect you to *literally* open up and bare all; and tell them everything you do, and everywhere you go, and everyone you know. They all act smooth and protecting, but y'know what…? You get under them and they're all the same. They're all just *dicks*. They'll wear different flavour coats, trying any flavour that will get your attention – any cover that looks appealing – just so they can fuck you. But underneath, they're all just identical, slimy *dicks*.' She flicks the condom into the air with her last word. It flies over my head and lands in a pathetic pile in the middle of the floor.

I can't help but laugh. She can turn anything into something you can smile about. I'm feeling better than I was. I know that I've done the right thing by going to get checked, and it's a weight off my mind knowing that I've done all I can. All I have to do now is wait for my results. I'm still scared – scared that now, it's out of my hands. But there's a weird comfort in that. It's like doing an exam in school. You try your best, but once it's done – you just have to sit there and wait for results day. There's no use stressing out over how you think you did. It's done. All you can do is wait for the results and hope for the best.
So, there's no point in thinking about it until I have to.
There's a weird peace in not having the control anymore.

I take my jacket off and fold it on the floor at the foot of the bed. Nancy's eyes fall to the plaster on my arm. 'Did they give you a blood test? Why didn't they do one for me?'

I scratch my arm, trying to cover the plaster. 'Oh, yeah. They asked me if I wanted one done, so I said I would. Only because I'll be worrying if I don't get every single test done. You know what I'm like.' I roll the sleeves of my checked-shirt lower. Having this plaster on show is almost like admitting what I had to do today.
Admitting what I've done.
Admitting that I'm in the situation I'm in.
I'd rather just keep it under wraps.

'Ah, right. Yeah, they offered me one. But they said I was at low risk because of what I've done – or something like that. So, I didn't bother. Maybe I should've, actually.' Her eyes wander. She sifts through the ingredients of a condom cocktail, trying to find more exotic flavours. She picks up the instructions of how to put a condom on, her face twisting as she reads it. She unfolds it and flattens out the creases over the bed. As she reads from it, she pinches her thumb and finger together on her right hand. Her left hand rolls an invisible condom down below. 'Fucking hell, you might as well keep these things. You'll get more use outta them than me. I ain't bothering with boys anymore. They're too much fucking hard work. I wish I was a lesbian. Things would be so much easier. Should we just start going out with each other?' She laughs to herself.

At some point, I'm going to have to go onto Facebook and change my Relationship Status. After me and James first had sex, he made me put that I was in a relationship on my profile. He wanted it advertised on Facebook; that way, all my friends and all his friends can see that we're together.
I'm strictly off limits… And everyone should know that.
I'm *James' girlfriend*. Nothing else.
That also means – when I change my Relationship Status and put that I'm single – all our friends will see it. I might just remove that feature from my profile, so it's not visible if I'm with anyone or not. Listing that I'm single would be a big statement. I don't want

to rock the boat. If the tests come back negative, we could still sort some stuff out between us. We could even end up getting back together at some point. Maybe. I don't know what's around the corner. But I do know that I don't want to start rowing with him. Plus, I think he's still got photos of me. I can't piss him off while he's got that hold on me. I don't think he'd do anything with them, but I don't seem to know him at all anymore.

It's not worth the hassle. I'll leave things as they are online.

'You've got me worried, now. D'you reckon I should've got a blood test done?' Her face looks different. It looks the way it did when her number was called. Her eyes squint and her face inflates with a deep breath she takes in and holds. She bites both of her lips together.

'Well they said I should do another one, so…' I've said too much. I need to explain this. '…Just so they can double check that everything is clear. Something to do with me having sex too recently, so the tests might not be as accurate or something. I'm gonna go doctors and get that done, so why don't you come with me? Book an appointment.' Saved myself from more questions.

'Yeah, yeah. I'll definitely come with you and do one. When you having it done?' She looks relieved, now. It's the same feeling I'm running on; the feeling that I'm doing all I can to get my life back to how it was.

'End of next week. I don't wanna drag this out. I wanna get it done and out the way as soon as. I wanna put all this behind me and leave it in this year. Go into next year with a clean slate, you know what I mean?'

That's what I'm living for at the moment.
A clean slate.
A fresh start.

48. LOBBY - WESTFIELD, STRATFORD CITY

It's been a slow couple of days. We haven't done much – just been floating between Woolwich and Stratford, not really knowing what to do with ourselves. I managed to get Nancy her Christmas present while we've been down here. I told her to wait outside while I got it and made sure she didn't know what it was. She should like it. I thought it was really cute. Managed to get a gift receipt, in case she wants to change it or get a different size. It was hard buying something for mum. My heart wasn't really in it because of the way she's been acting. Plus, what do you get for a woman who never leaves the house? I settled for a bottle of perfume that was on sale and a few box sets she's been wanting to watch. I don't know why I bothered – not after how she's been. But racking my brains and hunting for something to buy her was keeping my mind off the test results.
Nancy has seemed nervous about what they'll be, but I'm sure she's got nothing to worry about.

Every journey we've made, we've been looking out; waiting for James to make one of his over-the-shoulder appearances that he'd always do in Westfield if we were meeting.
There's no way he'd be here unless he was meeting me. He rarely leaves the house, but I'm still on my guard. Just in case.
Thinking back, except meeting me when I'd be with Nance, I can only remember one time that we went out properly.

As I was tidying my room a few days ago, one of my fluffy toys fell off of the bed and landed – face down on the floor.

It was a cream-coloured bear, no bigger than my hand. He was holding a red heart made of silk, with white stitching that said – *Always*.

It was for our one-month anniversary.

James was really embarrassed about giving it to me. I know a lot of girls will laugh if a guy does something romantic, and that must be embarrassing. I thought it was really sweet, though. He gave it to me when we got back to his, after we went out for the evening. We went into the West End for dinner and cinema.

It was a really nice night.

I felt a bit overdressed. I made an effort because I didn't know where he'd be taking me; I'd rather be overdressed in a normal place than underdressed at a posh place.

It was summer, so it was still warm enough to dress nicely and not have to kill it with a massive coat. I wore a pair of black jeans I'd bought especially, black pumps, a monochrome mesh top, and a statement necklace. I thought it'd look nice to wear a chunky necklace on top to break up the outfit a bit. It looked nicer in my head because I was mentally dressing someone who was nicer looking than me, but I was happy with how it turned out.

Nancy saw me beforehand and said I looked really nice.

James looked smart and I could tell he'd made an effort. He wore a blue quilted jacket that I'd bought him for his birthday; a printed T-shirt that I'd picked out for him in Topman; light jeans; white trainers.

I check my phone.
No texts.

Nancy cuts my reminiscing. 'What d'you wanna start going jogging for, anyway? I wish I had your body! Slim, with big boobs *and* a nice bum. Lucky bitch.' She's a good liar.

The two of us have just finished wandering around the aisles of a big sports shop. We'll both be on the health-kick in January. We're going to start going jogging. We've planned the route; now we just need all of the accessories that go with it. We've been looking at running shoes and sports bras. There was a watch that measured your heart rate, how many steps you do, and how many calories you burn.

That's what I need to work out. Calories.

I barely seem to eat, but I'm still fat. There'll be times when I think I'm not *as fat* as others. At best, I get *skinny fat*… My frame gets thinner, but I hold all the wobbles in the same places as when I'm *fat fat* – and can't even get away with being curvy because I'm not the right kind of fat anymore.

It wouldn't hurt to do a bit of exercise and get in shape. I'd love to have Nancy's figure. I've got no idea why she's jealous of mine. She's like model-material.

I check my phone.

No texts.

It feels weird to have my phone back. For the last few days, I kept forgetting that I didn't have it with me. I'd be patting myself down quickly – panicking and thinking that I'd lost it. I'd get flustered and start frisking myself or crawling through my bag, then I'd remember my life and why I didn't have it with me.

I've only just started using it again properly since we've been out today.

Before we left the house, when I'd not started using my phone, Nance was asking if I'd been thinking about him or been tempted to text him at all. I had to put up a bit of a front and make out that he hadn't really been on my mind.

'Who? James? Oh, James! Nah. I actually forgot about him, to be honest.'

She could see right through me. I can't lie to her.

I got her to switch my phone on for me in the end, to shelter me from the worst stuff that might've been said.

I was so nervous when she finally turned it back on. My stomach was knotted, and I was so anxious to know what he'd said to me. I was itching to know what was on there. It frantically vibrated with a million texts when she first turned it on. I kept my watch fixed on her to see if her expression changed.
As her face lit up and her eyes scanned through each message, nothing changed.
Eyes.
Mouth.
Nothing flinched.
I walked over to her and pretended to do something beside her, so I could try to get a look – but I couldn't see anything. I didn't really want to know what he'd said. Horrible morbid curiosity was driving me. It wouldn't have been *my* James speaking; the James who told me to close my eyes and stuttered over his words when he nervously gave me that little bear and first told me he loved me.
It would've just been anger and name-calling. I don't want to think of him like that.
It was hard, but I had to occupy myself with something else while she read the messages that I'd missed. I didn't want it to look like I was waiting to hear what was said or that any of this really bothered me anymore.

Nance made my mind up for me. She asked me before she did – but she deleted the texts from him. After she'd read them, she told me that there was no point in me reading them. It wouldn't help the situation. They were hurtful and spiteful. If I'd read them, I'd just get upset and panicked – or worse, I would've wanted to reply.
I gave her control of what was best. I told her to delete his number and block him on WhatsApp, too. I know that, if I have his

number, I'll find myself texting him eventually. I'd make up some fake excuse that Nancy took my phone and wouldn't let me reply, and that's the only reason I'd been off the radar for so long. Then, I'd be taken back into a big argument, end up apologising for something I hadn't even done, and be in the same mess all over again.

I'm not doing that.

I'm not ready to speak to him yet. I'm still hurting.

I've still got photos of him on my phone, but I want to hold onto them.

As much as I don't want to think about him right now, I'm not ready to let go of him.

This whole thing will change me.

It already has.

My trust has gone.

For one stupid minute, I started questioning why Nance was acting the way she was.

Why did she want to delete the texts?

Why didn't she want me to see them?

Did they say something about him and her?

Did they do anything together?

Is *Charlotte*, Nancy?

Did he just save her under a different name in his phone?

That's why they don't talk to each other.

That's why she wanted to get checked.

That's why she wants a blood test with me.

If I've got something, she's got something.

That's why she doesn't like him – because they've done stuff together.

That's why he doesn't like me seeing her – in case she says anything to me about the two of them.

If I've got something, she's got something.

49. FOOD COURT - WESTFIELD, STRATFORD CITY

Nancy's been spinning her phone in her hand.
Constantly.
All week.
Every time I see her, she's lighting up the screen to see if she's got any texts.
I haven't seen it go off. We're both waiting for the same thing.

I had to think myself out of her and James doing stuff. I noticed that I was acting a bit cold with her. I wasn't really making conversation and was only giving one-word answers whenever she'd ask me something. She started to notice and kept asking me what was wrong – if there was something on my mind and telling me that if I wanted to talk about anything, I could.
I couldn't, though.
How could I explain that train of thought?
Saying it out loud would sound ridiculous. In my head, it's a brilliant plan between the two of them. It makes perfect sense. But I know – as soon as the words would leave my mouth – they'd make no sense.

I played the conversation in my head.
I would tell her that I was worried she had been sleeping with James behind my back.

I would tell her that I think she's worried James gave her
something, as well as me.
I would tell her that I'm basically not grateful for anything she's
done for me.
I would tell her that James has destroyed our friendship because
he's destroyed my ability to trust anyone.
I would watch her face wrinkle with confusion.
She would tell me how stupid it was to even think that.
I would agree with her.

It's a ridiculous thought and doesn't have to be said out loud.
Don't think about it, and don't make it real by talking about it.
I decided not to say anything.

'I know I keep going on, but d'you reckon we'll both get the
text at the same time? We did it together, so it should come
through at the same time, right?' Her eyes don't know where to
look. I can tell the reality of it has hit her recently. I keep trying to
reassure her about it, but the truth is – I really don't know any
more than she does.
'I'm not sure. If we got tested at the same time, they'd probably
get sent away and looked at on the same day. So, I would've
thought the results would come through together. I don't know a
hundred percent, though.' I've adjusted to the helpless feeling. I'm
used to not being in control, but Nance has always been more
independent than me. It's killing her to have to wait for these
results and not be able to do anything.
'Surely, they must've looked at them by now, though... How
can it take a week to look at a fucking jar of vag juice? What are
they doing? A taste test?' She holds in a laugh. She's trying to be
as serious as she can, but we've both just imagined a group of old
snobs at a wine-tasting. 'How are you staying so calm about it?
Ain't you worried?' Her voice gets lost in itself and she sounds
weirdly vulnerable.
Worried is an understatement.

'Yeah, course I am. But what's the point in worrying about it? It's done, now. It's out of our hands. You'll be fine, anyway. You ain't had sex with anyone recently, have you?'
I get ready to pick apart her answer and look for hidden meaning that isn't there.

'Ha! With the losers round here? Are you serious? There's more chance of me lezzing off with you than going out with any of the boys from this area.' Confident sass comes back to her voice.

Before I have the chance to talk myself into thinking she's lying, a text comes through on one of our phones.
Another text follows straight after.
The whole of Westfield hears it. Every shop falls silent to know who it is. Nancy's eyes dart down to her phone to check it. The generic text sound could have come from any of us. Westfield is still moving around us, but no one is making any noise. There are hundreds of robotic shoppers, programmed to move past each other in silence. I took my phone off vibrate. I didn't want to miss it if the clinic called for any reason.
I didn't realise I'd had my phone in my hand, too.
The two of us have been sitting at a table in the Food Court.
No food.
We just sit – mirroring each other's anxiety in fiddling with our phones.

Her eyes crawl back up to me.
It was my phone.
Two texts.
Two numbers that my phone doesn't recognise.
The first is a normal, long number.
The second is a short number.

I open the first text.

Lipgloss

'Don't think I forgot about you.'

That must be from James.
I can tell it's him from the way it's written.
I pick apart the text and look for hidden meaning that isn't there.

Don't think I forgot about you – I still care about you.
Don't think I forgot about you – I'm going to find you, eventually.

I prepare myself to reply to him. I need to know what that meant.
Is this him being nice about the situation, so we can talk
everything through? Or should I be scared?

While my fingers hover over the keys, I feel Nancy's eyes on me.
The whole of Westfield comes back to life and I remember I've
got another text to read.

Nancy's voice shakes over the crowds around us. 'What does it
say?' She's biting both of her lips into her mouth and her body has
tensed up in front of me.

If I've got something, she's got something.
That's why she's nervous.
If I've got something, she's got something.
My thumb hovers over the button to open the text.
If I've got something, she's got something.
We're in this together.
If I've got something, she's got something.
Open.
If I've got something, she's got something.

*'Your Results for Chlamydia, Gonorrhoea, Syphilis and HIV are
all negative (normal).'*

I read it over, making sure I focus on every word.

I need to make sure it's right before I commit to any sort of reaction.
Negative.
Normal.

My head falls back onto the chair. A clean, new breath leaves my mouth, chasing away all my worries into the air.
I got lucky. I took a risk in doing what I did.
That could've been so much worse. Luckily, my only punishment for being so stupid is a lesson learned. There's no way I'm doing anything without protection. Ever.
I probably won't even have sex again. Not after all this.
It's not worth it.

'Babes?' Her voice shakes. 'What does it say?'
I don't know how long Nancy's been asking me that. The world went away for a moment. Now, I'm back in it.
Clean and uninfected.
'All negative.' I can't help but smile. Those words feel so good to say. It's good that they actually say *'normal'* at the end of the text. Otherwise, I'd probably still panic.
'*Negative*? Is that the good one?' She's still worried. Her face is twisted and I can see her forehead wrinkle through thick foundation.
'Yeah, yeah. Negative means they didn't find anything.' I'm so relieved. I always expect the worst. It feels good for things to be going right for a change. Nancy deflates with an exhausted breath that follows mine into the air.

If I've got something, she's got something.
What was I thinking? There's no way she would've done anything with him. I can tell she's happy for me; not because my result means that she should be fine. She's relieved because she's my friend. And no matter what we go through, we care about each other.

She pushes her hair back and runs her fingers through it. 'Well done, babes. I'm so relieved for you. I'm glad you ain't got anything. Now, all we gotta do is wait for mine. The last time I had sex, STDs weren't even invented, so I should be fine. Shouldn't I?' She's stronger than me, but there are times when I can see real worry and nerves in her. It's good to know that everyone – no matter how strong you are – can be worried at some point.

'Oh, yeah. Hundred percent, you'll be fine. Guaranteed. I'm still gonna go for this blood test, though. Just to make sure – after what the doctor said. I don't wanna go into 2012 with any of this hanging over me. Let's just go into next year fresh. We've booked the appointment, so we might as well go still.' I haven't said a sentence that long for days. I've been so preoccupied with playing mind-games with myself – and losing. I've not been normal.

At the very least, I've known that I've not been normal.
Hopefully, that means I'm not on the way to turning into mum.

This is the closure I needed.
Things can start to get back on track, now.

50. FOOD COURT - WESTFIELD, STRATFORD CITY cont.

We're both in such a good mood. Her results came through about an hour after mine. She had the exact same text as me. We haven't been this relaxed for ages. We are crying with laughter over the most stupid things; things we'd never usually find funny. It's nice to just enjoy having no worries. We're only seventeen. Every day should be like this. The last couple of weeks have taught me that you never know what's around the corner. So, you might as well enjoy the care-free times while they last. Worrying about stuff when things are going good just wastes time. And you miss that time when things are actually going bad.

A text comes through to one of our phones.
Nancy doesn't look at hers; she just places it flat on the table.
It's mine.
James' eyes hover over my shoulder as my phone lights up.

'Sorry. Our last text was wrong. You're actually a dirty little slag.'

It's from Nancy.

She starts laughing as soon as I open it. Her eyebrows rise through a mask of powdery foundation. 'Too soon?'

I throw a bit of rubbish at her from across the table, but she swings her head down to avoid it. It hits a guy's shoulder behind her and he slowly turns around to see us laughing.

He's middle-aged – with an earring.

That shouldn't be allowed.

He's got tattoos going up his red neck and they stop under his veiny, bald head. His whole family look over with him. They look rough and he looks angry. I turn around with him, acting like the rubbish came from somewhere else. There's only an old woman sitting behind me, trying to tackle a hamburger that's twice the size of her. Bless her. I mumble to myself, curious about who threw that bit of rubbish that just flew past me.

Nancy's looking away, squinting her eyes shut and pinning her mouth from exploding. The guy can see her body vibrating with silent laughter. He turns back around.

'You stupid bitch. You see the size of him?' I playfully slap her hand and whisper into her. 'Even his daughter looked like she could have us, and she was only about ten.' We both aim our laughter at the table.

'I can't help it if I got reflexes like a cat. Come, let's go. I just wanna get a nice pair of bottoms for jogging and I'm done. Could you properly see my knickers through the other pair I tried?' She chucks a scrunched receipt onto her tray.

We both stand up, leaving our rubbish on the table. Nance doesn't give me a chance to clear it myself. She's started walking away, so I trail beside – speaking after her.

'Yeah, it was quite bad. But they were proper thin, so you're always gonna be able to see through them.' We walk past tables of families surrounded by bags of presents that their kids are trying to look through.

I wish I could stay that age.

Everything was easier. No worries at all as a kid. The only thing I had to think about was what game to play at lunchtime. Or – the biggest challenge – who'd be the first one out to claim the swing that went really high; and didn't have to go on the one with the horrible, rusted chain and chomped, rubber seat.

I feel like I was tricked into growing up quickly. Everyone was in a rush to get older when I was little. It was a race to mature and be a *proper woman.*
I'm still not even there yet.
It's got worse recently. At least, when I was younger, I could flick through the Argos catalogue and look for some toys that I'd want to put on my Christmas list. Now, little kids are looking for a phone contract to ask Father Christmas for.
I feel like I belong to the last generation of kids.
There was me; with my glitter jelly-shoes, unmatching clothes, and permanent cherryade stains around my mouth at the sheer age of ten. Now, the *'young people'*... Can't call them kids anymore – bad for their self-esteem or something – are better coordinated and put together than me. The whole idea of an awkward, ugly phase doesn't seem to be a thing. I remember mine and Nancy's awkward phase at about twelve or thirteen – hadn't quite grown into our faces and always looked like we got dressed in the dark. You can't really afford to get caught slipping like that when everyone has a camera on them to capture it forever. You've got to make sure you always look photo-ready.
Younger kids just seem way more grown up than I was at that age. I walked past a nursery the other day and they were having an end-of-term party in the playground. They were all singing along to the lyrics of this song, and they were really sexual. Obviously, the kids didn't know any better. But it was weird to hear a bunch of kids singing about having *hands on their body*, and how *a kiss can turn them on.* And they were doing some dance where they were rubbing their bodies, bending over and pushing their bums out, and sticking their tongues out at the camera.
It was all just too noncey for me.

All the songs I hear by girls are about being with a guy, and all the songs by guys are about being with a girl. It's the same with programmes on telly; so many are designed to try to get people to get with each other on screen.

I don't know why everything is about being paired up with someone so quick. As if it's a bad thing to be alone. I've always been made to feel like being without someone is worse than being with someone – no matter who it is. It's better to be with the wrong person than not be with anyone. And the outcome is what I've just been through.

It doesn't help that so many people are famous just because they slept with someone, and their new relationship is *'couple goals'*. It will have an effect in a few years, when the only people to look up to are all reality stars that haven't done anything; competing for who can be the most outrageous and embarrass themselves on telly to get the most publicity.

It's bad, really. You get used to the idea of sex at a young age through what you see before what you're taught, and it means that you don't appreciate what a big thing it is. You don't get a proper understanding of the vulnerability and responsibility of what it actually is – outside of some recycled song lyrics.

Girls especially are getting sexualised younger. It's a normal thing to lose your virginity at an even younger age.

It just means you're an *early bloomer*. Or a *slut*, depending on who you ask.

'Yeah, true. And if I'm on, you'll be able to see my pad crunching about between my legs. I'll sound like a packet of crisps running down the road. I could wear a thong… That wouldn't be *that* noticeable, would it? But then, I'd have to keep pulling out a wedgie every two minutes. Nah, I'll just get a pair of tracksuit bottoms. Even though they'll make me look like a skanky chav *hoe*.' She stretches the last words over all the shoppers walking past us. 'But I can't hide from my true self, can I?'

251

As we walk along more tables, I see the kids getting older. Their attention used to be on the bags of presents and how big the world was around them. They were all too busy running around and playing to notice much else.

As the kids along the tables get older, their world gets smaller. They stop looking and questioning the world around them.

As the kids get older, their heads get lower. They bury themselves in their phones. The only way you can tell they're alive is by their occasional blinking, as the phones light up their faces and blind them to the world around them.

I'm part of this group, so I can't even hate it. Well, I was until a couple of weeks ago. Then, real life gave me a slap and woke me up.

The only time you notice the world is when something goes wrong in it. That's why everyone walks around looking so miserable. Everyone – including me – tries to hide from real life. It's easier to just ignore it.

Phones are the filters of real-life problems.

The problems online are easier to deal with than the ones in the real world; that's why everyone is so quick to be a hero online – plus, it makes you *look* like a good person… Which is all that matters.

If a friend is upset and opens up to you in real life, you have to actually make the effort to console them; thinking about your words and tone of voice. All while sitting in an awkward position – hugging them and getting pins and needles in your arm – trying to be sensitive to their problem and giving them hard advice that they probably don't want to hear.

Online, you can just give them a like, a sad face, and some meaningless words.

'Thinking of you.'

'PM if you wanna talk.'

I'm done with it.

I guess that's my life-long dream of being an *'influencer'* out of the window – because that's an actual ambition for people.

Lipgloss

I'll settle for being a good friend instead.

I'm having a social media detox after all this. I can't put a filter on my whole life.
I'm not good looking.
I'm not always on holiday.
I don't have money to eat in restaurants all the time.
I don't have wise quotes to share with you.
I'm just normal.
I can't lie anymore. I don't want to be involved in all of that. Even though, by being young, I'm in that group automatically – I have to be anti-social just to have a social life, when the social life isn't social.
Makes sense.

The whole thing makes me anxious.
I'd always be scared to put a different status or picture up.
If it gets no likes, it's just embarrassing. It makes you look sad. It means that even your *better* personality – the one you advertise online – isn't appealing.
Refresh.
Refresh.
Exit.
Scroll down.
Refresh.
And repeat.
I see some girls getting into the hundreds of likes on their pictures. I'm lucky if I get ten.
But when you see me in real life, at least I actually look the same.
Sorry – I don't have a cute bunny nose, floppy dog ears, or a starry halo background permanently around my head.
Some of the filters Nancy puts on us make us look incredible – but nowhere near real.
Our skin smooths.
Our eyes pop.

Our cheekbones rise.
Our lips plump.
It looks like we've had surgery and makes us look so much better
– so, why not get surgery to look like that permanently?
It can really mess with you.
If someone's picture gets more likes than mine, they're better looking.
If someone's got more friends than me, they're more popular.

Even though it can be nasty, I'm going to try to stay in the real world. When I lived online, I was a different person. Even my profile picture wasn't a real reflection of me.
It was… It is… A picture of me and James. I've got a smile painted on my face and he's doing a scowling frown, pulling me into him.
That's not me, and that's not the boy I was seeing.
That's not the girl I need to care for, and that's not the boy I fell in love with.

The last couple of weeks have been the jump-start that I've needed to start living my life and making it better for myself.

No one else is going to do that for me.

51. TOILETS - WESTFIELD, STRATFORD CITY

The smell of industrial disinfectant in the toilets took me to James' block – after its weekly clean. The fake, sweet smell mixes with the harsh, dull metal. Suddenly, I'm at James'. Because he's got the outside flat on the ground floor, I don't have to go into the block. But as soon as someone pushes through the heavy security door, with its broken magnetic lock, the smell escapes.
It's not the nicest smell in the world.
'It stinks of shit in here.' Nance couldn't tell a lie if she tried. I look at her quickly, pinning in a laugh and pointing to the only closed cubicle door. I signal to her to be quiet.
There's nothing worse than having to use the toilet in public.
…Especially, if it's more than just a wee.

The toilets are completely silent. Whoever is in there is holding it in, waiting to hear when we walk out.
They need to get the technique right.
I usually listen out for how many times the door opens and closes. If it opens once, someone's inside. If it opens again, they've left; and it's safe to make all the noise in the world.
It gets a bit more confusing when the door opens too soon after it was first opened. That means someone else came in after the first person.
I'll put tissue in the toilet, so there's no… Splash. I usually wait until someone uses the hand-dryer before I unleash hell.

It's a really strategic plan. I should be in the army.
The two of us are looking in the mirror, talking at our reflections.
Nance is applying more foundation and I'm blowing my snotty nose.
I'm so attractive.

We can't talk about anything serious. Neither of us wants the girl behind the door to know our life story. Even though she's got her knickers around her ankles and squatting over the rim, she's still got the upper hand. Somehow – she's beating us at life.

Mumbling from the cubicle gets louder. 'There you go. All done.' The voice behind the door echoes around the toilets. The two of us look away from our reflections and turn straight to each other.
Her expression is mirroring mine.
Eyebrows lowered with confusion.
Forehead crinkled.
Mouth open, half-smiling.

Who's she talking to?
What's *'all done'*?

Nance mouths some silent words to me and signals with her hand. 'Is she tossing someone off?'
I break the silence and burst out laughing. I slump over the sink and let my head fall between my arms, trying to contain myself. My elbows rest in small puddles of water around the basin; splash-back from thousands of people today.
As I raise my eyes, I see the cubicle door open in the mirror's reflection.
Here comes the walk of shame. The worst part about going to the toilet in public…

A mum comes out, walking after her little girl.
She's so cute. She can't be older than four.

She's bouncing from foot to foot, bopping over in her pink Converse.
She's got a little rucksack on and a set of pink dungarees that would fit a teddy bear.
Her hair is light brown, almost blonde. It curls past her tiny, gold earrings and dangles over her big, blue eyes.
She looks like a little cherub.
It's the baby from Oxford Circus – grown up in just days.
She hops carelessly over to us and waves, trying to say hello through chubby, rosy cheeks.

'Hello!' I kneel down and reach my hand out to her. My voice gets higher, climbing to the pitch of an excited primary school teacher. I look up at her mum. 'She's gorgeous.'
She jumps up and turns around, showing us her Dora the Explorer rucksack.

I could cry.
She's a cartoon of what a little girl should look like.
She's just so happy and excited.
How can she be so cute?
I don't want her to grow up.
I want to take her home.
I don't want the world to take over her.
Why can't she just stay at this age forever?

Her mum fingers her hair. 'Poor thing messed herself. She couldn't wait to get in here… We just didn't make it on time. She's alright now, though. Aren't you?' Her mum ruffles her curls some more and they bounce under her fingers. It looks so soft. I want to touch it, but I don't want her mum to think I'm weird. Nance is still preening herself in the mirror behind me, licking herself like a cat. Her mum takes her hand. 'Come on, you. Let's get you home. Say *'bye'* to the nice girl.'
The small angel makes a sound to me and waves, then toddles off alongside her mum.

'Bye.' My voice lowers, fading back to my own. I'm still kneeling down, alone in the toilets.

Nance talks into the mirror as the door swings shut. 'That's a plus, as well. It's one thing getting an STD, but having a kid...'

I don't say anything.
I can't.

She stops playing with her hair, but still talks to the mirror. 'At least we've avoided that one, eh?'
I still don't know how to react.
I stay kneeling on the floor, looking at where my little girl once stood. Too long has gone past for me to get up and react normally to what she's just said.

Nance turns around to face the back of my head. 'We *have* avoided that, babes... Haven't we?'

52. LOBBY - WESTFIELD, STRATFORD CITY

Westfield is suddenly empty. Nancy is holding my hand, charging towards Boots. Anyone who's in our way doesn't exist. We go through hundreds of invisible shoppers, getting smashed by elbows and bags that aren't attached to a body.
I've blocked out everyone else. They all know where we're going and why we're going there.
My head is down, eyes aimed at Nancy's shoes. They're steaming straight ahead, occasionally darting to the side to avoid a pram. We don't want to face one of them.

Boots is next door.
Before I know it, we're outside.
The crowds thin out as we go in. It doesn't make a difference to Nancy. She shoves past anyone strolling down the aisles or taking their time. As we walk down the middle of the shop, we barge through our old selves. I see myself in front of Nancy. She's rummaging through her bag, holding some gum out for me. In the next aisle, I'm standing with a water bottle. I've dropped a promotional display card and a sales assistant is coming over to me.

We reach the Pharmacy.

Nancy turns me to face her, and the world behind her blurs out of focus. 'Babes, listen. If you think there's even the slightest chance of you being pregnant, we gotta do a test. Now.' She's blunt. The bounce has disappeared from her voice.
She hasn't let go of my hand since we left the toilets.
I don't say anything.
I was hoping she wouldn't say the word. That makes it real.
Everything has happened so fast up until now.
Now, I'm controlling the pace.

Hours pass.
I finally nod.

Now, our pace has slowed.
Nance has been wired to move slower, now that we're here. Her usual strut has gone. She moves as if she's running under water, each step is slower than the last.
She'll stop soon.
She has to. She'll need air. Then, we can leave here.
Get on with our normal lives.

She resets and plays at normal speed. 'Here. This one. It has to be the best. It's the most expensive. We ain't cheaping out on something like this. I'll pay for it, don't worry.' She hands me a box. I don't look down to see it. I recognise the feel of it from last time. I don't need reminding. She pulls a second box from the shelf and hands it to me. 'Best to be sure.'

We walk towards the till beside each other.
She's not leading me anymore.

I stop and take her hand, still looking straight on. 'Nance… I can't do this.' My eyes are fixed on the till. I can see the sales assistant looking at me. It's the same person who sold me the last test I bought. She looks different, but it's the same person. She's serving another customer, smiling. Every so often, she'll look over at me, waiting for me to come over. She recognises me and knows exactly what I'm buying. She's wondering if I even used the last one – or if I'm such a *whore* that I've had another scare two weeks later. I can't do this. 'She recognises me, Nance. Can you get it for me?' My eyes are fixed on the girl's grin. She's goading me over, but I won't go.

Nance steps in front of me, shielding me from view. 'Who does? Recognise you from where?' She whispers into me.

I can still see the girl over Nancy's shoulder. She's pretending she hasn't seen me, in case Nancy notices. 'Please, Nance.' She doesn't know that I snuck away and bought a test the last time we were here. And I'm not going to tell her that now. She knows I've taken a test and didn't check the result.
That's all she needs to know.

She tightly squeezes my hand for a moment, then her grip loosens. 'Alright, babes. You just wait outside, yeah? I'll meet you out there in a bit.'

53. NANCY'S

'You ain't coming outta there until I hear piss.' Nancy's voice muffles through the toilet door. 'You hear me?' She's pressed her body against the door, so I couldn't get out if I tried. I locked it when I came in, but she's made sure I definitely can't come out. Her mum isn't in, so we went straight upstairs to do the test. She wanted me to do it in the toilets in Westfield, but I'd rather do it here. I feel safer. As soon as we got in, she called out for her mum to make sure she wasn't home. Then, she marched me upstairs, following behind me. We had a little talk outside the bathroom door first. She said that I had to do it – I needed to know. It would be easier for me to bury my head in the sand, but that could make things a lot worse in the long run. We had a teary cuddle and I went inside. 'Don't forget… Don't put the box in the bin. If mum sees it, she'll go mad. Bring it out here after and we'll take it to the bins on the corner.'

It took me a while to even sit on the toilet seat.
I was pacing for a while, wondering how I could get out of this.
I can't.
I just need to do it.
The sooner I do it, the sooner it's done.

'Any luck? D'you want another drink?' Her voice is damp as it seeps through the heavy, wooden door. She gave me a big drink of water when we came in, just to get me started. I had a sip, but I felt too sick to drink. 'Run the taps if you want. And the bath. Run the bath.'

I didn't feel like I needed to go at first.

Now, I definitely need to go because of the nerves, but my body won't let me. It's like it knows what the result will be, so it's trying to let me enjoy my life as it is – while I can. The second this result comes through, my life could change. The next five minutes are going to shape the rest of my life.

I didn't have an STI. The chances of getting an STI must be higher than the chances of getting...

Some people try for years and can't.

What makes me so special that I would be... By accident?

I can't be.

I won't be.

I can't be.

My whole body tenses up, trying to hold in the flow that's coming through me.

I've started.

It echoes around the toilet bowl as I frantically take the test out of the box. I didn't prepare it beforehand like last time. This time, I've done everything I can to draw things out. And now, it's over. I've got to do it. There's nowhere left to run.

The ripped box drops to my feet with the instructions still inside. I ease it between my legs for the final time in my life. I'm never going to have to do this again. I'll make sure of it. From the last time, I've got a rough idea of where I need to place it.

I shouldn't know how to do this. Not at seventeen.

The flow into the toilet turns into a pat on the surface of the stick. I hold it there until I'm finished.

The flow gets weaker. The last few drops land, and I keep the stick hidden under me. I want to get every bit that I can. I don't want to have to do this, again.

I've brought this on myself. I declined the test at the clinic. I lied about unprotected vaginal sex.

I don't know why I did.

I'm a passenger in my own head.

The last drops stop.

Everything is quiet.

Nancy isn't at the door anymore. It's just me and my result.

I started this alone and I'm going to finish it alone.

I ease the test out from between my legs.

I close my eyes.

The familiar cramp of anxiety begs me not to look.

My hand shakes as it rises.

Drops trickle onto the floor, hammering down louder than they should.

I lean forward.

My head rests on my left hand – pushing my hair back.

I hold the stick in my right hand – face down, between my knees.

Hours pass.

My eyes open.

Pregnant.

The stick drops to the floor.

My head collapses between my legs, pouring water from my eyes, nose, and mouth.

My body goes limp under me.

The door rattles against the frame and the brass handle shakes with the force. 'Babes! Babes! Open the door! Let me in!'

54. NANCY'S cont.

'Are you gonna tell him?' We're lying on Nancy's bed. I'm resting my head on her chest and her arms are wrapped around me. Her hands are clenched tight, locking me into her.
We did the test a few hours ago.
I was sat crying in the bathroom for ages. The door stopped making noise after a while. It just wobbled against the hinges in silence as Nancy pounded it from the other side. After a while, I managed to pick myself up and let her in. The whole flat was rattling around me from her barging against the wood, trying to knock it through. Nance burst in and launched into me. We sat on a damp bath mat and propped ourselves up against the bath. She cradled me for days. I didn't want to drag her into all this. I don't like to burden everyone else with my stupid problems. I'd rather just keep them to myself.
I can't. Not now. There's no way I can get through this alone.

'Y'know… As much as I don't like him – and as much of a prick he is for what he's done to you – he's got a right to know. Before you…' She pauses. '…Decide what to…' Pause. '…I don't know.' She doesn't know what to say.
It doesn't matter.
It's better to be here and say the wrong thing, than to not be here at all.
I lift my head up, wiping my eyes before I look at her. 'I can't. I know I need to, but I can't.'

I can't go a whole week without speaking to him and come out with this.

'Listen.' She holds my face, pointing it at her. 'Listen to me.' She wipes my eyes with her sleeve. 'This is not your fault. Okay? You ain't done nothing wrong. You didn't do this on your own. You both did this together. It's no one's fault, but you both need to sort this out. If you don't wanna tell him, I'll support you. But as much of a prick he is, I'd want to know if I was him. You need to know what you're doing, before it gets too late.'
She's avoiding the real words.

'Can you tell him for me? Please?' I look pathetic. Her face changes as my eyes water. I don't recognise her through my squinted vision.

'D'you want me to text him for you? And say it's me, texting off your phone? Or d'you wanna ring?' She sits up on the bed, trying not to disturb my body on top of her. 'Have you got your phone? I'll text him for you.' She composes her body, wriggling her shoulders and straightening her back. She's hiding it, but she's nervous about speaking to him. She's trying to be strong for my sake.

I roll over and dig my phone out of my bag. I don't look at it as I give it to her. At the last moment, before it lands in her hand, I pull it back. 'Wait – I deleted his number.'
We're both holding the phone.
I know we could just reply to the text he sent me earlier, but I don't want that to be an option. She still doesn't know he messaged me.

Don't think I forgot about you.

I grasp the phone tighter. 'Haven't you got his number on your phone?' I ask her – not knowing what she'll say.
If she's Charlotte, she's got his number.

She answers quickly. 'Nah. You gave him my number – in case he can't get hold of you. Remember? I don't have his. He's never text me or nothing. D'you not remember his number off by heart?' I thought he might've texted her in the last few days, when he had no reply from me… I guess that would mean he cares.
Without realising, I've opened my messages and my phone is out of my hands.

Don't think I forgot about you.

'Is this him?' Nance studies the screen. 'Sorry, I wasn't going through your phone, I swear. That was the first thing that was open on the screen. Is this him, though?' She points the phone at me, shielding it from her eyes. 'Right. Are you sure you want me to text him?' Her voice shakes. 'What d'you want me to say?' She sits completely upright and braces herself, holding the phone between her legs.
I haven't moved since I gave her the phone.

I don't know what she can say.
I'm no good at this.
I wasn't meant to speak to him.
Not so soon.
Not like this.

'Just tell him the truth.' I turn my body – face down. The pillow swallows my face and I don't let myself breathe. There's only darkness around me. I can't tell if my eyes are open or closed. There's no difference. There's no light in any direction.
I haven't given myself a way out.

Don't think I forgot about you.

There's no escape.

55. GP SURGERY

'Okay – sharp scratch.' The doctor takes more of Nancy's blood. She withers away behind the needle, getting sucked of all her life. Her body shrivels and her skin becomes vacuumed around the bones of her face. She's an empty shell of who she used to be… Before I dragged her in here. Her essence drains from her arm with an impossibly dark red, still beating as it collects. It gets plugged into a tiny bottle and stuffed into a clear bag – marked with hundreds of bright warning labels. 'And that's it. We're all done. You should get your results within a few days. We'll reach out to you when they're back, so there's nothing for you to have to do.'
We managed to get back-to-back appointments, so the doctor let both of us come in and have our tests done together. I'm sitting behind Nancy. My thumb is scrolling through my messages. Nance sent the first one and James replied straight away.
I asked her to show me what he said.
It wasn't the James that I know.

Among the paragraphs of messages, certain sentences keep jumping to my eyes.

'It's Nancy.'
'Forget about the last couple days.'
'Your girlfriend is pregnant.'
'Do the right thing.'
'Forget about your problems and be with her.'

'Yeah yeah course good timing.'
'Probably ain't even mine.'
'Know your friend when she's tryna get attention.'
'Fucking flush it or something because no way that thing is mine.'

Nancy's call rejected by James.

'Don't try ring me with this shit.'
'Not heard nothing for days then this.'
'Sort it out yourselves.'
'Stop getting involved.'
'Nothing to do with you so fuck off.'

'I was with her when she did the test actually.'
'Not here to argue with you.'
'She ain't done nothing to you.'
'Do the right thing or you'll regret it for years.'

That was sent a couple of days ago and I still haven't had a text
back. My neon pink thumbnail keeps hovering over the button to
reply, but I know I shouldn't.
He's made up his mind. He doesn't want anything to do with me.

I get lost in a conversation with James.
I've texted him and he's replied.
Everything's okay. We're going to forget about the last few weeks.
We've both done some stuff wrong, but we're going to write it off
and forget about it. There's no use blaming each other for what's
happened. We can get back to normal. There's been no lasting
damage done. The two of us are going to move forward and start
again – nine months ago, but as new. It'll be as if we've just met.
We'll forget all the things we've done to each other and meet each
other again for the first time. We'll go back to the bus stop. We
won't know anything about our past or future. We'll discover each

other all over again. Learn new things about each other every day.
We'll make new memories. New private jokes. New plans for the
future.
I get off the bus – packed with school kids, running and screaming
along the aisle of the top deck. I can still hear them from the
street. James is walking in front of me. I hang back a few paces
behind him. I don't want us to have to walk next to each other in
an awkward silence.
He slows down. *'You following me?'*
I look at him and smile. *'Don't flatter yourself.'*
He asks me if I'm free after school the next day to go to the cafe.

My eyes water from concentrating on the screen for too long.
The rustling of papers from the doctor's desk wakes me up. He
clatters his keyboard before turning to us. 'Okay, we'll telephone
the both of you when your results come in. Allow for a few extra
days because of the weekend. You'll have them this side of
Christmas, though. Is there anything else I can help you with?'
The doctor looks straight to me.
He knows what I've been talking about with Nancy over the last
few days. Now, he's just waiting to see if I'll act on it.
Am I going to carry on being a talker? Or am I going to act on
what I say and finally follow through on a promise to myself?
I can't keep living in my own head. I have to do what needs to be
done.
He looks through me for longer, burning a hole in my stomach.
His stare is making me cramp with nerves and tension.
He's waiting for me to say it.

As I breathe in to force my words out, Nancy looks over her
shoulder at me.
She knows what sounds I'm about to make.
We've already spoken about it.
She's prepared herself for it.
She reaches a hand out and places it on my knee.

I breathe my words out at the doctor.
    'I want…'
Stop.
    'I need… To have an abortion.'

56. AT MINE

My eyes follow a crack in the ceiling. It's never been there. It's just appeared and fractured my room in half.

I had to close the blinds. The world was watching me through the slits, looking down on me with disgust.

My fluffy toys have fallen off the foot of the bed. Their empty, marble eyes are looking away. They can't look at me with comfort. They can't surround the girl I've become.

My room has turned into mum's room. I'm shut off from the rest of the world. There's no sense of outside or feeling of escape. A hint of light is making big shadows of the smallest objects. All the shadows are climbing up the walls and hanging over me from the ceiling. My hands are resting on my belly under the duvet, gently rubbing each side. I'm protecting myself from the world around me; the world that's waiting to collapse under the new crack above my bed.

I won't be able to stand the weight when it falls through the ceiling.

I don't know what's on top, but it will crush me for sure.

My hands shield my belly.

My mind hasn't left the house for days, not since my blood test. The results for that were normal, but I wasn't thinking about them. With everything else going on, they were hardly worth worrying about.

My body has had to go to meetings with consultants and discuss options, reasons, methods... I wasn't able to understand a lot of it, but Nancy was there to guide me through. They've just been speaking words at me, not making proper sentences. Nancy has been translating their language for me and explaining what the next few days will be like.

Everyone else is just ticking boxes. I'm being taken through a conveyor belt of steps and stages. Thousands of girls have been carried on it and thousands more will be after me. At the end of the belt, there's just a drop. If you haven't been there yourself, you don't know where you will fall to. When it comes to falling off, no one else has to.

Just me.

No one else really cares about it.

To everyone else, this is just a procedure.

And I'm just a statistic.

I haven't let myself know the specifics. I don't want to know what will happen or how it will happen. If I go where I'm told to go, do what I'm told to do, everything will be easier. I've programmed my body to respond to what they want me to do, to get through this as quickly as I can.

Nancy told me that I'm further along than we originally thought, so that's going to change the way...

I had to be on my own tonight. I've been with Nancy constantly throughout all this. For this night, I need to be alone. I need one night to get my head and body back together.

All this week, I've been a zombie.

They've pointed me where to go – I've walked.

They've given me a time and a place – I've gone.

Tomorrow, when it's real and not just words, I need to be in control of myself. I need to make sure I'm doing the right thing for me.

I don't know if mum is in.

I haven't looked out for her or made an effort to find out where she is.

We're both locked away in our caves.
They mirror each other, now.
She cradles her photos and bottles.
I cradle myself.
We're both clinging to what's keeping us down, desperately
holding it closest to us.

I'm mum. Trapped in my own world, not knowing anything about
what's happening around me.
The days are going past with no sign of one ending and another
beginning.
It's always dark, now.

Tomorrow, if I can tell when that is, my body will change.
It will change in a way that it won't ever recover from.
Once tomorrow is done, it can't be undone.

57. CLINIC

From the Walk-In Medical Centre, I've learnt not to stare at the walls. The posters just remind me of where I am.
My eyes are on the floor.
I'm picking at the neon pink nail varnish. It's stayed on all this time, but now I'm picking at it. It would've been fine, but I ruined it. I chipped one piece, and the rest began to flake off. I could've left it, but I kept on digging; trying to go under the layers of nail polish, protector, undercoat… The thing I thought would last has flaked away and fallen to the floor.
Pink petals drop and pile at my feet. The last shreds of my childhood – and anything innocent or girly – have come away from me.
I'm empty.

I would never have put myself here. Ever. I'm supposed to be a primary school teacher. A placement in a nursery next year, taken on as a paid teacher's assistant, then getting qualified as a full teacher. I shouldn't be here.
I try to imagine myself away, but my stomach cramps and brings me back to my chair – locking me in amongst the pink petals, stacking higher around my feet and swallowing me from the bottom.
Nance told James what was happening today.
He didn't reply.

He helped put me in this situation, but apparently this is a *women's issue*. He can do whatever he wants and everyone's happy for him to have no responsibility because it's my body. My body. My choice. My responsibility. My problem.
He can just not reply.
I'm so grateful for Nancy. She's stayed with me through all this...
But I'm still on my own because this is my situation.
Am I a bad person for doing this? Does this make me evil? I'm killing something. Someone. Would it be a boy or a girl? I can't kill something that's not alive. Then – why is this so difficult?
It still doesn't seem real. I'm waiting for them to come out and tell me they've made a mistake. When could this have happened? They said how long ago it must have been. I can't remember what they said, but they're wrong.
Is this selfish? There are people who can't have kids. They try for years and can't have any. I can – and I'm doing this. What kind of person am I? I put myself in this position, and rather than face up to it and be responsible, I'm still running away from it.

Nance is rubbing my back. If she stops, I think I'll walk out of here. I'm waiting for a reason to go. I don't know where I am, but I'll make my way home. I wish I could be her. Her mind is so clear. The only thing she has is worry for me. She breaks the heavy silence. 'I love you. You know that?' She pulls me across the arm rest and our heads nestle together. 'I wish I could do this for you. I really do.'
We both stare straight ahead.

The room gets bigger and emptier, until the only things left are our two chairs – side by side; floating lifelessly on the sterile, blue floor.

I close my eyes.

They call me in.

58. NOWHERE

My eyes open.

The two of us stand up on unstable, wobbly legs. Our hands are locked together, holding each other up from falling.
I turn to her. She brings me into her with a tight, warm hug.
Neither of us can let go.
It feels different to any hug she's ever given me. We aren't sure what will happen when it breaks. We get tighter into each other and she sniffs into my shoulder.

I let her go. Both my hands crease down the arms of her jacket to her warm fingers, linking them at the end.
Her eyes are shaking under a coat of water. She won't let the tears drop down her cheek. She'll hold them up until I turn away.
That's what she does. No matter what the world does, she'll stay strong for me. She won't move from here – no matter what. She won't let go of my hands until she knows that I can walk away without her.

Hours pass. Finally, my fingers slip out of hers.
As I turn away, I see her head fall and her fingers trail up to wipe the tears before I can see them.

A stranger walks me forward and takes me to a room.
My stomach cramps, begging me not to go in.

I get led inside. They speak to me in silence, explaining what will happen. I nod, not knowing what I'm nodding to. They ask me to go behind a curtain, take off the bottom half of my clothing, lie on the bed. They pull back the curtain. I'm exposed. I'm another teenage girl, killing another baby. A baby that never had a chance. A baby that wouldn't have a chance.

My feet rest on two metal plates, forcing my legs open. They drape a heavy sheet over my knees – cold and sterile. Someone disappears under it. My knees jerk together, closing my legs. A head comes up from under the sheet and says something to me in a soft, reassuring voice.

Someone comes to my side and takes my hand. It's cold. It doesn't have the warmth and softness of Nancy's.

A voice tells me the area is getting numbed. It already is. My whole body has been numbed. Another hand rests on my knee, relaxing it from shaking. My whole body is shivering with cold that isn't here. The head comes back up from under the sheet.

A machine gets wheeled over. Some prongs and sticks disappear between my legs. My body stays tensed.

I try to imagine myself away, but there's nothing else.

There's nowhere left to go. Nothing else to imagine.

My stomach cramps.

The machine starts.

I've been told hundreds of times what it will do, but I block it from my mind every time. There's a deafening clanking of invisible iron and steel machinery inside me, hammering its way through my body to my head. My body builds up, waiting to break down. All my muscles tense together.

I try to control my breathing by not breathing at all.

Relax.

Just relax.

Keep breathing.

Relax.

Lipgloss

I close my eyes.

I see myself from above.
I watch a young girl, vulnerable and exposed.
Her stomach cramps. Her stomach kicks. I felt a kick. My body
comes to life. 'Stop. Stop. Stop, please. Stop. Don't do it. I can't do
it. Please, stop. Please.' I sit up and my legs close together. 'I'm
sorry. Please, don't. I can't do it. I'm sorry, please.' The machine
stops. Voices tell me that they will not continue. They didn't start,
so it isn't too late to stop. The young girl rushes out to Nancy and
the two hold each other in tears.

My stomach cramps and forces my eyes to open.
I'm lying on the hospital bed. My legs are open. The machine
continues to rattle ferociously. The hand on my shaking knee
weighs down. A head emerges from under the sheet.
Everything stops.
The room freezes and I feel a loss.
I've never felt this.
I feel like I've lost something I've always had.
Something I've always wanted.
Something I've always needed.
I've always had it and now it's gone.
Empty.
The room stays. Everyone is fixed where they are.
My thoughts slow and I could drift away to sleep – like there's
nothing left to stay here for.
There's no reason for me to stay awake.
To move.
Even to breathe.
There's nothing left for me.
Everything slows to a still.
My body moves like it's under water.
I'm under water and running out of air.
But I don't panic.

I don't care anymore.

The room jolts. Everyone comes back to life, moving faster than normal.
The machine gets wheeled out quickly.

Nothing.

I close my eyes.

My sincerest thanks to you for sticking with this until the end.

I truly appreciate you taking the time to come on this journey with the characters.
I hope the story gave you something in return.

If you found it at all meaningful, please encourage others to give it a read and/or leave a review on the marketplace from which you found it.

Until the next one…

Liam Gammalliere

Printed in Great Britain
by Amazon

55373708R00180